"What happened?" Christie asked. "You seemed fine for a second there, and then *bam*!"

Aubrey winced. Had her fall been that bad? "I got distracted."

"By what?"

"The *perfect* boy," Aubrey said, glancing across the frozen lake again. "Unless I imagined him in all the head trauma. He was over there, but I don't see him now. He was tall, chiseled, blond. Total ski-instructor type."

"You just described every other guy on this mountain. But don't worry. If it was meant to be, you'll see him again," Christie said confidently. She grinned in a sly way. "Maybe we *will* have some romance to talk about on this vacation."

Other books by Emma Harrison

Tourist Trap
The Best Girl

EMMA HARRISON

Snow Queen

HARPER TEEN
An Imprint of HarperCollinsPublishers

HarperTeen is an imprint
of HarperCollins Publishers.

www.harperteen.com

Library of Congress catalog card number:
2009931190
ISBN 978-0-06-171490-0

Typography by Andrea Vandergrift
10 11 12 13 14   OPM   10 9 8 7 6 5 4 3 2 1

First Edition

For Brady

Chapter 1

"*W*here's the snow? I was promised snow."

Aubrey Mills stared out the window of the Spotted Owl Inn's white shuttle van as it climbed the mountain just outside Darling, Vermont. She saw lots of things. She saw piles of dead brown leaves. She saw acres of bare, spindly trees mixed in with tons of gorgeous evergreens. She saw a bright sun and a clear blue sky so cloud free it was blinding. What she did not see was snow.

"This *is* Vermont, right? There's supposed to be snow."

In the front seat, Aubrey's best friend, Christie Howell, laughed with her cousin Charlie, who was behind the wheel of the creaky old van.

"Not *always*," Christie replied, turning around in her seat so that Aubrey could see her teasing smile. "They do have seasons here, you know."

Christie's black hair was pulled back in a tight French braid, which showed off her jet-black eyes and perfect complexion. Along with her red snow jacket, she wore a cozy-looking white scarf with matching mittens and earmuffs. She had donned all of this the second they had stepped off the plane from Fort Lauderdale. Aubrey, meanwhile, was freezing her butt off in a pink zipped hoodie and Tampa Bay Lightning baseball cap. She had realized it was going to be cold in the Northeast, but having never been out of Florida, she hadn't known exactly what that cold was going to feel like. And it felt biting, like a million tiny pinpricks all over her skin. Why hadn't anyone told her to carry her new winter coat onto the plane like Christie had? She was sure that cuddling into the thick, down puffer jacket would have been like heaven on earth right about now, but unfortunately it was still balled up at the bottom of her suitcase at the rear of the van.

Aubrey rolled her big blue eyes. Her seat let out a loud squeak as Charlie drove over a bump, and the spring beneath her poked her in the butt. "Yeah, right. Not in August, maybe, but it's February. So where's the snow?"

Charlie turned the van in to a wide driveway. The painted wooden sign stuck in the ground at the curb read SPOTTED OWL INN, JUST UP THE HILL.

"It's been a pretty flake-free winter," Charlie said, glancing at Aubrey in the rearview mirror. "But it's in the forecast for the end of the week."

"And in the meantime, all the slopes have snow machines," Christie added.

Aubrey huffed and slumped down in her seat, sliding left to get her butt cheek free of the offending spring. "I did not sign on for man-made snow."

Normally, Aubrey wasn't one for pouting, but she had never seen snow in her life except on animated Christmas specials and broadcasts of the Winter X Games. Every year, Christie spent two weeks in February up here in Vermont at her grandparents' inn, and every year she came back with stories of snowball fights and sledding down hills and racing snowmobiles. All her life, Aubrey had been jealous of Christie's close relationship with snow, and she had always wanted to see Vermont and its white, wintry vistas. So this year, her junior year, she had begged her parents for months to let her tack an extra week onto her February break—just like Christie always did—so that she could come along, and her parents had agreed. All Aubrey had to do was keep her room clean (a major imposition), get straight B's or higher (she usually did this anyway), and promise to visit her own grandparents when she returned (always boring, but doable). And now, here she was in Vermont—finally—and no snow.

"Speaking of snow, Charlie, how are your boarding skills coming along?" Christie asked.

Charlie took one hand off the wheel and shoved up the sleeve of his bright-yellow jacket. There was a long, jagged scrape from his elbow to his wrist, which was just starting to scab up.

"Does that answer your question?" he asked with a wry smile.

"Ew! Cover it up!" Christie said, grimacing and turning toward the window.

"Whoa! How'd you get that?" Aubrey asked, sitting forward.

"Slid off the course and over about thirty

yards of rocky terrain," Charlie replied with a hint of pride. "You should see the one on my leg."

"No thank you!" Christie said, holding up her hands in surrender. "I'm sorry I asked. Maybe you should stick to skiing."

"Never. I will master the snowboard if it kills me," Charlie joked.

Charlie's parents, Christie's aunt and uncle, had moved to his mother's homeland of Norway when he'd graduated from high school, but Charlie had come to stay with his grandparents. He was twenty years old and was taking business classes at the local community college while learning how to run the inn—a job he would take over one day when his grandparents retired. Aubrey had learned all of this on the plane ride from Florida, but Christie hadn't mentioned his snowboarding obsession. Aubrey had to admire his determination. Not everyone would get right back up on a snowboard after sustaining injuries like that.

Charlie pulled the van around a bend and Aubrey got her first look at the famous Spotted Owl Inn. She had heard so many stories about it over the years it may as well have been a fairy-tale castle, and the sight of it caused a little catch of excitement in her chest, even without the snow. The huge lemonade porch, dotted with rocking chairs of all shapes and sizes; the double fieldstone chimneys puffing smoke into the sky; ski slopes—white strips of man-made powder stark against all the brown—rising up behind the wide, colonial-style structure as the ski lifts whisked pairs of skiers skyward. Aubrey pressed her forehead against the scratched window to take it all in. She was here. She was finally here.

"Welcome to the Spotted Owl," Charlie said, putting the van in park. It bucked forward and let out a loud wail as he did so, as if it was slowly dying from the effort. "Hope you ladies enjoy your stay."

Aubrey and Christie squealed with excitement and jumped out of the van, the rusty door hinges groaning. As Charlie unloaded their bags from the back, Aubrey took a deep breath of the fresh mountain air and got a fragrant whiff of the wood burning in the fireplaces, too. When she let the air go, it made a big puff of steam in front of her face. Her breath had never done that before, and she laughed giddily, feeling like a little kid. What other new cold-weather oddities was she going to experience in the next two weeks?

"Christie, it's exactly like you said," Aubrey mused. "So beautiful."

"Isn't it, though?" Christie sighed.

The beeping sound of a truck backing up caught Aubrey's attention, and she walked around the front of the van to see what was going on. Down a small hill and across the road was a wide-open field where dozens of trucks were either parked or maneuvering into place. Half of them were flatbeds carrying pieces of carnival rides—big bulb lights, Ferris wheel seats, gears, and colorful placards and signs advertising hot chocolate and deep-fried Oreos. Apparently preparations for the winter carnival had already begun. The carnival was a huge event thrown each year by Christie and Charlie's grandparents to raise money for the inn and its yearly renovations. The weeklong festival included rides, shows, contests, and crazy amounts of food. It was a favorite event of locals and tourists alike, and the Spotted Owl was always booked solid for the week of the carnival.

"Where do they hold the hockey shot contest?" Aubrey asked excitedly. The only female on her school's roller-hockey team, she was planning on signing up for the event as soon as possible. The hockey goal would be covered by a board, which would have five holes cut out of it—one at the bottom center and one at each corner. The idea was to hit all five holes using fewer than ten pucks. Aubrey had been practicing for weeks on the asphalt back home and wanted to hit the ice as soon as possible so she could check her skills on the new surface.

"See that pond way out there at the back of the field?" Christie said, standing on her toes and pointing at a wide patch of frozen water. "That's the spot."

"I can't wait to try out my new ice skates," Aubrey said, grinning. She had never been on ice skates before, but she figured they couldn't be all that different from Rollerblades. And she was a natural on her Rollerblades. A stiff wind blew Aubrey's long, straight, strawberry-blond hair back from her face and she zipped her hooded sweatshirt all the way up to her chin. "Do they always set up this early? I thought the carnival didn't start till next week."

"It takes a while to get everything ready. I told you, the thing is huge," Christie replied.

Aubrey watched as a guy directing one of the trucks to back up seemed to forget what he was doing and almost got himself run over. She kept one eye on him and the other on Christie and Charlie.

"Yeah, and it's going to be bigger than ever this year," Charlie said, joining them. He had Aubrey's backpack slung over one shoulder and one of Christie's many totes on the other. He nudged Christie with his elbow. "Rose says you guys already signed up for the pa—"

"So, Charlie, how's Daniela?" Christie interrupted rather loudly. "Are you guys handling the long-distance thing okay?"

Aubrey tore her eyes from the near miss on the field and glanced at the two cousins. She marveled again at how very different they looked, Christie tiny and slight with her dark eyes, dark hair, and Korean features and Charlie with his blond hair, freckles, and broad build.

Their fathers were brothers, and Charlie's dad had married a Norwegian ski instructor, while Christie's father had married Christie's mother, who was Korean. Aubrey would have loved for her family to be that international, but alas, every single one of her relatives was as auburn-haired and pale as she was. Which was not good for a family that lived exclusively in Florida. The sunblock costs alone were staggering.

"Yeah. We're dealing," Charlie said, appearing confused by the sudden change of topic. "My girlfriend's studying abroad in Russia for the semester," he explained to Aubrey. "Come on. Let's get all this stuff inside."

As they turned to go, a large, modern, black bus with tinted windows rolled along the road down below. The words CHAMBERLAIN SKI RESORT AND SPA were emblazoned across the side in gold script. Christie and Charlie suddenly looked sour.

"Okay, what is this resort and spa thing?" Aubrey asked, wresting her suitcase from Charlie's grip. He was a tad weighed down by Christie's many bags, and Aubrey had never been one to make other people carry her stuff.

"I saw at least five billboards for that place on the way here."

"It's just this hotel on the other side of town," Christie said, waving a hand. "It opened about ten years ago and totally ramped up the tourism in town. Which is a good thing," she added, almost defensively.

"Yeah, Rose and Jim were worried about it when it was first being built, but it's actually brought in more business," Charlie explained as they approached the steps to the porch. "We get a lot of their overflow, plus all the people who prefer quaint and friendly to ostentatious and bitchy."

"Charlie!" Christie admonished.

"What? You know they make their employees suck on lemons all day so they'll be perpetually pissy," he joked. "That's why their faces are all pinched." He sucked in his cheeks and pursed his lips in an unattractive way.

Aubrey laughed, but Christie sighed. "You're so negative," Christie said.

"She thinks I'm funny," Charlie replied, pointing at Aubrey as he backed through the wooden door with Christie's things.

He held the door for Aubrey and Christie. They had barely stepped foot inside the cozy lobby, when they heard a shout.

"Christie!"

Aubrey was so startled by the volume she jumped. An older man and woman came bursting out from behind the reservation desk and rushed to wrap Christie up in their arms.

"Beware. They get a little crazy with grandkids they haven't seen in a while," Charlie warned.

"I see that," Aubrey replied.

She watched as Christie and her grandmother jumped up and down in each other's arms. These people were grandparents? Impossible. They were way too spry and cool looking to be grandparents. Rose Howell had short blond hair and wore a turtleneck sweater and jeans over hiking boots, while her husband, Jim, was tall, solidly built, and clad in a plaid flannel shirt and cords. Aubrey had seen pictures of the Howells before, but she had expected them to have aged somewhat. Instead they looked like they had given up the whole aging business at fifty-five—and maybe started going backward. Meanwhile,

Aubrey's grandparents were hanging out in a retirement villa in Palm Beach, wearing tacky polyester and griping about Drew Carey taking over *The Price Is Right*.

Maybe I should bring them up here next year. Maybe the fresh mountain air makes people all peppy, Aubrey mused.

"Rose, Jim, this is my best friend, Aubrey," Christie said as she leaned into her grandfather's side, his arm clenched around her shoulders.

"Nice to finally meet you, Aubrey," he said.

Aubrey put her suitcase down so that she could shake hands with him. His grip was warm and strong and steady. "Nice to meet you, too."

"We hear nothing but 'Aubrey' this and 'Aubrey' that," Rose added, giving her a hug.

"Thanks. I've heard a lot about you, too, Mr. and Mrs. Howell," Aubrey said.

"Oh, please. Call us Rose and Jim," Rose said with a wave. "Everyone does."

"Okay, Rose and Jim," Aubrey said happily. Her own grandparents demanded to be called "sir" and "ma'am." Yeah. She really needed to get them to Vermont.

"I should get this stuff upstairs," Charlie said.

"Don't forget to put them in room ten this time," Rose said.

"Got it," Charlie replied, disappearing up the stairs.

"Wait, why ten?" Christie asked, her brow furrowing. "Did you guys book someone in my room?"

Rose and Jim exchanged a look. "No, hon. You know we'd never give away fifteen if we knew you were coming," Rose said. "It has the nicest view in the place," she explained to Aubrey.

"We had to shut down a few of the rooms out back because of some issues with the pipes," Jim said.

"But those are the best rooms. That can't be good for business. Especially with the carnival next week," Christie said worriedly.

"Don't worry your pretty head about it," Jim said, kissing Christie's forehead. He cleared his throat and glanced at Rose. "It'll all be sorted out soon."

"Okay. As long as everything's all right," Christie said.

"Everything's fine," Rose assured her, running her hand over Christie's braid. Something in Rose and Jim's tone gave Aubrey the feeling that everything wasn't as fine as they were saying, but Christie didn't seem to notice.

"Is Jonathan around?" Christie asked, trying to sound casual. Jonathan Price was the crush of Christie's life. He worked at the Spotted Owl, and every year Christie jetted up to Vermont hoping to finally get him to ask her out. Every year she came home disappointed. Aubrey was dying to meet this guy who was oblivious to her best friend's awesomeness.

"He's not working today," Jim said. "But he'll be around tomorrow."

"Oh. Okay," Christie said, obviously disappointed.

"Hey, this way you get to clean up from the trip before you see him," Aubrey said in Christie's ear.

Her friend perked right up. "Good point!"

"So! It's finally here!" Rose said, her blue eyes shining as she took both of Christie's hands. "The year my little Christie girl here wins the Snow Queen crown!"

Christie glanced somewhat warily in Aubrey's direction, which was odd. Aubrey had heard all about the Snow Queen Pageant. Christie had been obsessed with the event for years. A girlie-girl to the core, Christie had been daydreaming about winning the Snow Queen crown ever since she'd first attended the pageant in first grade. Practically every one of her daydreams revolved around having that crown placed atop her head—and Jonathan kissing her under the moonlight afterward. Aubrey knew very well that Christie intended to compete in the pageant now that she was sixteen and finally eligible, and she had promised to help Christie rehearse or do whatever pageant girls had to do. So why did Christie look so nervous all of a sudden?

Then Rose turned and, still hanging on to Christie with one hand, took Aubrey's hand up as well.

"I hope you girls have your gowns pressed and your interview skills sharpened."

"My what and my what, now?" Aubrey asked, confused.

Christie stared at Aubrey pleadingly. Aubrey felt a nasty blush of realization start to creep up from her chin.

"Wait a minute—"

"I signed us both up to compete in the Snow Queen Pageant!" Christie announced, her voice strained. "Surprise!"

Aubrey took a step backward and Rose dropped both their hands. "Please tell me you're kidding."

Christie said nothing. She just looked as if she'd swallowed one of those lemons from the Chamberlain Ski Resort and Spa.

"Christie! I've never even watched a pageant on TV. I would never enter one!" Aubrey wailed.

"Oh, please, please, please just do it with me!" Christie clasped her hands together under her chin as she begged. "I've been looking forward to this forever but there's no way I can get through all the rehearsals and everything by myself. I know I'd get too nervous and intimidated and I'd drop out."

This was not an unfounded argument. It had happened when Christie had resolved to try out for cheerleading and lasted through one day of pre-tryout practice before deciding she wasn't good enough. It had happened when she'd actually tried out for the musical, made the chorus, and then chickened out before opening night. And it had happened when she'd applied to be a camp counselor and run away from the interview in tears when they'd asked her how she would handle an allergic reaction to a bee sting. She had managed to make the color guard as a baton twirler last fall, but only because she had been the lone new hopeful trying out. Plus, their school's football team was awful, so there was never much of an audience for the halftime shows. The girl was not great under pressure, but she had always wanted to be Snow Queen.

"And, hey, you can win tons of money!" Christie continued. "The winner gets ten thousand dollars and there are prizes for second and third place, too."

Aubrey blinked. "Wow. Where do they get that kind of money?"

"From those bastard Chamberlains," Jim said with a scoff.

"Jim!" Rose admonished.

"I'm just saying," he replied, lifting his hands. "They're the ones who run the contest and they have that kind of money," he explained. "But I have to say I don't think you girls should bother.

Lillian Chamberlain started up this whole event ten years ago just so that her daughter, Layla, could win it when she turned sixteen, which she did a couple of weeks ago. The fix is in."

"Oh, Jim!" Rose said, smacking his arm as she made her way back around the reservation desk. "Don't discourage them."

"What? Those people even put their son on the judging panel a couple years back. You can't tell me they're not fixing the results," Jim argued, picking up a perfectly stacked pile of magazines and restacking them. "If she doesn't win I'll eat my hat. No offense, Christie. You know I think you can wipe the stage with that girl."

"None taken, Jim," Christie said with a fond smile.

"Girls, do not listen to him," Rose instructed. "Jim has a conspiracy theory for everything. He's decided our lack of snow this season is due to some Canadian scientists who've figured out a way to keep the weather north of the border so they can steal all our tourists," she added, rolling her eyes.

The girls laughed.

"What? It's possible! I read an article!" Jim protested. "And do you know how much snow they've had in Montreal this past month? Three feet!"

The door behind Aubrey swung open, letting in a blast of cold air. A girl in black spandex snow pants, a black snow jacket with plush fur lining, and huge sunglasses had just stepped into the lobby. Her brown hair, streaked with blond highlights, bounced around her shoulders in big, lush curls, and her lip gloss sparkled even from across the room. She looked around with obvious distaste, sighed loudly, and removed her sunglasses.

"Is my brother here somewhere?" she asked, with no greeting whatsoever. "He's not picking up his cell. *Again*," she added in an exasperated tone.

"Hi, Layla!" Christie said brightly, stepping forward.

Layla looked Christie up and down, her expression blank. "Oh. It's you again."

Hello, rude, Aubrey thought. *Who is this rhymes-with-witch?* No one was ever rude to Christie.

Probably because she was the sweetest person on earth.

"Layla Chamberlain, this is my friend Aubrey Mills," Christie said, gesturing at each of them.

So she was a Chamberlain. The Chamberlain who was going to win the Snow Queen Pageant, according to Jim. Interesting.

"Hi," Aubrey said.

Layla looked Aubrey over and said nothing. Aubrey was starting to understand why Jim didn't like this family.

"How've you been?" Christie asked in the same friendly way. "How's school? Are you still on the cheerleading team?"

That was Christie. Always nice to everyone, no matter what.

Layla heaved another sigh and pulled a sleek cell phone out of her pocket to check the screen.

"Fine, fine, and yes," she said in a bored way as she quickly typed in a text. "I heard you and some other FL chick are competing in the pageant." Her eyes flicked toward Aubrey. "You, I assume? Too bad I'll be winning it," she added, before Aubrey could even open her mouth to respond.

Christie laughed. "I think we all have a good chance of—"

"I tried to convince my mother that it wasn't fair, you guys competing," Layla continued. "I mean, it really should only be open to people who *live* here."

Christie's face drained of color. "What? No. You can't—"

"Now, now. Christie's been a part-time Darling resident for years," Jim said defensively, putting his arm around Christie.

"Whatever. My mom said it was too late to change the rules now anyway, so I guess you two are in," Layla said. "If you see my brother, tell him I'm looking for him." Then she snapped her phone closed and sauntered out, her hair bouncing behind her.

"Oh. My. God," Aubrey said, splaying her fingers out in front of her. "If that is the kind of girl competing in this pageant then I will *definitely* not be participating. I'll help you beat her, but if I had to go up against that girl, I might have to kill her. So thanks anyway, but I'm out."

Aubrey had a serious competitive streak, which had only grown stronger playing on an all-boys team in an all-boys league. She knew that if she were to go up against someone as clearly egotistical as Layla, things could get ugly. Fast.

Jim laughed as he turned and walked back behind the reservation desk, where he started to sort through some papers. "Smart girl."

"She's not *that* bad," Christie said.

"Oh, please!" Aubrey replied, picking up her luggage again. "She was totally rude. She looked at you like you were the mud stuck up in the treads of her overpriced boots."

"No! That's just the way her face is!" Christie said, earning a laugh from both her grandparents.

"Oh, Chris, I so love how you always see the good in everyone," her grandmother said.

Christie shrugged and Aubrey sighed. She loved her best friend more than almost anyone, but the one thing that had always bugged her about Christie was her lack of self-worth and backbone.

"One of these days I am going to get you to

stick up for yourself," Aubrey promised.

"Hear, hear!" Jim cheered, raising a fist.

"But right now, I want to see our room and change into something *a lot* warmer," she said.

"Okay! Let's go up!" Christie said cheerily. She led Aubrey over to the stairs. "But you are going to reconsider the pageant, right?"

"Um, no," Aubrey said.

"Please? I need you! You have to do it!" Christie begged as they mounted the creaky old stairs. "Please, please, please, please, please?"

Aubrey rolled her eyes. It was going to be a long couple of weeks.

Chapter 2

"Ow! Okay, that one's gonna leave a mark," Aubrey said as the cold wetness of the ice seeped through the rear of her jeans. Pain radiated up her back as she reached her hands up toward Christie. "Is it just me, or is ice way harder than asphalt?"

After dinner with Rose and Jim, Christie had suggested a skate on the lake at the center of Darling, and Aubrey had jumped at the chance to try out her new ice skates. What she hadn't realized was that the lake was going to be kind of a scene. Kids of all ages were gathered in packs on and around the ice, and a bunch of mom types were selling hot chocolate and snacks through a window in a quaint log cabin just off the lake.

Christie gave her a sympathetic look. "Are you sure you want to keep doing this? You're going to be bruised beyond belief."

She hoisted Aubrey up, and Aubrey fought to keep her feet beneath her. Once she felt steady again, she let go of Christie's hands. "I'm fine. I've only fallen three times."

"Try eight," Christie corrected.

Aubrey laughed under her breath. "Gee. Thanks for keeping such good track of my klutziness."

"I'm just a good friend like that," Christie joked.

From the corner of her eye, Aubrey saw a guy skating toward them at top speed. He was on a collision course with Christie, but he was moving so fast Aubrey didn't even have time to warn her. Christie turned around and flinched, but the guy managed to stop short right in front of her, spraying up ice chunks all over their ankles.

"Hey, Christie. I thought that was you," he said. His cheeks were all flushed, and his brown eyes sparkled happily as he looked down at her. He was handsome in a boyish way, his head covered by a leather aviator hat with wooly earflaps.

"Hi, Jonathan," Christie said.

She bit her lip as she glanced at Aubrey with wide eyes. So this was him. The boy Aubrey had been hearing about nonstop since she was twelve. Aubrey could totally see the attraction. Jonathan was tall, obviously athletic, and had an easy smile. The boy didn't *look* stupid, so why hadn't he asked Christie out yet?

"I'm Aubrey Mills. Christie's best friend," Aubrey said.

"Oh, right. Sorry!" Christie said, smacking herself in the head. "Aubrey, Jonathan, Jonathan, Aubrey."

Jonathan laughed. "Welcome to Vermont," he said in a friendly way, tugging on a pair of chunky knit gloves that looked as if they'd seen better days. "I'll be working all day tomorrow, and Rose and Jim told me to take good care of you guys, so let me know if you need anything."

He looked at Christie. She blushed and stared at her feet. This was not normal for

Aubrey's gregarious BFF. Why was she acting like such a doof?

"Okay. Thanks!" Aubrey said.

Jonathan hesitated a second, clearly waiting for Christie to say something. When it became blatantly obvious that she was going to remain mute, he skated backward a bit. "Okay, then . . . See ya!"

He skated off toward a group of guys on the other side of the ice, all of whom greeted him in a raucous way.

"Okay. What the heck was that?" Aubrey asked.

"Nothing. That was nothing," Christie replied, skating ahead a bit. She turned around to face Aubrey and offered her hands. Aubrey tucked her own hands under her arms.

"That was not nothing," Aubrey said. "Why didn't you talk to him?"

The blush deepened. "I don't know! I just . . . I get all nervous around him."

Aubrey was starting to understand why these two had yet to hook up. If Christie always acted that way around him, he probably thought she was a kook.

"Why? He clearly likes you," Aubrey said.

"No! He does not!" Christie replied with a scoff. Then she glanced over her shoulder at Jonathan and his friends. "Does he?"

"Oh my gosh, yes! He came over here just to say hi to you, didn't he? He wanted to talk to you, but you barely said two words!" Aubrey pointed out. Over Christie's shoulder, Aubrey saw Jonathan glance back at her friend, checking her out. "I am so getting you two together on this trip. It'll be fun to have a little romance to talk about."

"No! Aubrey! Promise me you will not say anything to him. It would be so humiliating," Christie whispered.

"Why? If I can help, then I want to help!" Aubrey said.

Christie fluttered her knees nervously. Aubrey could see that her friend was getting agitated by the pressure and decided to back off. But she would never understand why Christie didn't go after the things she wanted. "Can we talk about something else?" Christie asked. "Why don't we skate?"

Aubrey sighed and let Christie take her

hands. "Fine."

Up ahead, Layla Chamberlain and one of her girlfriends stepped out onto the ice. They took off around the circle, gliding like pros, chatting and laughing and not even paying attention to where they were going. They made it look so easy they may as well have been walking. Aubrey gritted her teeth, forgetting all about Jonathan and Christie for the moment. If Layla could do this, so could she.

"Okay. I think you can let go of me now," she said, suddenly feeling like a moron being tugged along by Christie.

"You're sure?" Christie said.

"Definitely," Aubrey replied, even as her ankles wobbled. "I'm ready."

"Okay," Christie said, carefully releasing Aubrey's hand. "It's all you!"

In a moment, Christie's fingers were gone and Aubrey was on her own. She felt a twinge of trepidation but brushed it aside.

You can do this, she told herself. *Just take it easy.*

She took two tentative glides and felt pretty secure on her skates. Behind her, Layla's voice grew louder. Aubrey forced herself to tear her eyes off her feet and watch where she was going. She wanted to appear as if she knew what she was doing. When she looked up, she looked right into the eyes of the single most gorgeous guy she had ever seen in her life. He was tall—definitely over six feet—with blond hair that was parted to the side, but in a messy, spiky 'do. He had a tiny bit of stubble all over his chin and a slight tan, probably from skiing the slopes all day. He was standing across the lake, but he was watching her, and when her gaze caught his, he didn't look away. He merely smiled and lightly clapped his hands in her direction, as if he'd been watching her all night and realized these were her first steps on her own. Aubrey's heart caught, and she smiled back.

That was when her right foot slipped forward and her stomach swooped. In a nanosecond, the gorgeous boy was gone and all she saw was the starry sky above. Aubrey winced, anticipating the crash as her feet flew up in the air. Her back and butt slammed into the ice while the hood of her brown puffer jacket flew up to cradle the back of her head before it could crack in two.

"Ow," Aubrey whimpered.

Already the wetness was seeping through her jeans again and clinging with its freezing-cold fingers to her bare skin beneath. She could hear the laughter coming from all corners of the lake and her face burned.

He saw that happen, she thought miserably. *Just kill me now.*

Within seconds Christie's face hovered over hers. "Are you okay?"

Aubrey heard a loud laugh growing louder as it bore down on her. Suddenly Layla's face appeared next to Christie's. Her hair tumbled over her shoulder and hung toward Aubrey's nose.

"Yes, *are* you okay? That looked *so* bad," Layla said with a grin. "There's an ambulance in the parking lot. Want me to get them to bring the stretcher?"

"That won't be necessary," Aubrey said.

Layla's friend joined them. She had a long nose and dyed-blond hair pulled back in a high ponytail. "Maybe it was that jacket that threw you off. It looks like it weighs a ton. Did you borrow it from your dad or something?"

Damn. She had *told* her mother this was too much coat. But her mom had been all stressed out about her being cold. Which, she had to admit, she was not, thanks to the coat. Except for the moments in which she was lying on the ice.

"Rebecca!" Layla said in a faux-scolding tone. Then she laughed as she looked Aubrey over again. "Actually, it *is* rather lumberjack-y," she said, wrinkling her nose. "Did it come with a free chainsaw?" Her friend giggled, and the two of them slapped gloved hands.

Aubrey hoisted herself up, shrugging off Christie's offered hand, and turned over onto her knees. Her kneecaps instantly froze, but she didn't care. She was getting up off the ice by herself if it killed her. She pressed her frigid fingers onto the lake surface and managed to push her way up to standing without falling on her ass again. Taking a deep breath, she willed her feet to stay in one place as she tugged down on the hem of her admittedly oversized coat. One glance over Layla's shoulder told Aubrey that the gorgeous boy was gone. He'd probably convulsed from laughter and passed out somewhere behind the skate rental counter.

"Maybe I was *going* for the lumberjack look," Aubrey said confidently.

Layla and Rebecca exchanged an amused glance. "Honey, no one is actually *going* for the lumberjack look," Layla said. Then she and her friend hooked arms and skated off together in perfect synch. "See you at rehearsal!" Layla sang over her shoulder.

Aubrey rolled her eyes and carefully slid over to the edge of the lake, where a bench had just been vacated by a couple and their young kids. She sat down gingerly and took a deep breath.

"What happened?" Christie asked. "You seemed fine for a second there, and then *bam*!"

Aubrey winced. Was it that bad? "I got distracted."

"By what?"

"The *perfect* boy," Aubrey said, glancing across the lake again. "Unless I imagined him in all the head trauma."

"Where?" Christie sat up straight, her head swiveling around like an owl's.

"He was over there, but I don't see him now," Aubrey replied, pointing. "He was tall, chiseled, blond. Total ski-instructor type."

Christie deflated slightly. "You just described every other guy on this mountain."

Aubrey sighed. "I figured."

"But don't worry. If it was meant to be, you'll see him again," Christie said confidently. She grinned in a sly way. "Maybe we *will* have some romance to talk about on this vacation."

Yeah, right, Aubrey thought miserably. *As long as he doesn't mind dating a bruised, balance-impaired lumberjack.*

After all the traveling and skating and falling, Aubrey should have been exhausted, but she had a restless night. Every hour or so she woke up and found herself staring at the glowing green numbers on the digital clock, which sat on the nightstand between her bed and Christie's. She had never been good at sleeping in strange places, and the fact that Layla's taunts kept echoing in her head did not help.

Normally Aubrey didn't let other people get to her, so it bothered her even more that she was letting Layla get under her skin. Maybe it was because she had thought she would pick up ice skating with no problem. It was frustrating that she had found it so hard, and it put the whole hockey shot competition in jeopardy. If she didn't learn to ice-skate before next week, she wasn't going to be able to compete, and she'd been so looking forward to it. Maybe that was why the fact that Layla and Rebecca were naturals on the ice, and the fact that they felt the need to rub that in her face, was really bothering her.

Not to mention the fact that Gorgeous Boy had seen her deck. *That* was painful to think about.

Although maybe it was better that Gorgeous Boy had seen her fall. The last time she had tried the romance thing, it hadn't worked out too well. She had been crushing on David Markson, a guy on her roller-hockey team, forever. Last summer, after months of pining, she had finally gotten up the guts to tell him. Much to Aubrey's shock, he said he felt the same way, and they spent the rest of the summer playing video games in his basement, going surfing together, and stealing kisses on the beach. But as soon as roller-hockey practice started up again, David began to act all distant, and three days into the season he told her he thought it would be better if they went back to being friends. Aubrey was devastated, and she could only imagine that he had taken a beating from the guys on the team for dating her when she was essentially one of them. One of the guys. Another roller jock.

She tried to talk to David about it again. After all, she wasn't *that* tomboyish. She wore light makeup and bikinis and denim skirts and the occasional pink T-shirt. And he hadn't thought she was so masculine when he was kissing her under the boardwalk all those evenings as the sun went down. But David avoided any further explanations, and by the end of September he'd started dating Jenna Warren, one of the perkiest cheerleaders in school.

In fact, Layla kind of reminded Aubrey of Jenna. Big hair, big attitude, annoying laugh. And just like that, Aubrey was right back on the ice, with Layla mocking her. She balled up the well-worn quilt under her chin a little bit more, just as she'd been doing all night whenever her spectacular fall came to mind. By the time the sky was turning pink outside the Spotted Owl's windows, she had balled it up so much her wool-socked feet were exposed.

"That's it," she said to herself, sitting up straight. Adrenaline rushed through her veins, just as it always did when she was presented with a new challenge. The next time those people saw her skate, she was going to be a pro.

She shoved the covers off and swung her legs over the side of the bed. Moving as quietly as possible so as not to disturb Christie, Aubrey dressed in clean, dry jeans, a wool sweater, and sneakers. She put on her black wool hat and grabbed her skates, but hesitated as her hand hovered over her brown coat. With a glance over her shoulder at Christie's slumbering form, she picked up her friend's stylish red jacket instead. Not that anyone was going to see her, but maybe Layla's friend had been right. Maybe the puffer was throwing off her equilibrium.

The inn was perfectly quiet as she slipped downstairs and out the front door. Charlie was hanging out behind the front desk, sipping coffee, and he shot her an inquisitive smile as she made her way through the lobby, but he didn't bother her with questions. She would have stopped to say hello, but she was on a mission and she hoped he would understand.

Outside, the air was frigid but crisp—the light still dim as the sun made its way up from behind the mountains. Aubrey zipped up her friend's jacket and removed the gloves from the pockets, slipping them on. She jogged down the steps and across the street to the carnival grounds, where all the hulking equipment sat in half-constructed silence. Five minutes later, Aubrey sat on the cold dirt at the edge of the pond Christie had pointed out to her the day before and laced up her skates. Her breath was coming short and shallow from all the excitement, and the brief run had warmed her up considerably. As she stepped onto the ice for the first time on her own, she felt exhilarated. She could do this.

And after a few moments dealing with wobbly ankles, it seemed that she *could* do it. Why had this been so difficult last night? Aubrey wasn't sure what had changed, but before long she was gliding across the ice, feeling more and more confident. This wasn't that different from Rollerblading. She tried a few quick turns, skating backward, then forward. When she attempted a stop she almost flew off balance but managed to steady herself by waving her arms around. As soon as she had her equilibrium again, she laughed to herself.

"Glad no one was around to see *that*," she said, bracing her hands just above her knees for a moment to catch her breath.

Then a sharp whistle cut through the silence, startling a flock of birds from the nearby trees. Heart in her throat, Aubrey whirled around. Gorgeous Boy was walking toward her out of the trees wearing hiking boots, a gray and silver jacket, and a black ski band that covered his ears but not his hair. He was even more beautiful up close than he had been from across the lake. But where the hell had he come from, and what was he doing here? Maybe she was still in bed and had finally dozed off, and this was just a very hot dream.

"Nice work!" he cheered, reaching the edge of the pond. He placed a backpack on the ground, and Aubrey saw that a pair of well-worn hockey skates were tied to the outside. "Mind if I join you?"

Say something, Aubrey told herself. *Say something smart or funny. You actually have a second chance to make a first impression.*

Taking a deep breath, Aubrey stood up straight, more than ready to make this guy fall for her. But she moved too fast. Her feet slipped out from under her and *she* fell instead. Right on her seriously sore butt.

Chapter 3

*G*orgeous Boy was laughing at her. He was standing over her, laughing at her. So much for the second first impression.

"Wow. They really teach you how to be a gentleman up here in Vermont," Aubrey joked, trying to mask her embarrassment.

"Sorry," he replied, offering his hand. "I've just never seen anyone go down like that. One second you're standing and the next second, horizontal city."

"Glad I was able to entertain you." Aubrey briefly considered refusing his hand, but she kind of wanted to touch him. She reached up and he clasped her forearm, lifting her off the ice so easily she may as well have weighed nothing. Aubrey was so surprised by the speed she tripped forward into his chest. He smelled like soap, pine, and a tiny bit of sweat. Totally perfect.

"Sorry," she said, blushing. She pushed away from him and willed herself not to fall.

"It's no problem, really," he replied, smiling down at her in an amused way.

Her face stung. How could she have let him see her deck twice? "That was the first time I fell all morning. Just so we're clear."

"Okay." He was still amused. His eyes were light blue and they danced with merriment.

"I'm serious!" Aubrey stated.

"I believe you!" he exclaimed. He turned and walked across the ice in his boots like it was nothing. Dropping down next to his backpack, he quickly changed into his skates. "I'm Grayson, by the way."

"Aubrey," she said. The fact that he owned hockey skates that were that beat-up made him even more attractive. She wondered what position he played. He was tall enough for defense, but lean, like a forward.

"You're a friend of Christie's?" he asked as he tied his laces.

"Yeah. You know her?" she replied, intrigued.

If Christie knew this guy, maybe she could get the inside dirt on him. Like whether he had a girlfriend, what his last name was, and why he was appearing out of nowhere and surprising her at the crack of dawn.

He nodded. "For a few years now."

Interesting . . . How did he and Christie know each other? Was he a friend of Charlie's or something?

"So, what're you doing out here so early?" Aubrey asked.

"I'm a hiking guide," he replied. "Kind of freelance. I run hikes for the Spotted Owl and for the Chamberlain Resort. I was just checking out the trail for this morning, making sure there were no new obstructions . . . fallen tree limbs, stuff like that."

"Oh. So you work for Christie's grandparents. That's cool." Aubrey skated in a small circle, still practicing. A freelance hiking guide. Who knew a person could do something that fun for a living?

"Yeah. It's a good time. Usually I do snowshoeing, too, but that's not really happening so much this year," he said, looking around at the bare ground.

"Yeah, what's up with that?" Aubrey asked, turning her palms up. "Where's all the snow?"

"It's in the forecast for the end of the week," he told her.

"So I keep hearing," Aubrey replied, looking back at the sun as it rose higher in the perfectly clear sky. Didn't seem like snow weather to her. She may have been from Florida, but even she knew it took clouds to make snow.

Grayson yanked on his laces to make sure they were tight, then got up and glided over to her effortlessly. Aubrey felt a pang of envy. Was everyone in this town a natural on the ice?

"So, Aubrey, learning to skate?" he asked, moving around her in a tight circle.

"No. I know how to skate. Just not on ice."

"Ah." He nodded and stopped in front of her. "Well, it's pretty much the same concept as Rollerblades. You're probably just thrown off because your ice blades have less surface area to balance on."

"What are you, a physics major?" Aubrey joked. She skated away from him, silently praying that she wouldn't fall again. Her knees felt like Jell-O, but she had a feeling it was more from his ridiculously hot presence than from any lack of confidence on her part. "Thanks for the tip, but I'm fine."

Grayson laughed. "Tell that to your butt. I bet it's black and blue by now."

Aubrey's hands instantly covered her backside. "Who said you could comment on my butt?"

Skating by her so fast he was a blur, Grayson raised his hands. "Sorry. I guess that wasn't very Vermont-gentlemanly. But if I may say, it's way too nice of a butt to be bruised."

Aubrey blushed hard and came to an awkward stop. For a second she felt off-kilter and she threw her hands out, managing to regain her balance. Suddenly Grayson came skating up from behind, grabbed one of her outstretched hands, and tugged her along. Aubrey's heart skipped, both from the sudden contact and the sudden speed.

"What are you doing?" she blurted as the

scenery whipped by.

"Don't think about it," he instructed her. "Just skate."

Aubrey was tempted to close her eyes out of fear. The trees and the carnival trucks and the rocks alongside the pond were going by way too fast. But she couldn't be a wuss. Grayson was watching. And he was also holding her hand tightly in his. As if it belonged there.

Don't think. Just skate.

Aubrey took a deep breath and imagined herself back on the roller-hockey rink outside her high school. She saw herself doing laps around the rink before practice, running drills with the guys on her team. She was so confident on her Rollerblades she never thought about her form. She just skated. So she tried to do the same now.

"See? You're a natural," Grayson said, letting go of her hand.

Aubrey leaned into a turn and came out of it with no problem, standing up and sailing across the pond. Grayson skated behind her, keeping pace with her, and Aubrey was reminded of the speed-skating competition in the Olympics.

Suddenly she felt perfectly safe and able and athletic and free. Then Grayson stopped and waited for her to make one lap around the pond. As she approached him, he didn't move. He just stood in her way like an extremely handsome road block.

"What're you doing?" she shouted, zooming closer.

Somewhere in the distance she heard the engine of a car revving.

"Getting you to stop," Grayson replied.

Oh crap. She hadn't considered stopping. Suddenly she couldn't remotely imagine how to do it. "Move!" she shouted.

"Nope," he replied with a grin.

"Move!"

She was right on top of him.

"Not gonna happen."

It was too late. There was no way she could stop properly now. But she gave it a try anyway and dug her blades into the ice. Her forward momentum was too much, however, and for the second time, she found herself buried in Grayson's chest. Her feet skittered out backward and she clung to his jacket with both hands. He clamped his arms around her to keep her from falling to her knees and hoisted her back up onto her blades.

For a second, Aubrey felt as if this wasn't the worst place in the world to be, even if her heart was still pounding with fear. Then, she heard the car engine roar again and someone leaned on a horn. The sound was way too close for comfort.

"Grayson! There you are!"

Aubrey slid back a few inches and looked past Grayson's shoulder. Layla Chamberlain was sitting behind the steering wheel of a pristine black BMW, which was idling in the grass right next to the pond. There were two tread marks cut into the earth behind the car, extending all the way around the carnival grounds to the road. Grayson sighed and tipped his head forward before turning around, as if he was briefly praying for patience.

"Hey, Layla," he said. "Have you met Aubrey?"

"Yes. We've met. Hello again," Layla said politely. More politely than Aubrey would have predicted, considering how rude she'd been the last two times they'd met. The girl got out of her car and crossed her arms over her chest, shooting Grayson a questioning look, as if she was silently beckoning him to her side.

Aubrey recognized that look. It was the proprietary-slash-confused look of a girlfriend who had just caught her boyfriend with another girl. Aubrey suddenly felt sick to her stomach and warm all over. Oh, God, no. Grayson—Gorgeous Boy himself—was Layla Chamberlain's *boyfriend*? She swallowed a large lump in her throat and skated backward a bit farther, putting some distance between herself and Grayson. Why were the hot guys always going for the bitchy girls? It was like David and Jenna all over again.

"Are you coming? We're going to be late," Layla said.

"Keep your pants on. I'm in the middle of something here," Grayson answered with a laugh.

Aubrey smirked involuntarily. That would have been funnier if she wasn't so annoyed.

"So, want to schedule another lesson?" Grayson asked Aubrey.

"First of all, you are not my skate tutor," she

replied flatly. "And secondly, I don't want to keep you from your girlfriend."

Grayson blinked and glanced over his shoulder, where Layla continued to stare. Then he laughed. He laughed hard. He laughed so hard he doubled over on his skates and had to press his fingertips into the ice to keep from falling. Layla rolled her eyes and trudged out across the pond. She walked right past them and over to Grayson's things, which she picked up with a disgusted scrunch of her nose.

"She's not my girlfriend," Grayson said through his laughter. "She's my sister."

Aubrey's jaw dropped as Layla joined them, handing Grayson his backpack and muddy boots. Aubrey looked from Grayson to Layla and realized she could see a bit of a familial resemblance. Although Layla's beauty was overly manufactured and fake with all the makeup and hair spray and highlights, Grayson's hotness was all-natural. But how could Grayson be a Chamberlain?

"Wait. You're a Chamberlain, but you work for the Howells?" Aubrey said.

"Don't even get me started," Layla put in.

"Yeah. My parents don't love the situation, but I'm eighteen, so there's not much they can do about it," Grayson said, earning a hugely exaggerated sigh from his sister. "I love to hike and I want to share what I know about this place with the people who come to visit, so I'm not going to discriminate against people who want the small-inn experience." He leaned forward and whispered, knowing full well that Layla was going to hear. "Actually, I kind of prefer the old Owl to my family's place. Much more my style."

Aubrey grinned and Layla clucked her tongue.

"Okay. Enough with the welcome-committee act," she said, grabbing his arm. "Fabrizia's flying in this morning, and Mom told her we'd all be there to have breakfast with her. Sorry to cut this short, Aubrey," she added with a smile, though her eyes told a different story. Aubrey could tell that she wasn't sorry at all to be pulling her brother away from the new girl. She wondered if Layla really thought that her nice act was fooling anyone. She certainly hadn't bothered to put on a show yesterday, so why now? Was it all for Grayson's benefit? If so, it seemed odd.

Grayson was her brother. Wouldn't he know her well enough to realize it was all a façade?

Grayson rolled his beautiful eyes. "Fabrizia," he said with a laugh. "She's the director of the Snow Queen Pageant. Have you heard about my family's little pet project?"

Aubrey opened her mouth to respond, but Layla cut her off.

"Actually, Aubrey's going to compete," she said with an amused smirk.

Grayson laughed. "No."

A searing heat stung Aubrey's face, as if she'd been lying out in the Florida sun way too long. Had he just *laughed* at the idea of her competing in a beauty pageant?

"Is that funny for some reason?" she asked.

Grayson paled and his eyes went wide. "No! No, absolutely not. Of course not."

But the damage was already done. Aubrey felt his reaction in her nerves, her bones, her skin. Why was the thought of her as a beauty queen so outright hilarious? Did Grayson think she was that unattractive? Layla, meanwhile, smiled triumphantly. She could clearly tell how upset Aubrey was, no matter how hard Aubrey was working to hide it. Then a very familiar feeling took over. Her adrenaline started to rush through her veins and her fingers curled into tight fists.

Her competitive streak was about to take over.

"I just meant—" Grayson began.

"I'm not only competing in the pageant, I'm going to kick butt in the pageant," Aubrey blurted defensively.

"'Kick butt'?" Layla said, showing her sarcastic side for a split second. "It's not a karate match."

"Whatever. Just don't be surprised when I win," Aubrey replied, her face burning. Not that she wanted to win. She wanted Christie to win. She did. But they didn't need to know that. Besides, Aubrey had a problem with challenges, in that she never backed down from one.

"Great! Yeah. I'm sure you will," Grayson said awkwardly.

Layla groaned. "Come on, Gray. Mom and Dad will freak if we're late." She turned and strolled toward her car across the ice—again, as if she was merely walking on dirt. "Bye,

Aubrey! See you at the first pageant meeting this afternoon!" she sang.

Grayson shot an apologetic look over his shoulder as he skated after his sister. "I'll see you around?"

But Aubrey didn't respond. She was too busy fuming and feeling annoyingly self-conscious at the same time. Did he think she wasn't pretty enough? Not poised enough? Not girlie enough?

Well, guess what, Grayson Chamberlain. You are about to be proven wrong.

"Aubrey! Where have you been?" Christie cried, jumping up from the thick wooden table in the family's private kitchen, which was right next to the inn's spacious catering kitchen. "I was so freaked when you weren't in your bed!"

There was a big, untouched bowl of oatmeal at Christie's place, and Rose was at the old-fashioned iron stove making scrambled eggs. Jim sat at the head of the table, reading a newspaper and eating his oatmeal, and Jonathan was over at the huge refrigerator, rifling through the contents. That explained why Christie was already showered and perfectly coiffed.

"Sorry. I'm fine," Aubrey mumbled, dropping Christie's jacket and gloves on an empty chair. She pulled out the seat next to Christie's and plopped down. "Just went out for a skate."

"I love a morning workout," Jonathan said, emerging with a Snapple bottle and popping it open.

"I run! In the morning!" Christie piped in overly loudly. "Sometimes."

"Yeah? We should go together sometime," Jonathan said, taking a sip of his drink.

Christie laughed so hard she let out a snort. Then she slapped her hand over her mouth and sat down at her oatmeal again, looking horrified. Aubrey sighed. She was never going to get these two together if Christie couldn't get comfortable around him. At least Jonathan was still smiling at Christie, so the snort hadn't totally turned him off.

"How was it? Your skate," Jonathan asked.

"Okay. Good," Aubrey said flatly, glancing at the clock on the wall. "I can't believe I was out there for over an hour."

"Then you'll have worked up an appetite," Rose said. "What do you like? Eggs? Oatmeal?

I can make pancakes."

"I'm totally in for pancakes," Jonathan said, pulling out the chair on Christie's other side and sitting down. Christie's blush deepened and she took a bite of her oatmeal.

Aubrey's stomach grumbled at the thought of a big stack of pancakes, but she reached for the bowl of fruit salad at the center of the table.

"I'm good with this," she said, serving up a heaping helping.

"No! You need more than that. It's cold out there. You need something warm in ya," Rose said, turning away from the stove for a moment to squeeze Aubrey's shoulder.

"Yeah, Aubrey. *Just* fruit salad?" Christie asked. "I've never seen you turn down a carb in your life."

Aubrey took a deep breath and toyed with the fraying edge of the red cotton placemat under her stoneware plate. She did not relish the thought of going back on her word. It was something she rarely, if ever, did. But if she had to, she might as well get it over with.

"Well, I don't want to be all bloated for the pageant," she said, casting a quick glance at Christie.

Her friend's dark eyes widened so fast Aubrey was afraid her face might break. "What?" Christie squealed.

Jim started and looked up from his paper as if he'd just realized there were other people in the room. "What just happened?"

"Aubrey's going to do the pageant!" Christie exclaimed. She threw her arms around Aubrey and squeezed her so hard she almost choked. "Thank you, thank you, thank you, thank you!"

"Wow. I guess you really wanted her to do the pageant," Jonathan joked.

"Oh, you have no idea!" Christie replied, forgetting to be nervous in all the excitement.

"Let go of her, dear. She's having trouble breathing," Rose said kindly, nudging Christie's shoulder. She placed a cup of steaming hot coffee in front of Aubrey and smiled.

"Oh my God. Sorry!" Christie leaned back and covered her mouth with both hands for a moment, her eyes dancing with glee. "What changed your mind?"

Aubrey's skin tingled at the memory of Grayson's laugh. The amused and triumphant look on Layla's face. "Let's just say I want to help you win and see you put Layla and that whole stupid family of hers in their place."

And maybe I'll come in second, she added silently. *Just to annoy them even more.*

But she promised herself right then that her only goal in all of this would be to help Christie win. Her friend had been dreaming about that crown for years, and Aubrey was not about to get in her way.

"Hear, hear!" Jim cheered, lifting his coffee mug.

"Don't we all," Rose muttered under her breath as she returned to the stove.

"What, Rose?" Christie asked, turning in her seat.

"Nothing!" Rose replied cheerily. She served up some eggs on two separate plates and added two slices of wheat toast, then placed the plates in front of Aubrey and Christie. "But you two are going to need your energy if you're going to take down Layla Chamberlain."

"The fix is in!" Jim added, his eyes back on his paper.

Jonathan laughed as Rose rolled her eyes fondly at her husband.

"Please. Christie can beat Layla any day of the week and twice on Sunday," Jonathan said.

Christie blushed so deeply Aubrey thought her friend might spontaneously combust. It was so obvious Jonathan liked her he may as well have had "I (heart) Christie" tattooed on his nose.

"Thanks," Christie said, so quietly it was barely audible.

"And you too, Aubrey," he added quickly, blushing as well.

"Yeah, yeah," Aubrey said lightly.

Rose patted Aubrey on the back. "Eat up."

Aubrey's willpower flew out the window at the sight of the scrambled eggs. Rose was right. If she was going to endure a full day of rehearsals with Layla and a whole mess of girls like her, she was going to need her strength.

"Thank you, Aubrey, really," Christie said, putting her hand over Aubrey's on the table. "This is going to be *so much fun!*"

Aubrey managed a smile. She wasn't sure about that assessment, but she knew there was one part of this whole endeavor that she would enjoy—seeing the look on Christie's face when she won that crown.

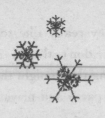

Chapter 4

The Chamberlain Ski Resort and Spa was built into the side of the mountain, its twelve-story façade rising up into the sky, its hundreds of plate-glass windows reflecting the glistening sun. Turrets and shingled roofs and private verandas overlooked the extensive grounds. Everything was pristine and beautiful.

The first things Aubrey noticed when she walked into the huge lobby were the two tremendous stone fireplaces flanking the room. The second thing she noticed was a large calendar of events for the month, posted on the wall across from the check-in desk. It seemed that there was something going on every day and night—events ranging from indoor water-polo matches to square dances to a silent auction and something called a Winter Ball.

"Wow. They really like to keep you busy around here, don't they?" Aubrey said to Christie, noting that tonight there was going to be a cocktail party and private concert in the main lounge.

"That's the Chamberlain for you," Christie said. "It's all about seeing and being seen." Her eyes narrowed as she looked over the schedule. "That's weird. They forgot to put the carnival on there."

"Why would they? Isn't it your grandparents' thing?" Aubrey asked.

"It's really a whole-town thing," Christie replied. "People come to Darling just for the carnival, so the Chamberlain always runs a shuttle over there. And it's also why they schedule the pageant for this week, because they know there will be tons of people around to buy tickets."

"Huh. Maybe you should tell someone it's not on there," Aubrey said.

"Yeah . . . maybe later," Christie said, glancing at her gold watch. "I don't want to be late for the first meeting."

Christie led Aubrey through the lobby and out the back door. Aubrey hesitated at the threshold, clinging to her white cotton cardigan.

"The meeting is outside?" she asked.

"It's at the amphitheater, where the pageant is always held," Christie said. She shot Aubrey a look of concern. "I told you to wear your coat."

Just suck it up, Aubrey told herself as a pair of chatting girls in furry boots and snow hats slid past them onto the cobblestone pathway outside. *How bad can it be?*

Aubrey held her breath and stepped outside, clutching her personal information form as if it could somehow keep her warm. On the form were written her name, birth date, year in high school, and some other vital information, including her measurements—something the pageant needed for some costume she had to wear. She hadn't had a clue what her measurements were, so Rose had taken them for her after breakfast, which was when Aubrey had learned that she had zero curves. None whatsoever.

"I didn't think I'd *need* a coat," Aubrey said as a stiff wind nearly blew the breath right out of her. The last thing she'd wanted to do was show up in her lumberjack gear and invite more insults from Layla and her friend Rebecca. Not to mention the fact that it didn't exactly seem like the type of outerwear a pageant girl would wear. She had thought she'd just have to go from the car to the hotel, not sit in the cold for an hour. "Why do they hold this thing outside? Doesn't everyone freeze?"

"They'll have heat lamps the night of the event," Christie said, looking perfectly toasty and warm in her own jacket. "Are you not wearing your coat because of what Layla and Rebecca said about it? Because your comfort is way more important than what other people think."

"I know," Aubrey said defensively, annoyed all over again that she had let Layla get to her. "That's not why I'm not wearing it," she lied. "I just thought we'd be inside."

They had just come to a fork in the path and the girls ahead of them veered off to the left. Aubrey could see the huge stone amphitheater down the hill with at least fifty rows of seating facing the stage. She gulped, imagining the place packed with spectators. Was it too late to back out of this?

"This thing doesn't, like, sell out, does it?" she asked Christie.

"Oh, every year," Christie replied casually. "Standing room only. That's why I'm so glad you're doing this with me. If you weren't, I'd definitely chicken out."

Right. You're doing this for Christie. Remember that, Aubrey told herself. *And so that she can win and Layla can watch it happen. And so that you can prove to Grayson that you can be a pageant girl.*

Every time Aubrey thought about the encounter with Grayson that morning, she felt a thrill of excitement followed by a rush of annoyance. The flirting had been fun, but why had he laughed about her being in the pageant? Was the idea of her as a beauty queen that hilarious? She had told Christie about the whole thing while they were getting ready to come to the meeting, and Christie had been thrilled that Grayson Chamberlain was the gorgeous boy from the lake. She had insisted that Gray was an incredible guy and was sure that Aubrey had taken his laughter the wrong way.

Aubrey hoped her friend was right, but Christie hadn't been there. She hadn't seen how humiliating the whole thing was.

Christie wrapped her arm around Aubrey's, which served, at least, to warm one side of Aubrey's body, and started down the hill toward the seating area. There were already about a dozen girls crowded into the center of the front row, Layla and Rebecca included, so Aubrey slipped in behind them and settled into a chair in the middle. Layla glanced over her shoulder as they sat. She was looking cozy in a gray fur jacket and matching earmuffs.

"Hey, FL, I know you surfer girls are supposed to be ditzy and all that, so I'll give you a helpful hint. It's called a coat."

Apparently Bitchy Layla was back in action. As she and the girls around her giggled, Aubrey tried to look unaffected by the cold. But her fingertips were starting to go numb. How long, exactly, did it take a person to develop frostbite?

"Ladies! Welcome one and all to the tenth annual Darling, Vermont, Snow Queen Pageant!"

Aubrey looked up at the stage to find a diminutive woman in a long, purple, faux-fur cape waltzing toward center stage. She wore a matching fur hat that stood up a good foot off her head, and so much makeup her face could have been a Halloween mask. Long, white silk gloves covered her arms, and her knee-high, mustard-colored heeled boots were decorated with long fringe. Her accent was somewhere between French and Russian, which made her ridiculously difficult to understand. The first words that popped into Aubrey's mind were "total nut job."

"*I* am *Fabrizia!*" she announced.

So this was the person Grayson and Layla had rushed off to greet that morning. That must have been one interesting breakfast.

"I will be your director, your guide, your mentor, and your big sister throughout the next two weeks," Fabrizia said, bringing her hands together. Every gesture she made was elegant and drawn out, like a dancer's, and each of her words took a good three seconds to sink into Aubrey's brain. She felt as if she was deciphering code as she listened to the director talk. "But before we get started, I would like to introduce to you my assistant director and the emcee for this year's pageant, Mr. Grayson Chamberlain!"

Those last two words, Aubrey understood perfectly. Her heart caught as Grayson strode out from the wings, wearing a black wool coat that made his blond hair look even lighter, and carrying a clipboard. He lifted a hand to acknowledge the smattering of applause from the audience.

"Thanks, everyone. It's good to be here, helping Fabrizia out," he said. "As most of you know, I usually act as a judge for this event, but since my little sister is competing this year . . ." Here he paused to point Layla out and she sat up straight, preening. ". . . I thought it would be best if I removed myself from the panel. So if you guys need anything, just let me know."

Grayson looked right at Aubrey and widened his smile. As irked as she still was by his reaction to her pageant-girl status that morning, Aubrey couldn't help smiling back. He was just that swoon-worthy. Then Layla turned around and gave Aubrey a sour look—which wiped the grin right off Aubrey's face. She sank in her seat slightly and then stayed there, realizing that the lower she sat, the more the wind was blocked by the seats around her. Grayson looked at her with a slight wrinkle in his brow and she started to feel conspicuous. Could he tell she was turning into an ice sculpture of herself out here?

"Now, to go through the order of events for this year's pageant program," Fabrizia said, lifting her own clipboard. She donned a pair of tiny, frameless glasses and looked down her nose at her schedule. "First will be the opening dance number, in which you will all participate."

"Dance number?" Aubrey hissed to Christie. "I don't dance."

"It'll be okay. I'll help you," Christie whispered back.

"Shhh!" Layla hissed.

Grayson jogged down the steps at the side of the stage and started walking up the aisle. All the girls were listening to Fabrizia but watching him. Not that Aubrey could blame them. No one could ignore a guy that perfect. Grayson's eyes were on Aubrey, however, and Aubrey alone. Her heart started to pound. What was he doing?

"Then we will have your introductions, followed by the evening-gown competition, the snowsuit competition—"

Snowsuits, okay, Aubrey thought as she began to shiver uncontrollably. *That's better than swimsuits, at least. I'd die out here in a swimsuit.*

Grayson slipped into the empty row of seats behind her and Christie. He shrugged out of his coat and slid it over her shoulders. Aubrey instantly warmed from head to toe. Part of her wanted to shrug the jacket off and hand it back, independent girl that she was, but the coat was all toasty from his body heat and she couldn't bring herself to remove it. The very idea that Grayson's warmth was now warming her made her giddy all over.

"Better?" he whispered in her ear.

A pleasant tingle ran all up and down the right side of her body.

"Much," she replied.

Christie shot Aubrey a giddy, impressed look, which made it much more difficult for Aubrey to keep from grinning. Layla, meanwhile, started to tap her foot in annoyance. Which just made the whole thing that much nicer.

"Then the talent competition," Fabrizia continued.

"What?" Aubrey blurted, sitting up straight.

Everyone laughed at her sudden outburst, including Grayson, who was now sitting behind her.

"Apparently someone has no talent," Rebecca said loudly, earning another round of giggles.

"Rebecca!" Layla scolded, glancing back at Grayson.

Aubrey bit her tongue to keep from snapping at the girl. Now she was *certain* that Layla was putting on a nice-girl act for her brother. There was no doubt in her mind that if Grayson had still been up on stage and out of earshot, Layla would have said the same thing as Rebecca had, or worse. But instead, she was acting as if Rebecca was being immature—and making sure that Grayson noticed.

Did Grayson know that his sister had two faces?

"Ladies, please! Let's settle down," Fabrizia said, holding her clipboard up. "And finally the interview portion."

"What am I supposed to do for talent?"

Aubrey whispered to Christie, glancing at Grayson out of the corner of her eye.

"You can sing. You're in the choir," Christie replied.

"Yeah, but there are a hundred other people in the choir, too. I just blend," Aubrey said through her teeth. "I've never done a solo."

"We'll figure it out. I promise," Christie said, keeping her eyes trained on Fabrizia, who was still talking. Something about etiquette and being a good sport, all of which was lost on Aubrey. She sat back in her seat, fuming. What had Christie gotten her into here? She had thought this was a beauty pageant. A lot of walking and posing and smiling. Not dancing and performing talents that she did not possess.

What I wouldn't give to be playing hockey right now, Aubrey thought, as the girls around her whispered and giggled and fixed their makeup.

For the rest of the meeting, Aubrey sat and stared at the vaulted roof over the stage, trying to imagine herself singing in front of hundreds of people. She couldn't think of a single song to which she knew all the words—other than "Jingle Bells" and "Happy Birthday." There was no way she could do this. Just no way.

Maybe Grayson had been right to laugh at her this morning. Clearly, she was not pageant-worthy.

"Okay, then, my little princesses! I will see you tomorrow for the first rehearsal!" Fabrizia said finally.

"Why is she calling us 'princesses'?" Aubrey asked.

"We're all snow princesses until one of us is named Snow Queen. That's how it works," Christie replied.

Great. Just what Aubrey had always wanted to be—a princess. Ugh.

"Make sure to give your measurements to my assistant director on the way out!" Fabrizia added.

Aubrey looked down at her crumpled piece of paper. She had to give this to Grayson? Grayson was going to know her measurements? Could this get any worse?

Everyone stood up. Aubrey and Christie

turned around to face Grayson.

"Hi, Gray!" Christie said with a smile. "How was your year?"

"Can't complain," Grayson replied. "I decided not to go to college this year, which of course made my father's head explode," he said. "That's actually why I'm emceeing the event. The guilt trip my mother laid on me was massive. Somehow my taking such an active role in her pet project is supposedly going to make up for my utter failure as a son."

Christie blinked, as if she was having trouble seeing the logic there. Which was, of course, the point. There was no logic there. "Well, it's going to be cool to have you around every day," Christie said finally. She glanced at Aubrey. "So I guess you've met my friend."

"Ah, yes. I've had the extreme pleasure," he said, looking at Aubrey in a way that made her heart flutter. "So. Measurements?" he said, holding out his hand. Suddenly there was a wicked smile on his face. Aubrey could only imagine how a hot guy like him enjoyed this part of his job. A couple dozen beautiful girls handing over the intimate details of their bods? It was probably a dream come true.

She narrowed her eyes at him. "I don't think so."

"Come on. I promise I won't look at it," he said.

"Sure you won't," Aubrey replied.

"Hey, haven't I proven I'm a gentleman yet? I gave you my coat," he pointed out.

Aubrey heaved a sigh. "Fine."

She grabbed Christie's sheet out of her hand, placed it on top of her own, and handed them both over. Grayson attached them to his clipboard without so much as glancing down.

"Hey, Grayson, on our way in we noticed that the carnival isn't on the calendar of events in the lobby," Christie said. "You should probably tell someone about that or the guests are gonna get confused."

"Forget confused, they're gonna revolt," Grayson said with a laugh. "Thanks for the tip." He looked at Aubrey. "So, the talent thing came out of left field for you, huh?" he asked as the other contestants walked by and handed over their sheets.

"That? Oh, no. I was just . . . thinking about

something else," Aubrey said, a blush rising to her cheeks. The last thing she wanted to do was prove his preconceived notions about her. She put her hands on her hips under his coat. "Of course I have talents."

"I'm sure you do. But just so you know, my parents have been forcing me to either watch this pageant or judge it for the last ten years," Grayson told her. "So if you need help coming up with something, I'm your guy."

Aubrey was sure her skin was about to melt off her face. How pathetic did he think she was? "I don't have to *come up* with something," she blurted. "I told you, I plan to kick butt in this pageant."

"I believe you!" he said, lifting his hand in surrender.

Why was it that whenever he said that, it seemed as if he actually *didn't* believe her?

"Come on, Christie," Aubrey said, hooking one arm around Christie's and using the other to whip Grayson's coat off from around her shoulders. The cold rushed in on her like a freight train, and she used every ounce of her self-control to keep from shivering as she handed the coat back to him. "Let's go home and start practicing. Rehearsing. Whatever."

"Bye, Grayson!" Christie shouted over her shoulder as Aubrey pulled her away.

"Why did you have to say good-bye to him?" Aubrey asked under her breath.

"I'm confused. I thought you liked him," Christie replied, stumbling to keep up.

"I do. Or I did," Aubrey said, struggling to explain. "Sometimes I do."

"Sometimes? You just met him," Christie pointed out.

"Can we analyze my insanity later?" Aubrey said, quickening her steps as they headed up the hill. "Right now all I can think about is getting inside."

And maybe snagging some hot chocolate and a nice wool blanket, she added silently.

Aubrey had to warm herself up as quickly as possible. Otherwise she was going to spend the rest of the day fantasizing about the warmth of Grayson's coat, the sweetness of his gesture, and the way he made her feel—both giddy and self-conscious. The way no other guy had ever made her feel before.

* * *

Late that night, Aubrey sat in one of the cush-
ioned chairs in the Spotted Owl's dining room,
staring out the huge plate-glass window at the
carnival grounds and the stars blanketing the
sky above. The view was as clear as crystal. Not
a cloud in sight. She heaved a sigh and rested
her chin in her hands, her elbows on the win-
dowsill. Still no snow, and no sign of any sort
of inclement weather. If the whole two weeks
passed without a flake, she was not going back
to Florida. She would hop the next flight to
Canada. Or Iceland. Or the Arctic Circle. However far north she had to go to see snow, she
would go there.

"Aubrey? A little help over here?"

Aubrey pulled her attention from the night
sky and turned around. It was after ten, so the
dining room was closed to guests, and Rose and
Jim had converted it into an arts-and-crafts
workspace for the evening. Strewn over the
inn's dozen dining tables were all kinds of art
supplies: colorful sheets of paper, jars of paint
and paintbrushes, glitter and foam and stencils.
Jonathan and Charlie were at a table across the

room, constructing the frame for a raffle ticket booth, while Aubrey and Christie were supposed to be painting signs. Instead Aubrey had spent the last ten minutes staring into space, and Christie was now struggling with the lid on a jar of red paint, her face screwing up unattractively from the effort of trying to open it.

"Sorry." Aubrey scooted off her chair and walked over to her friend, holding her hand out for the jar. "I've got it."

"Thank you," Christie sighed as she gratefully gave up the losing battle.

"Christie, why don't you go over and help Jonathan?" Aubrey whispered.

Christie's blush was instantaneous. "Just go over there? No. I couldn't."

Aubrey saw that her friend had already outlined all the letters for the raffle ticket sign and just needed the red paint to fill them in. She twisted the white cap, but it wouldn't budge.

"Why not? Charlie's over there if you need a buffer, and we're all just hanging out," Aubrey said. "You're not gonna find a more pressure-free moment."

Taking a deep breath and holding it, she tried

the cap again. Nothing.

"You think?" Christie said, biting her lip as she glanced across the room.

"Definitely." She grunted as she tried again. Her fingers were already smarting from the grooves on the lid. "There must be some dried paint under there or something."

"I'll go run it under some warm water," Christie offered.

"Oh no. You're not fooling anyone with that. You're gonna go talk to Jonathan. I got it. One more try," Aubrey said.

She held her breath, gripped the lid, and turned. The lid started to give and she smiled triumphantly just as Grayson sauntered through the door.

"Hey, everyone! Need some help?"

Aubrey was so surprised to see him, she forgot what she was doing. The lid twisted off and spun right out of her sweaty grip. Then it all happened in a flash. Aubrey grabbed for the lid, the jar of paint tipped, she saw that it was going to spill all over Christie's sign and tried to stop it, but managed only to fling it faster, which caused the paint to spatter in a huge arc, taking out not only the unfinished sign, but tons of paper and supplies as well. Christie and Grayson jumped back, out of the spray, but for the table it was too late. Everything was ruined.

Aubrey's heart pounded. Everyone in the room froze. Then Grayson dropped his hands at his sides.

"So. It's the postmodernist approach to carnival signage," he said dryly.

Aubrey felt a laugh bubble up in her throat. Across the room, Charlie and Jonathan cheered and applauded for Aubrey's stunning lack of coordination, although it was a tad difficult for Charlie, who was nursing a newly broken finger, thanks to another snowboarding mishap. Christie stepped forward carefully to survey the damage.

"Oh my gosh, Christie, I'm so sorry!" Aubrey said, bringing her hands to her mouth. "All that work!"

"It's okay," Christie said with a shrug. "I wasn't happy with it anyway. The lines weren't perfectly straight."

"Okay, Martha Stewart," Grayson joked, walking over and patting her on the back. He rubbed his hands together and looked down at the smears of red paint. "Want me to go get something to clean this up?"

Christie glanced at Aubrey. "No! That's okay. I'll go!" she said. She pulled a large garbage can over to the side of the table. "Why don't you guys toss anything we can't use and I'll go get some paper towels and water?"

"No. Christie!" Aubrey said through her teeth. She knew her friend was trying to get out of talking to Jonathan *and* trying to leave Aubrey alone with Grayson at the same time. But Christie was already on her way out of the room. "Hey, Jonathan! Why don't you go help Christie!" Aubrey shouted.

Christie froze and shot Aubrey a look of death.

"I'm on it!" Jonathan said, dropping his side of the booth so that Charlie had to struggle to keep it from crashing to the floor.

"Um . . . thanks," Christie said, ducking her head as she rushed out. Jonathan followed like a little puppy dog. Aubrey grinned triumphantly.

"What's up, Gray?" Charlie called out, doing

that whole chin-jerk thing guys all over the world seemed to do by way of greeting.

"Hey, man." Grayson placed his hands in his pockets and copied the chin jerk. Aubrey expected him to go help Charlie, especially since Jonathan had deserted him, but instead he stepped up to the table and swept a whole mess of paint-spattered poster board into the trash. Interesting. Apparently she was more appealing than Charlie. "Not having a very 'green' moment here, are we?" he joked.

Aubrey clucked her tongue. "I feel so bad. I hope they have more supplies."

"Don't worry. The Howells are always prepared. They're like a boy-scout troop that way." Grayson grinned.

"Good to know," Aubrey said with a laugh. She picked up a tube of glitter that was covered in red and sloughed off the paint into the garbage can. "So, what are you doing here, anyway?"

Grayson shrugged. "Came by to help with the carnival prep."

"Really? Isn't there some big hoedown happening at your parents' resort tonight?"

Aubrey asked, remembering the cocktail party on the calendar in the lobby.

"Oh, there's always some big *something* happening over at the CSRS," Grayson said in a facetious tone. "All the more reason to be here."

Aubrey smiled to herself as she swiped some more paper into the trash. "So you weren't kidding when you said you liked the vibe here."

"Why would I be kidding? I am not an organized-activity type of guy," Grayson said, holding his arms out at his sides. "The Spotted Owl is much more my speed. Chill. Calm. Hoedown-free."

"Yeah. I like a good hoedown-free zone myself," Aubrey replied, grinning.

"So that's something we have in common," Grayson said, looking her in the eye. Aubrey's heart did a series of backflips and she tried not to blush. He glanced around the dining room and crossed his arms over his chest with a sigh. "It's just too bad that—"

He stopped talking abruptly and blushed. Aubrey eyed him quizzically.

"It's just too bad that what?" she asked.

"Nothing," he said, looking away. He closed his eyes and scratched his forehead, obviously stalling. "I lost my train of thought. Does that ever happen to you?"

"All the time," Aubrey said, though she was still convinced he'd simply been on the verge of saying something he didn't want to say. But she wasn't about to grill a guy she'd just met about such things. Instead, she decided to help him by changing the subject.

"I think we got it all. We just need those paper towels," she said, glancing past him toward the door where Christie and Jonathan had long since disappeared. Grayson appeared relieved, but then his eyes narrowed.

"Oh, uh, you got a little something there," Grayson said, wrinkling his nose and pointing at her face.

Aubrey's hand went to her cheek. That was when she realized her fingers were covered in red paint. She could feel the sticky wetness all over her skin. She must have left a streak there when she'd touched her hair, but now it was everywhere.

"Oh my God."

"Yeah, you just made it *a lot* worse," Grayson said with a laugh.

"Shut up!" Aubrey replied, laughing through her embarrassment.

"I'm back!" Christie announced, bounding through the door with a couple of rolls of towels. Jonathan followed behind with a bucket of water. Christie took one look at Aubrey and her face fell. "What did you do to yourself?"

"Here." Grayson reached for the bucket of water and took one of the towel rolls. He dunked a balled-up paper towel into the water and leaned forward as if to clean Aubrey's face. She looked him in the eye and they both froze. Aubrey didn't know what to do. Was Grayson really going to clean her face for her?

"Um, here," he said, backing off and handing her the dripping towel. "I guess you should do that."

"Yeah. Probably," Aubrey said, chuckling.

She wiped her face with the towel while Christie directed her, glancing over every now and again at Grayson. He pretended to be busying himself with wiping down the table, but he kept glancing over at her as well. And was that a blush on his handsome, stubbly cheeks?

"There is *such* a vibe between you two," Christie whispered to Aubrey.

"You think?" Aubrey asked, biting her lip.

"Totally." She clapped her hands together noiselessly, her back to Grayson. "Winter carnival romance!" she whispered.

"I'll just leave this here," Jonathan said, placing the bucket on the floor. He'd obviously grown weary of being ignored and he walked across the room to rejoin Charlie.

"Go after him," Aubrey said to Christie, her heart fluttering as Grayson glanced at her over Christie's shoulder.

"What? No. We have to redo the signs," Christie protested.

"Grayson and I can do it," Aubrey said loudly. "Right?" she asked him.

"Oh, definitely," Grayson said, holding up a pencil. "Don't worry about it, Christie. I am a stickler for straight lines."

Christie looked over at Jonathan and hesitated until Aubrey shoved her in the small of her back and made her move. "You can do this," she whispered in her friend's ear. "You're gonna be the Snow Queen, Chris. Any guy would die to have you."

Christie grinned at this. "You're right," she said, lifting her chin. "I'm going in."

Aubrey smiled as her friend walked across the room, her head held high. Then she turned to look at Grayson, her own heart skipping a beat. There *was* a vibe between her and Grayson, wasn't there?

"So, you wanna stencil or paint?" he asked, lifting his eyebrows.

"Paint. Definitely. I am *not* a straight-line girl," she replied.

"I'm not a straight-line guy, either. I was just trying to get rid of her," he joked.

Aubrey laughed and found a clean piece of poster board. Grayson whistled as he grabbed a ruler and stencil. He was different from any guy she had ever known. Self-assured, mature, sarcastic, funny. Plus he was obviously a strong-willed person like herself, not going along with every little thing his family planned. And yeah, maybe he was always catching her in ridiculous situations, but so far none of that had seemed to bother him. The guys back home would have been mocking her endlessly for her many pratfalls, but not Grayson. Grayson just kept looking at her as if she was the prettiest girl in the room, even though she had red paint in her hair and Christie was over there looking perfectly put together.

Trying to stifle a smile, Aubrey bent over the table to get to work, her leg brushing Grayson's. She had come here for the snow, not for a boyfriend. But if she couldn't have one, maybe she would try out the other.

Chapter 5

"*I*'m sorry, but could it be any more obvious that Fabrizia is trying to shove Layla Chamberlain in the judges' faces?" Aubrey ranted as she and Christie walked into the Spotted Owl's lobby on Monday afternoon. She dropped her duffel bag on one of the couches near the fireplace and wriggled out of her brown coat. "She made absolutely sure that Madeline had Layla front and center throughout the entire dance sequence!"

"Aubrey, calm down," Christie said, laying her hands out flat. She placed her pink dance bag down next to Aubrey's and glanced over at the front desk, where Jonathan was chatting with a couple of guests. "Madeline is a world-class choreographer. I'm sure she wouldn't change her work unless she thought the changes made sense for the piece."

Aubrey guffawed as she lifted her arm overhead to stretch out. Her roller-hockey T-shirt was stuck to her skin with patches of sweat that peeled off as she moved. She'd had no idea that a two-hour dance rehearsal was going to be so labor-intensive.

"You're crazy! Both those women are having their paychecks signed by the Chamberlains and they are making damn sure that the judges have their eyes trained on Layla as much as possible," she said, fuming. "You're the one who should be front and center. You're a way better dancer than Layla."

"You think?" Christie asked, turning pink with pleasure. She dropped down on one of the overstuffed plaid chairs facing the stone fireplace.

"*Beyond* better," said Aubrey, looking out the window at the bright-blue, snow-free sky. She toyed with the strings hanging from the open blinds, her mind working overtime. What if Jim's paranoia wasn't paranoia at all, but good instincts? What if the fix *was* in? There was no way she was going to let nepotism get in the way of Christie winning the pageant. "Tomorrow we have to find a way to get them to notice you and put you in the front line. You need to have the spotlight on you if you're going to win."

"What about you? You should be in front too," Christie said, sitting forward.

Aubrey laughed. "Please. If they put me in front I'd twirl the wrong way and fall off the stage. Trust me. No one wants to be watching *me*."

Christie smiled slyly. "That's not exactly true," she said in a leading way, gazing up at Aubrey. "There was one person there who couldn't take his eyes off you."

Aubrey blushed as she twisted the string around her finger. Grayson had been sitting in the audience throughout the rehearsal, and Aubrey *had* noticed that he seemed to be watching her quite a lot. Every time she looked over at him he had his eyes on her, actually. She had been both flattered and seriously distracted. In fact, now that she thought back, she wasn't sure if she could remember a single dance move she'd learned.

She looked over her shoulder at Christie and caught her staring longingly at Jonathan. "Why don't you go talk to him?" she suggested.

"I can't," Christie protested.

"Why not? It went fine last night, didn't it?" Aubrey asked. "You guys were cracking each other up for, like, an hour."

"Yeah, I guess . . ." Christie said, blushing. "So can't I just rest on my laurels or whatever?"

"No. You cannot. We're only here for two weeks. You rest too long and all you'll *have* is laurels," Aubrey said with a laugh. "Whatever that means." The couple Jonathan was talking to picked up their skis and walked off. "Look, he's alone now. Just go over and say hi."

Christie considered for a moment, then stood up with a grin. "Okay. But you're coming with me."

Aubrey rolled her eyes, smiling at her friend's predictability. "Fine. Let's go."

"Hello, ladies," Jonathan said as they approached. He grinned and tapped the desktop with his pen. "How was practice? You scare off the competition yet?" he asked, looking right at Christie.

Christie opened her mouth to respond, when suddenly they all froze. Angry voices rose up from behind the closed door behind the front desk. Aubrey glanced at Christie. Rose and Jim were in the office arguing with a third person, but because of the closed door, Aubrey couldn't make out anything. Then, suddenly, the door was flung open and out stormed a woman in a winter-white suit, her brown hair pulled back in a bun.

"That's my final word," she snapped, folding her wool coat over her arm. "If I were you I'd start thinking about a new source of revenue."

She blew right past Aubrey, Christie, and Jonathan without so much as a glance and stalked out the front door. Rose and Jim emerged from the office, saw the girls standing there, and exchanged a defeated look.

"What was that all about?" Christie asked. "Why is Mrs. Chamberlain so angry?"

Aubrey glanced at the front door. The woman with all the fury was Grayson's mother?

Jim took a deep breath and shook his head. "We have to tell her, Rose."

Rose clucked her tongue and looked away. Aubrey's pulse started to race. There was something very not good going on around here.

"Tell me what?" Christie asked, her voice growing tense.

"Mr. and Mrs. Chamberlain have decided to stop supporting the winter carnival," Jim grumbled.

"What does that mean?" Christie asked.

"It means they're not going to advertise it; they're not going to run their shuttle over here. . . . They're basically going to ignore its existence," Rose replied wearily.

"And schedule as many highfalutin events at their resort as possible next week so that all the guests will want to stay there and not spend their money here," Jim added, pressing his fists into the top of the desk.

"I don't believe it," Jonathan said. "But half the people who come to Darling next week come for the carnival."

"Well, the Chamberlains are hoping to change all that," Jim replied.

Christie looked as if she was about to cry. "But the Chamberlain is huge. If no one comes to the carnival from the resort . . ."

"We're screwed," Jonathan finished for her.

"You said it." Jim blew out a sigh as he sat

down on one of the high stools behind the front desk, right next to Jonathan.

"So . . . why don't you run your own shuttle?" Aubrey suggested. "You don't need their stupid vans."

"Actually, we do," Rose replied. "You've seen the state of our van. It's about ten miles away from breaking down for good. Plus Charlie has class at night, so we'd have to hire someone to drive it . . . *and* it's a gas guzzler."

"We'd need a new, larger van and someone to man it," Jim said. "And we just don't have the money to pay for either."

"I'll drive it," Jonathan offered. "I'll do it for free."

Christie beamed at him as if he was Superman swooping in to save them all.

"That's sweet, Jon, but you're already working enough hours before and after school," Rose said, placing her hand on his back. "Besides, like Jim said, we don't have anything for you to drive."

"We were planning on using the carnival revenue to fix the rusted-out pipes on the north side of the inn," Jim explained. "But with the carnival standing to make less this year thanks to the Chamberlains, we might not even be able to do that, let alone buy a van for next year."

Aubrey's heart felt heavy. No wonder Rose had seemed so uncertain that first day when she was talking about the plumbing. Aubrey had *known* that everything was not okay.

"And if we can't fix the plumbing in all those rooms," Rose said slowly, casting a sad look at Jim, "we may have to close the Spotted Owl."

"What?" Christie and Jonathan said in unison.

"Which is, of course, exactly what the Chamberlains want. Then they'd be the only hotel on the mountain," Jim said bitterly.

Christie's eyes filled with tears, and an awful, sour feeling filled Aubrey's chest. Did Grayson know about this? If he loved the Spotted Owl so much, why hadn't he warned Jim and Rose this was happening? Or had all of that crap about liking the vibe here just been a lie?

Then, suddenly, a warm rush of realization came over Aubrey. Last night, she and Grayson had been talking about how much he liked the Spotted Owl, when he'd looked around in a nostalgic way and started to say something, but stopped himself.

It's just too bad that . . .

That what? That the place was about to be shut down by his parents? Aubrey's face burned at the realization. No wonder he had clammed up. He didn't want Aubrey to hear about his parents' insidious plans and run back to the Howells with the news.

I'm crushing on a two-faced jerk, Aubrey thought angrily.

"But you guys have owned this place forever," Jonathan said.

"Yeah, they can't just run you out of business," Aubrey added, her fists clenching.

Jim and Rose looked at each other; then Rose took a deep breath. "Listen, you kids shouldn't worry about this. We didn't intend to burden you with our problems. We're sorry you overheard anything."

Jim stood up and cleared his throat, shoving his hands into the pockets of his corduroys. "Rose is right. This is our issue and we'll figure out a way to fix it." He touched his wife's arm. "Come on, Rose. Let's go take a look at those numbers again."

Rose gave Christie a hug before walking back into the office with Jim and closing the door.

"Are you okay?" Jonathan asked Christie from the opposite side of the desk, his expression concerned.

"I just don't believe this," Christie breathed, shaking her head. "I can't imagine not having the Spotted Owl. And I've never seen those two so stressed out."

"I'm sure they'll come up with something," Aubrey assured her friend. "It's gonna be okay."

Suddenly Christie snapped to, as if she'd just come out of a daydream. She looked at Aubrey and Jonathan, a brightness in her eyes. "Yeah. It is going to be okay. I'm going to make it okay." She walked past Aubrey, heading for the stairs.

"Um, how, exactly?" Aubrey asked, chasing after her.

Christie stopped in her tracks and whirled around. "I am going to win that pageant," she said firmly, lifting her chin. "And I'm going to take the prize money and give it to my grandparents. Let them use the Chamberlains' own money to fix the pipes and put a down payment on a shuttle van. That'll show those jerks."

"Nice!" Jonathan shouted after them.

Aubrey smiled. That *would* show those jerks. Mrs. Chamberlain, Layla, Grayson . . . *all* of them.

"Wow," Aubrey said. "I've never seen you like this before. I like it."

Christie smiled. "Me too. Now come on. We have a lot of work to do."

"Dana! You're supposed to move stage left, not stage right," Layla snapped, causing Dana, the petite blonde she was confronting, to take a few startled steps backward. "You're not even listening to Madeline."

Layla was wearing black spandex pants that were so tight they were lewd, and a cropped red sweatshirt over a white tank top. Her brown hair was up in a high ponytail, and gold hoops dangled from her ears. She looked more like a streetwalker than a snow queen.

"Sorry, Layla! Sorry," Dana said meekly, endeavoring to smile.

"No one *can* listen to Madeline because

Layla's too busy shouting at all of us," Aubrey said under her breath.

"You said it, sister," said the newly defiant Christie.

It was Tuesday morning and Aubrey was right smack in the middle of the dance rehearsal from hell. For the last hour she had watched Layla order girls around, adjust their arms for them, and criticize everyone within shouting distance, as if she was running the show. Every time the girl opened her mouth and no one said anything to stop her, Aubrey was that much more convinced that Fabrizia and Madeline were afraid of her—that, perhaps, Layla's parents had told the director and the choreographer to *let* the girl run the show.

Aubrey glanced out at the front row of seats where Grayson usually sat, but he wasn't there. If he had been in attendance, she was sure that Layla would not have been acting this way, and she wondered why he had skipped rehearsal. But then she remembered she wasn't supposed to care.

We're hating the Chamberlains, remember? she told herself. *All the Chamberlains.*

"And *why* did you put Christie in the front row?" Layla demanded of Madeline. "It's too crowded up here now."

"More like you're feeling threatened because she's a better dancer than you are," Aubrey said under her breath.

Layla shot her a look that could have melted the steel blades of her ice skates. Aubrey simply smirked in response. Before rehearsal had started she had made Christie go over the steps with her center stage, knowing that Madeline was watching from the wings. Christie had come off looking like a pro, and as soon as rehearsal had started, Madeline had moved Christie front and center, where she *should* be. Aubrey was still giddy that her plan had worked. And clearly, Layla was *not*.

"Shall we take it from the top?" Madeline asked from her position in front of the stage. The slight dance instructor had blond hair shorn very close to her head, and the biggest green eyes Aubrey had ever seen. At that moment, however, those big green eyes looked baggy and exhausted. Shocking, considering she was having to do her job around an obnoxious know-it-all like Layla Chamberlain.

"Yes, let's," Layla said.

Aubrey's fingers curled into fists. "She wasn't asking your permission."

Layla shot Aubrey another irritated look over her shoulder.

"Five, six, seven, eight!" Madeline called out.

The music started and Aubrey launched into her steps as best she could. She had never taken a formal dance lesson in her life and was still playing catch-up, while everyone around her seemed as if they could do the routine in their sleep— everyone except Dana, who was as mixed-up as Aubrey was. Aubrey felt almost grateful that she was dancing right behind Layla. At least the girl's big hair would camouflage her a bit.

Still, Aubrey was starting to get the hang of it. At the very least, she was improving. She'd just started to feel proud of herself, when she executed a spin move and found herself facing the wrong direction. Suddenly, a foot came down right on top of her pinkie toe.

"Ow!" Aubrey cried, lifting her foot.

Layla, the owner of the offending foot, threw her hands up. "I cannot work like this!" She turned toward the wings, where Fabrizia was watching the rehearsal, her trusty clipboard in hand. "Can we rethink the whole 'everyone has to be in the opening dance number' thing? Aubrey's serious lack of rhythm is messing everyone up."

Aubrey's jaw dropped. She was about to respond, but Grayson beat her to the punch. Apparently, he had just arrived when Aubrey's attention had been elsewhere.

"Layla, is that really necessary?" he asked, walking down the aisle toward the stage.

For a moment Aubrey felt as if she'd won some small battle as Grayson defended her to his sister. But then she realized he hadn't actually said that Layla was *wrong* about her lack of rhythm. And besides, she was supposed to be angry at him. She was supposed to be angry at the entire Chamberlain family and everything they represented.

"Sorry, Grayson," Layla said, her eyes wide and innocent. "It's just . . . I want this pageant to be the best it can be."

"I know. You're a perfectionist," Grayson said fondly, smiling up at Layla from the front row.

Layla grinned back, all sweetness and light.

Aubrey's jaw dropped. How could he be so totally blind to her bitchiness? Layla was so fake around her brother it was ridiculous. And he bought her act like it was five-cent candy.

But then, he was a two-faced jerk too. Maybe it was just a trait that ran in the family.

"All right, everyone, let's take a ten-minute break!" Fabrizia called out, raising her arms in the air.

Layla turned on her heel, her ponytail whipping around, and strode off the stage to the left. Aubrey pivoted in the other direction and, along with Christie, strode off stage right, which put her in the unfortunate position of having to walk past Grayson. He turned toward her as she approached, making it obvious he wanted to talk to her. Aubrey's pulse pounded in her temples and sweat slicked her palms. But she was not going to stop. Not for a Chamberlain. No matter how annoyingly gorgeous he was.

As she slipped by him, Grayson's smile turned into a crease of confusion.

"Aubrey, is something—"

She stopped in her tracks and Christie

barreled right into her, slamming into her arm. Aubrey stared him down.

"Sorry. I don't have time for lying hypocrites right now," she said.

Grayson's mouth opened, but no sound came out. Aubrey grabbed Christie's hand in solidarity and kept walking up the aisle. She should have known that someone that hot couldn't possibly be a good guy.

Chapter 6

𝒯he dressing room backstage was a long, wide, low-ceilinged space with two entrances, centered by a row of well-lit mirrors, each with a plush stool situated before it. Each of the snow princesses had claimed one mirror as her own, and the counter space in front of the mirrors was starting to become cluttered with all kinds of colorful, fragrant paraphernalia. Makeup kits, tubs of lip gloss and moisturizer, perfume atomizers, eyelash curlers, straightening irons, tubes and palettes and bottles and brushes. Tons of stuff Aubrey had never even heard of before, let alone used. Every time she walked inside the room, she felt a little bit more claustrophobic, a tad more intimidated, and a pinch more irritated that she had let herself get sucked into this world.

It wasn't that she detested all girlie things,

but this was girlie overkill.

"My feet are killing me," Aubrey said, dropping down on her stool and carefully removing her toes from her black, high-heeled sling backs. Christie had coaxed her into packing them back in Florida, saying they might go out for a nice dinner one night. Now, in retrospect, Aubrey realized she had been played. Christie had known she would need these shoes for the pageant. Who knew her best friend could be so sneaky? "How do people walk around in these things all day?"

"Come on. It's not that bad," Christie replied, perching on her own stool.

"Please. I've only spent two hours in these little torture devices and I'm ready to toss them in the Spotted Owl's fireplace when we get home," Aubrey grumbled.

Christie smiled and shook her head fondly. The day's rehearsal had just ended, and she and Aubrey were the first to return to the dressing room, but the place was gradually filling up with chatter and laughter and spritzes of deodorant and perfume. Aubrey dropped her shoes on the counter in front of her mirror along with the half-empty bottle of Gatorade, her Mariners baseball cap, and her small pink-and-white-striped makeup case, which she'd gotten free with a purchase at Victoria's Secret last fall. Green velour pajama bottoms. So comfy. Aubrey groaned in longing just thinking about them. She rubbed her aching arches and put her cheek down on the white lacquered countertop, feeling sorry for herself. The problem was, she couldn't quite figure out why she was feeling sorry for herself. It wasn't as if she had never had sore feet before.

"What's wrong?" Christie asked.

"I don't know. I feel all . . . blah," Aubrey replied, turning so that her chin was down and she could see just her eyes and forehead in the mirror. "What's my problem?"

"Um . . . maybe it's this sudden cold front between you and Grayson?" Christie suggested, touching some Vaseline to her lips. "What's going on there?"

"Nothing. And that's definitely not what I'm upset about," Aubrey said, sitting up straight. "Grayson Chamberlain can kiss my butt."

"What? I thought you liked him," Christie

said, dropping the tube of Vaseline on her counter. "Or are we back to 'sometimes'?" she joked.

"No. We're on 'never.' It's not like I'm going to be canoodling with the enemy," Aubrey whispered, glancing around. Luckily all the other girls seemed to be too involved trading makeup tips and gossiping about one another to care what she and Christie were whispering about. "What kind of friend do you think I am?"

Christie's pretty brow creased. "I'm confused. Why is Grayson the enemy?"

"Hello? His family is trying to shut down your family's business!" Aubrey whispered harshly.

Christie laughed and started to toss her makeup back into her big silver bag, one tube at a time. "So? That's not Grayson. That's his parents."

"Yeah, but he knew all about it and he didn't even warn your grandparents, who he supposedly likes and respects," Aubrey replied.

"How do you know he knew?" Christie asked.

"Just something he said. Or didn't say," Aubrey told her, sitting up and toying with the Gatorade bottle. "I don't know."

"Um, yeah. Whatever happened to innocent until proven guilty?" Christie suggested.

Aubrey scoffed. "Please."

"I'm serious! Grayson is . . . different from the rest of his family," Christie said under her breath, eyeing Layla in the mirror. The girl was standing near the wall a few feet away, checking out her eyebrows in a compact mirror. "Why don't you just ask him about it?"

"Just walk up to him and ask him if he knew his parents were trying to ruin your grandparents' lives," Aubrey said skeptically.

"Well, maybe not in *those* words. But ignoring him is just . . . immature." She glanced at Aubrey and bit her lip. "Sorry."

Aubrey blew out a sigh, but said nothing. She had an awful twisting feeling in her gut that was telling her Christie was right and she was wrong. And she hated that feeling.

"I'm gonna go down to the lobby. I'll meet you there," she told Christie. She shoved all her stuff into her duffel bag and turned around to go, slamming right into Layla, who had just stepped away from the wall. Layla's compact went flying and the mirror shattered into about a zillion pieces on the floor. A couple of girls screeched and jumped out of the way as if someone had just tossed a stink bomb into the room.

"Look what you did!" Layla blurted. "Why are you even here? Why can't you just go back to Florida where you belong?"

The room, which had been noisier than an NHL playoff game two seconds earlier, was now dead silent. Aubrey knew they were dying for a catfight, but she was not a catfight kind of girl. She rolled her eyes and walked past Layla into the hallway.

"I asked you a question."

Aubrey stopped in her tracks. She couldn't believe that Layla had actually followed her. She ever so slowly turned around.

"What?" she asked.

"Why are you even here?" Layla asked, her voice much lower. She was dead serious. She really wanted to know. "You may be fooling Grayson, but don't try telling me a tomboy like you really wants to be Snow Queen. You'd be much happier cross-checking some guy into the boards."

Aubrey hesitated, surprised and impressed that Layla even knew about cross-checking and boards. For a moment, she let her guard down. "I'm here for Christie, all right? I promised her I'd help her win."

And beat you, she added silently.

"Aw. That's so sweet," Layla said. She narrowed her eyes. "But I'm not buying it."

"But I—"

"Look, if you're here for Grayson, I'm just going to ask you once . . . politely . . . to back off," Layla said.

Aubrey snorted a laugh. Christie stepped out into the hallway behind Layla but held back in silence, recognizing that there was a standoff going on.

"How was that polite?" Aubrey asked Layla.

"Believe me, it was," Layla said. Aubrey stared at Layla for a moment, refusing to be the first to break eye contact. Then, out of nowhere, Layla's eyes softened and she quickly glanced away. "I'm serious, Aubrey. The last thing Grayson needs right now is to get played by some tourist."

Aubrey's jaw clenched. Her fingers tightened

around the handles on her duffel bag. "I'm not here for your brother," she said through her teeth.

"Good," Layla said, tossing her hair back. "I hope you mean that. Because I'm going to be watching you."

With a fling of her ponytail, Layla turned and brushed by Christie, who was strolling back into the dressing room.

"What was *that* all about?" Christie asked.

"That was about Layla bossing everybody around. As usual," Aubrey griped. "Come on. Let's get out of here." They started down the hall together, leaving the chatter of the dressing room behind. "So, what did Layla mean by 'the last thing he needs right now'?" Aubrey asked.

"Oh, she was probably talking about Sophia," Christie said, waving a hand as if it meant nothing.

"Sophia?" Aubrey asked.

"Grayson's ex. They were together for, like, *ever*, but I heard from one of the girls that she broke up with him before she left for school in August," Christie explained. "I guess Layla thinks he's not over it yet."

"Oh," Aubrey said.

"I know you think Layla's a total jerk, but she and Grayson have always been close. She really cares about her brother," Christie said. "I guess she doesn't want to see him get hurt."

"Well, I'm not going to be hurting anyone," Aubrey replied, running her finger along the wall as they walked. "But just out of curiosity . . . what was this Sophia girl like?"

"Oh, she and Layla were complete BFFs. Sophia actually won Snow Queen last year," Christie said. "She was *so* pretty. And smart. She goes to Brown now."

"Really?" Aubrey said, feeling a pang of jealousy in her chest. So Grayson really did like the pageant-girl type. Beautiful and poised and perfect. Good thing she didn't like him anymore. It sounded like there was no way she would ever be able to measure up to Grayson's ex.

Christie's face fell when she saw Aubrey's grim expression. "But don't worry. I never really thought they went together anyway," she added quickly. "Besides, I thought you didn't care about him anymore," Christie teased, nudging Aubrey with her elbow.

"I don't!" Aubrey said quickly, annoyed that she'd let her feelings show through. "I don't. I told you, he's the enemy. I am officially done thinking about Grayson Chamberlain."

"This place has the best selection of snow gear in town," Rose said, holding the door of Tucker's Ski Shop open for Aubrey and Christie. "You girls should definitely be able to find something for the pageant here."

Aubrey looked around the airy shop, and her tightly wound shoulder muscles instantly relaxed. She felt more at home here than she had during any of the other pageant prep stops. The dress boutique had made her feel itchy, hot, and unattractive, and the woman behind the makeup counter at the local department store—with all her talk of sun damage and freckles and dry skin—had made her want to sprint for the airport. But this . . . this felt like heaven. Hanging from the ceiling were hundreds of colorful snowboards, each with a bright price tag dangling from it. All along one wall were cubbyhole shelves filled with athletic gear—everything from Under Armour pants and shirts to Adidas jogging shorts to thick, reinforced-toe socks. They had ski boots and hiking boots and ice skates and even hockey sticks. Aubrey walked over to a display rack and took down a red and silver aluminum Easton stick.

"I think I've died and gone to heaven," she said, running her hand along its smooth handle.

"Yeah, yeah. You can look at that later," Christie said, removing the stick from her hands and returning it to the rack. "We're here for snowsuits, remember?"

Aubrey let out a sigh of longing.

"Hi, Rose . . . Christie."

A stocky man in a turtleneck sweater walked over from behind the cashier's counter, rubbing his hands together. He was balding on top, with some scruffy hair around his ears, and wore thick glasses.

"Hi, Jason," Rose said, giving him a quick hug. "How's business?"

"Good, good. Well . . . actually . . . not great," he said with a good-natured laugh. "No snow, you know? Not good for the ski shop."

"Sorry about that. Aubrey here's praying for

it every night, if that helps," Christie said.

Jason smiled at Aubrey. "Every little bit helps. So . . . you girls here shopping for the pageant?"

"Yep," Christie said, glancing around. "Looks like you have some great stuff this year."

"Well, I wanted to let you know that whatever you need . . . you can have it on loan from the shop for free," he said, blushing a bit as he made the offer.

"What? No. That's too generous," Rose said.

"Oh, please. I've known you and Jim my whole life. Christie, too," Jason said, the blush deepening. "Everyone in town is pulling for you to win, Christie. I hope you know that." Then he glanced at Aubrey. "No offense. It's just these folks have always been there for me and my family. We're kind of like one *big* family in this town."

"None taken," Aubrey said. "But if you're loaning stuff out for free, let's talk about this hockey stick." She ran her fingers over the Easton stick again.

Jason laughed. "Snowsuits only. Sorry. But happy shopping."

"Thank you so much, Jason. Really. This is

very sweet of you," Rose said.

"Anytime," Jason replied, nodding as he returned to the desk.

"That was cool," Aubrey said. "And the whole town is cheering for you!"

Christie grinned from ear to ear. "I guess it's good to have grandparents like Rose and Jim."

Rose clucked her tongue, embarrassed. "Come on. Let's hit the racks."

Christie dragged Aubrey away from the hockey area and into an aisle filled with vinyl and fur and neon accents. It was the only section of the store she would never have thought to peruse.

"The key is to get something colorful, but not too ostentatious," Christie instructed, carefully examining a hot-pink suit. She wrinkled her nose at it and moved on. "You want it to be formfitting but not too sexy."

"I can't imagine how any of these could be considered sexy," Aubrey said, pulling out a lime-green snowsuit with purple piping.

"Well, the judges will be able to spot you from a helicopter in case of an avalanche," Rose said, fingering the grainy fabric. "But I don't think mountain safety is one of the requirements."

Aubrey laughed and moved on to another rack. She spotted a light-blue snow jacket with white fur around the hood, which came with a pair of matching pants. The lining on the inside was silky and white, and when she slipped her arms into the sleeves, it felt all cuddly and warm. Not only would it look good onstage, but she could actually imagine wearing it again—if she ever came back to Vermont. Maybe she should buy instead of borrow.

"This isn't too bad," she said, automatically reaching for the price tag, which was dangling near her wrist. Her eyes nearly popped out of her head when she saw the handwritten numbers. "Five hundred dollars?" she whispered, thoughts of making a purchase flying out the window. "Wow. It's good Jason's letting us borrow this stuff."

"Seriously," Christie said. "But your mom said she'd totally fund your pageant run, right?"

"Yeah, but I don't think she wanted me to spend my college fund on it," Aubrey replied.

It had actually taken Aubrey a good fifteen minutes to convince her mother that she was not, in fact, kidding about the pageant. But once she'd been convinced, her mom had told her to get whatever she needed to compete. She'd been so excited she had asked Aubrey to put Rose on the phone and proceeded to beg Rose to film the event. Once Aubrey had realized what the two women were talking about she had grabbed the receiver and told her mother that there was no way she was letting Rose anywhere near a video camera. The last thing she needed was indelible evidence of this insanity.

As Aubrey walked out from between the racks to move on to the next aisle, the bells above the door jingled and Aubrey automatically looked up, then froze. Grayson had just walked into the shop with a very serious look on his handsome face. Aubrey stopped breathing. Her first instinct was to turn around—to completely ignore him—but she couldn't seem to make her feet move, and it was obvious she had seen him. If she ignored him now it would be, in Christie's words, immature. So she stayed right where she was, feeling insanely conspicuous.

"Hey," he said.

Her heart rate quickened at the mere sound

of his voice. He'd removed his knit hat and his hair stuck up around his ears in an adorably unself-conscious way. His face was ruddy from the cold and his eyes bright, if questioning.

You're mad at him, remember? Mad, mad, mad.

"Hey," she replied. Only because she didn't want to seem rude in front of Rose.

"Hi, Grayson!" Rose said cheerily, coming up behind Aubrey.

"Hi, Rose. Christie," Grayson said, lifting his hat in greeting. "You guys pageant shopping?"

"Yep," Christie replied.

"Cool. I just overhead Layla and her friends talking about how you're the one to beat, Christie," he said.

"Really?" Christie squeaked. "They said that?"

"You've got them on their heels," Grayson confirmed with a smile.

"Wow," Christie breathed.

"Why don't you stay?" Rose suggested. "You can give the girls a male perspective on snowsuits."

Grayson's eyes flicked to Aubrey. "I'd love to help, but I'm not sure if Aubrey wants me to."

Rose appeared confused and Aubrey wished she was anywhere but there.

"I spotted you from outside five minutes ago and I've been standing out there debating whether or not to come in," Grayson said to Aubrey. "Wasn't sure if you'd be up to talking to a lying hypocrite just yet."

Aubrey's face flushed red-hot. Christie walked to the very end of the clothing rack and slowly moved one hanger aside at a time, making sure the metal hangers didn't make too much noise. It was obvious that she was eavesdropping, but Aubrey was too distracted by the fact that she'd just been put on the spot.

"Why would anyone think you were a lying hypocrite?" Rose asked, obviously baffled.

"Huh. That's a good question," Grayson said, his jacket making swishing noises as he crossed his arms over his chest and tucked his hands under his arms. He adopted a curious expression. "Aubrey?"

"I . . . well . . . it's because of the thing with his mom the other day," Aubrey said through her teeth to Rose, unsure of how exactly to explain this. Rose's brow knit in confusion, but it was

Grayson who spoke first.

"What thing with my mom the other day?" he asked.

"Oh, it was nothing," Rose said, waving it off.

"No it wasn't! It was definitely something," Aubrey replied.

"It kind of was, Rose," Christie put in.

"Does someone want to tell me what's going on here?" Grayson asked, his arms falling to his sides.

Rose blew out a sigh and averted her gaze. It was obvious to Aubrey that the woman was uncomfortable and she felt bad for putting her in this position. But then, it wasn't really *her* who was doing it. Grayson was the one being all demanding. Like he couldn't take no for an answer. One more reason to be irked with him.

"Well, I suppose you're going to find out sooner or later, Grayson," Rose said. "But I'm sorry to be the one to have to tell you."

Aubrey swallowed hard. Was it possible that Christie had been right? Was it actually possible that Grayson knew nothing about his parents' plans to kill the winter carnival and, by extension, the Spotted Owl? That she'd misinterpreted what he'd said? Rose seemed to think that was the case.

"Tell me what?" Grayson asked, his voice growing tense.

"Your parents have decided to . . . scale back their support of the winter carnival," Rose said finally.

"What?" Grayson said.

"Not scale back," Aubrey corrected. "They're stopping everything. They're not going to run their shuttle to the carnival or even tell any of the guests about it."

"I guess that's why no one put it on the calendar in the lobby," Christie added, biting her lip.

"They know that if the carnival goes south, then Rose and Jim won't be able to make repairs to the Spotted Owl and they'll go under," Aubrey said in a rush. "They're trying to put the Owl out of business."

Grayson snorted a laugh. "Please. No. That's not possible."

He turned and walked out of the tight aisle, which finally gave Aubrey some room to breathe. She followed him and hooked a left to join Christie on the other side of the snowsuit rack. Rose went after Grayson, who paused near a row of wooden benches set up in the center of the store for trying on shoes.

"Grayson," Rose said in a placating tone.

"They wouldn't do that," Grayson said, turning to face her, his jaw clenched.

Rose hesitated. She folded her coat over her arm and held it in front of her. "I don't know what to say, hon. I'm sorry you had to find out this way, but it's the truth."

Grayson's gaze flicked over to Aubrey and Christie and he looked angry. Aubrey's heart all but stopped. Was he mad at Aubrey for bringing this up, or mad at his parents for what they were doing? Aubrey had no idea. Either way, he did seem shocked at the revelation. Maybe he *hadn't* known about his parents' plans.

"I have to go," Grayson said.

"Grayson, don't be upset. Maybe you should just talk to them about this," Rose suggested kindly.

"That's exactly what I'm going to do," Grayson replied, turning on his heel. Then, without so much as a "see ya" for Aubrey and Christie, he stormed out of the store, shoving the door open with the heel of his hand.

"See? I told you he didn't know," Christie whispered.

"But his parents are obviously evil," Aubrey replied. "How can he not see that?"

Rose turned around slowly, looking suddenly tired. "No one wants to see the bad in their family, Aubrey. That's why I wanted to keep him from finding out until we could find a solution."

Aubrey gulped. Rose had been trying to protect Grayson and she had totally ruined it.

"I'm sorry, Rose," she replied.

"Well, there's nothing we can do about it now," Rose replied. She looked at the door. "What I wouldn't give to be a fly on the wall for that conversation."

Aubrey couldn't sleep. Every time she closed her eyes she saw Grayson's glare and she couldn't stop obsessing. Had he been angry at her? If so, why? So she had assumed he knew about his family's plans for the Spotted Owl. Big deal. He was the one who had been all mysterious and cagey that night when they were working on the carnival signs, which, of course, she was now even more curious about. Besides, where she came from, people knew what was going on in their families. They didn't assume their greedy parents were perfect role models and their bitchy sisters were little angels. Grayson couldn't go through life being so entirely naive. When it came down to it, she had done him a big favor.

So why did her stomach hurt every time she thought about him?

"Forget this," Aubrey muttered under her breath.

She got up and grabbed her coat, her hockey stick, and the sleeve of pucks she had bought at the sporting-goods store, and headed downstairs. There was a patch of iced-over concrete behind the inn where the garbage dumpsters were housed. If she wasn't going to sleep, at least she could get in some practice shots for the hockey shot competition. On her way to the stairs, she stopped at the drink machine next to the ice maker and bought two bottles of iced tea, figuring she could set them up as markers and shoot between them.

Down in the lobby, a young couple cuddled in front of the fireplace with mugs of hot chocolate. Jonathan was working the counter, and she gave him a quick wave as she headed for the door, but before she could get there, the door swung open toward her and Grayson stepped inside. Aubrey froze. Why, why, why had she left her hair in these two childish braids? And why had she simply shoved her feet into her snow boots while still in her thermal pj's with the smiley faces on them instead of changing into jeans?

"Oh, hey," Grayson said uncertainly. He looked her up and down and a smile lit his eyes. Aubrey's face burned. "That's a good look for you."

"What are you doing here?" Aubrey asked. All the paraphernalia she had cradled in her arms started to slip and she had to grip it tighter to keep it from crashing to the floor.

"I . . . uh . . . I came to apologize, actually," he said, pulling his knit cap from his head.

"To me?" Aubrey asked.

Grayson blinked. "Uh, *no*," he replied,

stepping past her toward the center of the lobby. "To Rose and Jim. I talked to my parents and it turns out you were right. Apparently they are trying to run the Spotted Owl out of town."

"Told you so," Aubrey said, before she could stop herself.

Grayson turned and looked at her, incredulous. "Did you just say 'told you so'?"

"Well . . . I did!" Aubrey replied. In her righteousness she lost her concentration, and all her stuff—hockey stick, pucks, and iced-tea bottles—tumbled to the floor. The cuddling couple looked up as one of the bottles rolled under their love seat.

Grayson laughed and dropped down on one of the couches near the center of the room. "You are something else, you know that?"

Aubrey didn't know what to do. Go after the errant iced-tea bottle, or just pretend it had never happened? She crouched and picked up the stick and pucks, at least, and placed them on the bench near the door.

"Something else good or something else bad?" Aubrey asked, walking over to hover near the end of the couch. She zipped up her coat so at least some of the smiley faces were covered up.

Narrowing his eyes as he studied her face, Grayson sighed. "It's tough to say." He leaned forward, resting his forearms on his knees. "So . . . before I apologize to Rose and Jim . . . was there anything *you* wanted to say to *me*?" he asked, looking up at her with a teasing glint in his eyes.

Aubrey's heart skipped in nervousness. This felt like a test, but she had no idea what the answer was. What was she supposed to say to him? Stalling for time, she walked over to the second couch, on the other side of the low coffee table, and sat, reaching underneath the table for one of the bottles. Grayson simply followed her with his eyes. He wasn't going to give her a hint.

"Like what?" she said finally, clutching the iced tea in both hands.

Grayson's laugh filled the lobby. Even the cuddling couple turned to look. "Like an apology of your own."

Aubrey blinked. She rarely, if ever, apologized. Apologizing meant admitting she was wrong—something she found very difficult to do. "For what?"

"For calling me a lying hypocrite!" Grayson replied, still amused. "Obviously I didn't know what my parents were doing. Therefore, no lying, no hypocrite."

"Oh." Aubrey's face turned the color of boiled crab shells. "That."

"Yeah. That," Grayson said, draping his arm over the couch and letting his legs fall open wide. He obviously felt at home here, even if his parents did hate the place and wanted to see it torn down. "Well?" he prompted.

"It wasn't my fault!" Aubrey protested. "The other night you started to say something about the Spotted Owl. Like you were going to miss it when it was gone or something. So I just assumed."

Grayson's jaw clenched and he looked away. "Oh. That."

"Was I right? I knew it! So what was that all about?" Aubrey asked.

Grayson sighed. "Fine. If you must know,

that was about college."

"College?" Aubrey asked, her brow furrowing.

"Yeah. College. I'm thinking about going next year, and what I was going to say that night was that I was going to miss this place when I was gone," he explained, keeping his voice down. "But I haven't told the Howells yet and I didn't want them to find out from you, so I stopped myself."

Aubrey swallowed hard. "Oh."

"So. Apology?" he asked.

Wow. He really wasn't going to give this up, was he? Suddenly it felt as if the fireplace, which was at least twenty feet away, was right behind her neck. She glanced over at Jonathan, half expecting to find him listening in, but he was busy with some kind of paperwork. The couple had returned to their cuddling. She took a deep breath. She knew she should admit she was wrong. She knew it. But she felt so stupid. Why did apologizing make her feel like such a loser?

"Look," Grayson said, shifting his feet and leaning forward again. "If you don't take back the lying-hypocrite comment, I can't ask you out," he said. "Because, really, what kind of tool would it make me to ask out a girl who thinks I'm a lying hypocrite even when it's already been proven that I'm not?"

Aubrey looked up at him. Had he just said what she thought he'd said? "Ask me out?" she repeated.

"Yep," he said, pressing his lips together. "But I can't do it unless I get an apology."

"Okay, fine! I'm sorry, okay?" Aubrey blurted.

Grayson's teasing smile turned into a grin. "I knew you wanted to go out with me."

Aubrey felt as if her face was going to explode. "Shut up!" she said, even though she couldn't stop grinning, either. Her insides were tied into a zillion tiny knots as she tried to decide if he was just messing with her or if he really was going to ask her out—or both. After this she was really going to have to shoot some pucks. Maybe a thousand. It would take that long to work off all this nervous tension.

Suddenly, Grayson stood up, straightened his jacket, and cleared his throat. "Well, I guess

I'd better go find Rose and Jim."

A flash of panic shot through Aubrey's chest. He *was* messing with her! He had no intention of asking her out. He'd just said that to get an apology out of her and humiliate her.

"Wait!" she said, standing up. She had to say something, anything, to save face here. Somehow make him believe that she *didn't* want him to ask her out. But standing there in her smiley-face pajamas with her big, brown puffer jacket making her arms stick out at an angle and her hair in stupid pigtails, she couldn't think of a thing to say that wouldn't make her look more childish than she already did.

"Oh, right! I almost forgot," Grayson said, taking a step toward her. "Aubrey, would you like to go out with me on Thursday night?"

Aubrey's jaw dropped open slightly. This had to be the most confusing five-minute conversation of her life.

"Seriously?" she asked.

"Seriously," he replied.

Her mind still trying to sort out the fifteen emotions she'd just felt in succession, Aubrey struggled for the proper response.

"Um, okay," she said finally.

"Good," Grayson replied with a smile. He turned and walked toward the front desk, giving Jonathan a nod of greeting, but he paused before getting to the office door. He turned around and gave Aubrey a flirtatious look. "Oh, and wear your hair like that, okay? It's beyond sexy."

The second he was gone, Aubrey collapsed onto the couch, feeling exhausted and exhilarated all at once. Grayson had asked her out. She was going out with Grayson! He hadn't known about his parents, and he was going to apologize, which made him a seriously stand-up guy—not a lying hypocrite. And he *had* been mad at her, but for the hypocrite comment, not for anything else. Everything was going to be just fine.

But one question remained.

Was he serious about the hair?

Chapter 7

"'*O*n my own, pretending he's beside me,'" Aubrey sang, staring at herself in the full-length mirror of the rehearsal room behind the amphitheater. She and Christie had booked it for one hour Wednesday morning so they could both practice their talents. Unfortunately, as Aubrey's voice bounced back at her from the soundproof walls, she was feeling anything but talented. "'All alone I walk with him till morning.'"

Behind her, Christie tossed her baton up in the air, tilted over to throw her leg up in a side split, then caught the baton again, between her legs. Now *that* was talent.

"I can't take it anymore," Aubrey said, hitting the pause button on the CD player in the corner. "I totally suck."

"You don't *totally* suck," Christie replied.

Aubrey's face burned. "But I *do* suck."

Christie's eyes widened. She held her baton in both hands and stepped toward Aubrey, her ballet flats soundless on the hardwood floor. "No! That's not what I said!"

"Yes you did! You emphasized *totally*, which means I don't *totally* suck, but I suck." Aubrey dropped down on the floor and hung her head in her hands. "That's it. I need to pick a different song. If I sing this, Layla and her friends are going to laugh me off the stage."

"Please, if anything they're going to laugh *me* off the stage," Christie said, tossing her baton from hand to hand. "Do you think I should try the one-handed cartwheel thing? I think it could really earn me some points, and if I want to win this thing over Layla I'm going to need all the extra points I can get."

"You mean the thing that you totally decked on during halftime at the Thanksgiving Day game?" Aubrey asked, picking at her fingernails.

"That was just one time. And I've been practicing a lot since then."

Aubrey's heart welled with sour guilt.

"Omigosh, Christie, I'm so sorry," she said, getting up on her knees. "I don't know what's wrong with me. I'm all negative today. But I'm sure you can do it. Why don't you show me?"

Christie grinned and stepped back to give herself more room. She tossed the baton in the air and executed a perfect one-handed cartwheel, then somehow caught the baton on its way down, landing in a split.

Aubrey whistled and clapped her hands. "Yes, you should *definitely* do that," she said. "In fact, I think it should be your grand finale. That trick is going to win you the crown."

"You think?" Christie asked, pushing herself up off the floor.

"Definitely," Aubrey said with a nod. She sat down again and slumped back against the mirror wall. "And we should make sure that they put you on after me so that everyone in the audience completely forgets about my totally off-key song."

"Come on. You're not off-key," Christie said.

"You have to say that because you're my best friend, but we both know I'm going to be publicly humiliated," Aubrey said, sinking lower against the mirror. "I don't know why I ever agreed to do this."

"Um, because you're a good friend?" Christie reminded her. Then, all of a sudden, her face lit up. "Wait. I have an idea. I saw it in a documentary about the making of this new musical on Broadway."

"What is it?" Aubrey asked, lifting her head hopefully.

"Lie on your back on the floor," Christie instructed.

Aubrey clucked her tongue and rolled her eyes. "Come on."

"Just try it!" Christie wheedled.

Aubrey sighed but did as she was told, hoping her red fleece V-neck didn't get too dirty in the process, since it was one of the very few warm pieces of clothing she had. The floor was predictably cold and hard, and the back of her skull hurt just lying there. "I feel like a moron."

"Okay, press your shoulder blades into the floor," Christie said, ignoring her comment and hovering over her. "It opens up your diaphragm or something."

One of the can lights in the ceiling was right

behind Christie's head and made a little halo around her dark hair.

"Fine," Aubrey said. She pressed her shoulder blades back and her chest did seem to open up a bit. She could even breathe better this way.

"Place your hands together in front of your heart," Christie instructed, laying her baton aside. "Like this."

Now the girl really looked like an angel, holding her hands flat together like she was praying.

"You're cracked," Aubrey said, but mimicked the pose anyway.

"Okay, sing," Christie instructed.

Aubrey took a deep breath, opened her mouth, and started the song. "'On my own, pretending he's beside me . . .'"

She paused and looked up at Christie, who was grinning from ear to ear. "See?"

"Wow. I really do sound better."

Someone laughed from the doorway, and Aubrey sat up and whipped around. Layla was standing there with one hand on the doorknob and one on her hip.

"Yeah, too bad you can't lie on the stage

during the pageant. I'm sure you'd win in a landslide," Layla said derisively.

Aubrey's cheeks heated up and she shoved herself up off the floor. She slapped her dusty hands against her jeans, then crossed her arms over her chest. "What're you doing here?" she asked, tossing her hair back and lifting her chin defiantly. "We have the room till ten."

"I heard you're going out with my brother tomorrow night," Layla said, keeping the heavy door propped open with her foot. "I thought I told you to stay away from him."

Aubrey tilted her head. "Yeah, I decided not to take your suggestion."

"You might want to rethink that," Layla said.

"Layla, we have the room until ten, so maybe you should go," Christie said with obvious effort. It was probably the most obnoxious thing Aubrey's sweet-as-pie friend had ever said in her life.

"Back off, Christie," Layla snapped. "This is between me and Red over here."

"You know what? You guys argue. I'm going to rehearse," Christie said. She walked over to the stereo in the corner and turned on her iPod, which was hooked up to the speakers. The dance music she'd selected for her baton-twirling act pounded through the speakers. Aubrey saw Layla checking out Christie's act through narrowed eyes and tried to step in front of the girl to obstruct her view. Layla's gaze flicked to Aubrey's face.

"I've been nice so far in the spirit of competition and all that, but—"

"Nice? This is you nice?" Aubrey demanded with a scoff. "You have a weird definition of the word."

"But you *really* don't want to mess with me," Layla said, finishing her sentence as if Aubrey had never interrupted.

Aubrey took a few steps forward, getting as close to Layla as she dared. Her competitive adrenaline coursed through her veins. "Maybe *you* don't want to mess with me. Ever think about that?"

Layla looked at the ceiling for a moment, as if she was pondering the question. "No," she said finally. "Actually, I haven't."

Then she backed up, letting the heavy door

slam right in Aubrey's face. Aubrey's fingers slowly curled into fists at her sides. Christie stepped up behind her.

"Aubrey, I know we're hating the Chamberlains right now, but when it comes to Layla, we should concentrate on just beating her in the pageant," Christie said over the music, reaching for Aubrey's arm. "Because the girl is right, you really don't want to mess with her."

But Aubrey didn't even hear her friend speak. All she could see was Layla's imperious expression, her judgmental gaze, her obnoxious smirk.

She turned and looked at her friend, ready for war. "Oh, it is so on."

"Just *wait* until you see my dress!" one of the girls cooed, walking past Aubrey and Christie, who were seated in two of the wooden chairs lined up along the back curtain. "It's *gorgeous*. And one of a kind. The designer said I had the perfect model's body."

Aubrey groaned and looked at Christie. "We really have to do some more dress shopping. We're running out of time and we need to find you something good."

"I know. There are a couple more shops we can try," Christie replied. "What about you? Have you found a new song to sing for your talent, or are you going to stick with 'On My Own'?"

Aubrey heard the question, but it didn't quite sink in. She was too busy looking past her friend at Grayson, who had just walked onto the stage and was now going over the programs with Fabrizia. It was slightly warmer than usual, so he was wearing a heavy wool sweater in gray with no coat, and he looked so handsome Aubrey couldn't take her eyes off of him.

I wonder if he's a good kisser, she thought, her entire body warming under her layers of clothing. She still hadn't gotten used to the cold, so for her, bundling up was necessary. *Who am I kidding? Of course he's a good kisser. Just look at him.*

"Aubrey? Hello?" Christie said.

Grayson laughed and Aubrey's heart fluttered.

Maybe he'll kiss me tomorrow night, she thought. *Maybe I'll kiss him.*

"Hello? Earth to Aubrey? Are you in there?"

Christie waved her hand in front of Aubrey's face.

"What? Oh, sorry," Aubrey shook her head, trying to focus. "What did you say?"

Christie rolled her eyes and giggled, shoving her hands into the pockets of her white zip-front fleece. "Nothing. But you'd better lick the drool off your lips," she joked.

Aubrey blushed. She turned her head away and surreptitiously wiped her glove across her mouth, just in case.

"Okay, my little princesses!" Fabrizia shouted, throwing her arms out and waggling her fingers. "I need my front-row girls front and center. We have a few kinks we need to work out."

"That's me," Christie said.

Then she got up, took one step, and tripped forward. Aubrey jumped up to try to catch her friend, but it was too late. Christie let out a shriek and landed flat on her face.

"Christie!" Grayson shouted.

Aubrey dove to her knees next to her friend's prone form. "Are you okay?" she asked, her heart in her throat.

Christie groaned and slowly lifted her head.

Her eyes were scrunched in pain and her cheek-bone was already turning red. "Ow."

"Where does it hurt?" Grayson asked, kneeling at Christie's other side.

"Everywhere," Christie said, pushing herself up slowly onto her hands and knees. Grayson lent her a hand, but as she tried to sit up, she hesitated. Her brow knit in confusion.

"What's wrong?" Aubrey asked.

"I can't move my feet," Christie said.

Aubrey blinked, her heart nose-diving. Was Christie seriously injured? She ducked behind her friend to take a look at her feet. Instantly, Aubrey's face turned red with rage. The laces on Christie's jazz shoes had been tied together. Layla. Layla must have done this. Fuming, Aubrey looked around and, sure enough, there were Layla and Rebecca, snickering by the back curtain.

Layla must have crawled up behind Christie's chair and done this while the two of them were chatting. Apparently, Grayson was right. His sister and her friends thought Christie was their main competition, and they had decided to make her a target. Talk about immature. This was a whole new level of low. Quickly, before anyone could see that Christie had fallen for such a lame prank, Aubrey reached down and untied the knots.

"Here. I'll help you get up," Aubrey said, standing and taking Christie's hands.

Once Christie was on her feet, Fabrizia scurried up next to Grayson to inspect her. She lifted her half-moon glasses to her nose and looked her up and down as if checking for defects.

"Ah! Here is the problem! Both your shoes are untied. You must have tripped on the laces," Fabrizia said. Christie looked down, confused, but the evidence was right there. Two completely undone laces. "All right, everyone. She's all right! We'll take another five so she can get cleaned up!"

From the corner of her eye, Aubrey saw Layla and Rebecca slip backstage.

"Come on," she said, taking Christie's hand. "I'll help you."

"No. It's okay. I don't need five minutes," Christie said. "I'll just tie my shoes and we can get back to rehearsal."

"Believe me. You want to come with me,"

Aubrey said, her grip on Christie's hand tightening. She tugged her baffled friend backstage, leaving Grayson and Fabrizia behind.

"There should be a couple of ice packs in the fridge in the office," Grayson called after them.

"Thanks!" Aubrey shouted in return. "We'll be right back."

Christie followed Aubrey backstage, then wrested her hand from her grip and dropped down to tie her shoes. "What is going on?" she asked. "What's with all the pulling?"

"Your shoelaces were tied together," Aubrey told her, crossing her arms over her chest as she looked down at the top of Christie's head. "Layla and her little friend did it."

"What?" Christie looked up, her eyes wide with shock. "Who does something like that?"

"Total bitches," Aubrey replied.

Christie stood and Aubrey led her behind the curtain, where they found Layla and Rebecca giggling together on their way to the bathroom in the wings. They stopped in their tracks the second they saw Christie and Aubrey, then instantly cracked up laughing all over again.

"How's your face?" Layla asked Christie, a

tear of mirth squeezing from the corner of her eye.

"It's . . . fine," Christie stammered.

"Despite your attempt to rearrange it," Aubrey said, standing between Layla and Christie. "You could have really hurt her."

"Please. I just wanted to remind Christie who her competition is," Layla said, glancing past Aubrey at Christie. "And show her that I'm not taking any prisoners."

Aubrey scoffed. "What did she ever do to you?"

"She's trying to win *my* pageant," Layla replied.

"So are a dozen other girls. Why not attack them?" Aubrey asked.

A flash of uncertainty lit up Layla's eyes and Aubrey felt a little thrill go through her. She had her answer. Layla was *really* intimidated by Christie. She was scared that Christie could actually beat her.

"You are so going to regret this," Aubrey said.

"Please," Layla said. "What are you going to do to me with all my friends around? Not to

150

mention my parents . . . my *brother* . . . You can't touch me."

"Oh, don't you worry about it. I have moves you can't even imagine," Aubrey said. "Moves that take a little more creativity than what you just did."

"Guys, come on," Christie said with a nervous giggle. "Can't we agree to stay out of each other's way and just leave it alone? Keep the whole pageant fair and square?"

"No. I really don't think we can, Christie," Aubrey said.

Christie grabbed Aubrey's arm and tugged her aside, pausing under a row of backstage lights. "Aubrey, *please*," she begged in a whisper, her eyes desperate. "I'm fine. It was a stupid prank. I'm over it."

"Yeah, but what if she doesn't stop there?" Aubrey whispered back. "We can't just let her get away with this."

"But . . . what are you going to do?" Christie said worriedly. "And what if you get disqualified or something? You can't leave me here alone with those girls."

"I won't. I promise," Aubrey whispered. "It's

not like I'm going to stoop to anything violent," she said loudly, glancing over her shoulder at Layla. "Some of us have too much class for that."

Layla pursed her lips at the insult and glanced at her friend. "Come on, Becks. She's got nothing," she said, walking toward the bathroom.

"Oh, you'll see," Aubrey replied. She had no idea what her retaliation plan would be, but she would come up with something. She had to. She had to defend Christie. "Just wait and see."

That evening as Aubrey and Christie made their way through the lobby of the Chamberlain Resort, the place was buzzing with activity. Aside from the usual commotion of guests checking in, skiers gathering their gear, and porters hustling about with luggage, a camera crew was setting up in front of the roaring fireplace. A young reporter stood still as could be as a hairdresser and makeup artist flitted around her and a burly man placed his camera and lights. Half the snow princesses had gathered around the area, trying to get a better look at what was going on. Meanwhile, two men stood atop two-story ladders, stringing a huge silver and white banner across the main entrance as Grayson's mother stood below, directing them.

Aubrey had no interest in the camera crew, but once the banner was unfurled she stopped in her tracks.

"'Tenth annual winter ball,'" she read. "What's that?"

"Didn't I tell you about that?" Christie asked.

Aubrey felt a thump of foreboding in her chest. Ever so slowly, she turned around to face her friend. "Another event you forgot to mention? What do I have to do for this one? Jump out of a cake in red lingerie or something?"

Christie laughed nervously. Aubrey could see that her friend's hands were clutching the strap on her pink bag.

"No. Nothing like that. It's just this formal dance the Chamberlains throw every year the night before the pageant," she said. Then she ducked her head and walked by Aubrey toward the rotating door. "And all the pageant contestants are required to go," she added under her breath.

"What? No!" Aubrey shouted.

A crowd of skiers glanced at her in a disturbed way as they passed by, headed for the elevators at the back of the lobby. Christie sighed, tilted her head, and turned around.

"It's not that big of a deal. All you've got to do is show up with a date who will escort you into the room when your name is announced," Christie said with a shrug.

Aubrey groaned and fell backward into one of the many overstuffed chairs that dotted the lobby. Her arms fell limp over the armrests and she tipped her head back to stare up at the huge wooden chandelier hanging overhead.

"Great. One more event to stress over and shop for," she complained.

"What's to stress?" Christie asked, sitting on the edge of the next chair and placing her bag on her lap. "You practically have a built-in date with Grayson."

As if Christie saying his name had conjured him up, Grayson walked through the front door of the lobby, in deep conversation with an older man in gray coveralls. Aubrey's heart skipped a beat at the sight of her supposed "built-in date."

"Please. We haven't even been on our *first*

date yet," she said, lifting her head. She bit her lip, imagining how mind-numbingly gorgeous Grayson would look in a tuxedo. She kept her eye on him as he and the older man crossed the lobby and walked back toward the resort's offices. With everything going on in the vast lobby, Grayson didn't see Aubrey, and she was able to watch him unabashedly. Grayson was gesturing emphatically and the older man kept nodding. When they turned the corner she saw that there was a patch on the back of his coveralls that read ACE PLUMBERS. "Do you really think Grayson will go with me?"

"Why wouldn't he? He obviously likes you," Christie replied. She looked down at her bag and toyed with the tassel on the zipper. "I wish I had a built-in date with Jonathan." She lifted her dark eyes to look at Aubrey hopefully. "Do you think I should ask him?"

"Of course you should ask him," Aubrey said. "What have I been saying all along? When you see an opportunity, you have to go for it."

Just then, the cameraman flicked his lights on, effectively blinding her even from twenty feet away. It took a few seconds for the spots in her vision to fade, but when they did, she saw that the young reporter was now interviewing none other than Layla Chamberlain, right in front of the camera.

"I understand that the grand prize for this event is quite a lot of money," the reporter was saying.

"Yes, it is," Layla replied, her smile all toothy and huge. "In fact, whoever wins the crown will take home a check for ten thousand dollars."

The idea occurred to Aubrey like a flash, and every bone in her body tingled with the sheer brilliance of it. Before she knew it, she was on her feet, leaving a confused Christie behind. As Aubrey made a beeline for the fireplace, the reporter asked the exact question Aubrey needed her to ask.

"Wow. So what will you do with all that money if you win?"

Aubrey stepped up behind Layla, slipped her arm around the girl's slim shoulders, and leaned in toward the microphone.

"Actually, my friend Layla here has decided that if she wins, she's going to donate all the money—every cent of it—to charity," she announced.

Layla's jaw dropped.

"Really?" the reporter asked. "And who might you be?"

"I'm Aubrey Mills, one of Layla's fellow contestants," Aubrey replied with a smile.

"Well, Layla, is what Aubrey says true?" the reporter asked.

Layla looked at the camera, her eyes wide. Aubrey knew what the girl was thinking. She couldn't say that no, in fact, she had never said she would give the money to charity. If she did that she would look like a selfish jerk on camera. Aubrey had effectively trapped the girl. Now, if Layla did win, she would *have* to donate the money or everyone would think she had lied.

It was the perfect revenge for Layla's attack on Christie. And so much more sophisticated than tying someone's shoelaces together.

"Yes, Robia, it's true," Layla said finally, looking at the reporter. She swallowed so hard Aubrey actually heard it. "I've always thought that it was important for those of us who are more fortunate to give back to those who . . .

aren't," she added awkwardly.

"Isn't she just the sweetest?" Aubrey said, giving Layla's shoulder a squeeze. "Have a nice broadcast."

Then she quickly backed away, removing herself from the camera's glare and striding back toward Christie. The grin on her face was so wide she felt as if her cheeks were going to crack. Layla may have scored the first blow in this little war, but Aubrey's blow had been much bigger. Ten thousand dollars bigger.

"I can't believe you just did that," Christie said, standing up as Aubrey grabbed her bag from the floor and kept walking.

"Believe it, baby," Aubrey said, gloating. "This is war."

Chapter 8

Thursday morning, Aubrey was up before the sun and out on the pond at the carnival grounds practicing her shooting skills. The night before, Jim had dragged an old hockey goal out of the basement of the inn and had helped her fashion her own target out of a paint-splattered tarp, so now she could really practice her precision. A few of the carnival workers even took a break to come watch, and some of them hooted and hollered when she made her last shot. She hadn't hit all five holes in ten shots yet, but she was getting closer. She was certain that by the night of the competition, she would be able to blow all contenders off the ice.

Christie had just emerged from the shower, when Aubrey returned from the pond, but by the time Aubrey left the bathroom all blow-dried and ready to go, Christie's bed was already made, everything perfectly tucked and smoothed, and Christie was gone. Aubrey glanced at her own bed, a big, rumpled mess, and decided to deal with it later.

Grabbing her skates so that she could get in a bit more ice time after pageant rehearsal and before her skate date with Grayson, Aubrey skipped down the back stairs and into the Howells' private kitchen. Christie was sitting with her back to the stairs, her hair pinned straight down her back, a bowl of oatmeal steaming in front of her.

"I am so going to win the hockey shootout," Aubrey gushed, crossing the room noisily and dropping into the next chair. "You should have seen me out there this morning, Christie! I—"

"Shhhhh!" Christie hissed, looking grim.

Aubrey's mouth snapped shut. "What's wrong?"

"I'm trying to hear," Christie whispered, glancing at the closed door that connected to the Howells' office.

For the first time Aubrey heard the tense voices coming from inside, and she realized with a start that one of the voices belonged to Grayson. She thought he had a nature hike this morning. What was he doing inside? And why did he and Rose and Jim sound so upset? Was he getting fired or something?

"Well, if you're going to eavesdrop, then do it right," Aubrey said, getting up out of her chair. She walked right over to the door and crouched down, putting her ear next to the old-school keyhole above the doorknob.

"Aubrey!" Christie hissed, her eyes going wide as she got off her chair. "Don't!"

"Shhh!" Aubrey said, waving her hand. Christie froze and suddenly Aubrey could hear everything the Howells and Grayson were saying.

" . . . tried everything I could. They just won't listen to me," Grayson was saying. "They're not going to back off."

"It's okay, Grayson," Rose replied. "We know you've done everything you can."

"Well, not everything."

Aubrey heard the rustle of some paper and there was a pause.

"What's this?" Jim said finally.

"It's a check. I cleared out my savings," Grayson told them. "I want you to put it toward the pipes. Or buying a new van. Whatever you want to use it for."

Aubrey's heart expanded inside her chest. She looked at Christie all gooey-eyed and Christie's brow knit. "What?" she mouthed.

"He's trying to give them money," Aubrey mouthed back.

"What?" Christie asked again, confused.

Aubrey rolled her eyes. "Forget it," she mouthed, trying to listen.

"No. Absolutely not," Jim replied gruffly. "We won't take charity."

"It's not charity," Grayson replied. "Most of it is money you guys paid me anyway. Why don't we just call it a refund for overpayment? Because you guys have been far too generous."

"Grayson, you know we can't take that," Rose said gently. "Please. Put the check away."

Grayson sighed. "I'm going to figure out a way to fix this."

"No offense, son, but it's not your place," Jim said. "It's our job to fix this. We appreciate everything you've tried to do, but now I think you'd better go, unless you want to be late for your first hike of the day."

Grayson cleared his throat, obviously chagrined. "Yes, sir."

Aubrey heard steps nearing the door and jumped up. She grabbed Christie and practically flung her back into her chair. When the door opened, she was halfway seated in her own chair, her heart pounding a mile a minute. Grayson hesitated as soon as he saw that he had an audience. Aubrey glanced at him, feeling guilty, although she didn't know why. It wasn't her fault that the kitchen was adjacent to the office. Anyone else in her position would have tried to listen in. He closed the door behind him.

"Good morning," Christie said cheerily. "Is everything okay?"

"Sure. Except that my parents are being totally unreasonable," he said, his jaw clenched. He walked over to the table and pressed his fists into its surface. "The other day I put the winter carnival up on the schedule in the lobby and they freaked out on me when they realized. This morning it was gone again. I don't know why we can't just keep things the way they were. It's like they're threatened by the Owl even though we've all been fine together for ten years."

He blew out a sigh and collapsed forward, letting his forearms rest on the table and bowing his head. Aubrey felt more attracted to him than ever at that moment. He was so obviously emotional over this whole thing, and she loved that he had such a strong loyalty to the Howells. How had his jerky parents managed to raise one bitchy, shallow daughter and one totally upstanding son?

"I'm working another angle, but it's still in the early stages," he said, lifting his head and resting it atop his fist.

"What angle?" Christie asked.

"I don't want to say until I know it'll work. Don't want to get your hopes up and all that," Grayson said with a sigh. "I just wish there was something more I could do."

"You could help Christie win the pageant," Aubrey piped up.

Grayson's eyebrows arched. "What?"

Christie blushed slightly. "I've already decided that if I win—"

"*When* you win," Aubrey corrected, patting her on the back.

"Right, *when* I win," Christie said, blushing even harder, "I'm going to give the money to my grandparents."

"Wow." Grayson stood up straight. "Christie, that's amazing. But I'm not sure they'll take it."

"Yeah, I thought of that, but they've never been able to resist me when I really want something," she said with a grin.

"Well, don't tell anyone I said this—especially not Layla—but I hope you do win," Grayson stated, reaching over to squeeze Christie's shoulder. "If it means saving the Spotted Owl, I'm definitely in your corner. No offense, Aubrey."

Aubrey grinned. "None taken. And you realize you could probably get fired for saying that, Mr. Assistant Director."

Grayson pondered this with a tilt of his head. "True. But that's a risk I'm willing to take."

He checked his watch and blanched. "Crap. I'm really late. I'll see you later, Christie," Grayson said, walking behind her toward the door. He paused next to Aubrey and leaned in close. "And I'll see *you* for our date tonight, right?"

A tingle of excitement raced down Aubrey's spine and she bit her lip to keep from shivering visibly. "I'll be there."

"I am completely impressed," Grayson said, skating up next to Aubrey as she slowly but steadily made the turn at the north end of the lake that night.

"With what?" Aubrey asked, holding back a smile.

Grayson skated ahead, then turned around on his blades so he could glide backward and talk to her. "With you! You're doing great. I would never know you'd never been on ice skates before this week."

"Thank you," Aubrey replied.

She knew all her hard work was paying off, but she liked to think that her new snow jacket and hat made her look more graceful as well. After her encounter with Grayson during her first trip to Tucker's Ski Shop, Aubrey hadn't been in the mood to try on snowsuits, so that afternoon she had gone back and purchased a royal blue jacket with navy accents that cut in toward the waist—the style gave her the illusion of the curves she now knew she didn't have. While she was there, Jason had offered to lend her the pants to go with it, which meant that she finally had a snowsuit for the pageant as well as an unembarrassing jacket to wear on her date. It not only kept her warm but also brought out the deep blue of her eyes. Topped off with a new white ski hat and gloves, Aubrey felt pretty out on the ice—pretty and steady and determined not to be the object of anyone's laughter. At least not this evening.

It was a perfect, clear night—still no sign of snow—and the lake was jam-packed with skaters. A troop of little girls celebrating a birthday kept skating by hand in hand, all of them wearing pink crowns over their warm hats. A few middle-school boys were shooting a puck around at the center of the ice, their parents hanging out near the snack bar, nursing coffees. Everywhere Aubrey looked there were groups of teenagers, couples clutching each other, families out for a night on the ice. It was a cozy, convivial atmosphere, and she felt light and happy and couldn't stop smiling.

She hadn't even thought about Layla or the

threat to the Spotted Owl or her stupid song for the pageant once all night.

Grayson turned around again and slowed down so that he and Aubrey were skating side by side. She glanced up at his profile and her heart skipped a couple thousand beats. It was hard to believe that a guy that gorgeous was actually there with her. Standing around the lake or skating across its surface were dozens of beautiful Vermont ski bunnies and fresh-faced tourists, but Grayson had chosen her, the awkward tomboy from Florida who didn't know how to dress for the weather. Did he still think she wasn't pageant-worthy?

The thought made her breath catch and she decided not to dwell on that right now. Why go all negative during the most perfect date ever?

"Hey, there's Christie and Charlie," Grayson said, nodding toward the edge of the lake.

Aubrey glanced over and saw Christie and her cousin lacing up their skates. Christie was staring off to her right and Aubrey followed her line of sight to find Jonathan yukking it up with a group of his friends. Why couldn't her best friend just get up the guts to ask the guy out already? And why hadn't Jonathan asked *her* out? Aubrey was sure he liked her. Maybe she should go over there right now and ask him what his problem was.

"Want to go say hi?" Grayson asked, sliding his hand into Aubrey's.

Aubrey nearly tripped in surprise and Grayson quickly gripped her arm with his other hand to steady her.

"Whoa. That was a close one," Aubrey said, embarrassed.

Grayson laughed and squeezed her fingers. "Why don't we go get some hot chocolate and take a break?" he suggested.

"That might not be a bad idea," Aubrey said, her ankles feeling wobbly after her near miss.

Grayson's holding my hand! she thought giddily. *Grayson is holding my hand!* If he was going to do that in front of all these people, he must really like her.

Trying not to smile too hugely, Aubrey clung to Grayson as they slowly skated toward the snack bar, on the opposite bank from where Christie was just moving onto the ice. Aubrey's matchmaking plans would have to be put on hold for now. She was too busy matching herself. And she was sure that if she asked Christie, she would agree that while on a date, she should concentrate on her date.

Grayson sat down on the first empty bench he saw and placed his plastic sleeves over his blades, then helped Aubrey put hers on. Together they toddled toward the snack bar line, which was full of middle-school kids all trying to figure out what they could afford with their allowance money.

"I can get popcorn, a small hot chocolate, *and* a chili dog," one kid bragged to another.

"So not fair! Why did I buy those stupid ring pops before?" the other kid groused.

Aubrey caught Grayson's eye and they tried not to laugh. The line moved ahead and they both stayed where they were, letting a bit of space open up between them and the boys.

"Ah, the problems of a sixth grader," Grayson joked under his breath.

"Should we tell them that in a few years from now they'll be trying to help bail out their employers from a hostile takeover by their own parents?" Aubrey joked.

The light went out of Grayson's eyes and he looked down at the asphalt. "Yeah. Maybe not," he said. "Wouldn't want to tarnish their youth."

Aubrey's heart squeezed. Why did she have to say that? Obviously Grayson was all conflicted and upset about it. Totally not a date-night topic.

"Grayson, I'm sorry. I—"

"Hey! Mind if we cut in!?"

Out of nowhere, Layla appeared, dragging another girl with her and filling up the space in the line. Aubrey bit her tongue to keep from saying something rude. She had already trashed her date's family enough for one night.

"Sophia?" Grayson blurted. Just like that, he dropped Aubrey's hand.

Aubrey's pulse seized up in her veins. In all her annoyance at Layla, she hadn't even bothered to look at the girl she was with. Grayson had, though. And he was frozen in his tracks, his jaw hanging open.

"Sophia?" Aubrey repeated. As in, Sophia his ex-girlfriend, Sophia? The girl, tall and lithe with thick blond hair and clear gray eyes, was wearing a suede coat with a woolly collar over a white turtleneck. She had perfect cheek-bones, perfect skin, and perfect earlobes with huge diamond studs glittering from them. She blushed and looked at the ground before meeting Grayson's gaze.

"Hey, Gray. It's good to see you."

"You too. What're you doing here?" he asked. He reached out a hand as if to hug her or shake her hand or something, but then retracted it awkwardly. Sophia chuckled in an embarrassed way. Layla looked at Aubrey, a satisfied purse to her lips.

"I invited her to come up for the week," Layla said, placing her hand on Sophia's back. "She's going to work on the pageant!"

She kept her eyes trained on Aubrey as she said this, and Aubrey knew with sudden clarity that this had been done for her benefit. When Layla had told her to stay away from Grayson, she had meant it—and this was her way of ensuring it would happen. Christie had told Aubrey that Sophia and Layla were best friends. Apparently Layla wanted to see her two favorite people get back together—and leave Aubrey out in the cold.

"Work? How?" Grayson said, looking confused and, much to Aubrey's pleasure, none too happy about this development.

"I'm going to help out backstage," Sophia explained. "And on the night of the pageant I'll pass the crown off to the new winner."

"Really? We've never had the former Snow Queen do that before," Grayson said.

"Mom thought it would be a cool idea," Layla put in.

I'll bet. Once you convinced her of it, Aubrey thought.

"Anyway, as assistant director, you'll be Sophia's boss," Layla said to Grayson. "Guess you two will be spending a lot of time together."

Aubrey's stomach turned as Sophia smiled. She found herself staring down at Grayson's hand—the one that had so recently been holding hers. Why had he let go of her? Did he not want Sophia to see that they were together?

"Um, hi," Sophia said suddenly, turning toward Aubrey.

"Oh, sorry. Aubrey, this is Sophia. Sophia, this is Aubrey," Grayson said. "Aubrey's visiting from Florida. She's competing in the pageant."

"Nice to meet you," Sophia said in a totally genuine tone.

"You too," Aubrey managed to reply.

"Well. Good luck. I bet Layla's going to be tough to beat," Sophia said, adjusting the strap on her expensive leather purse.

Layla preened. "Oh, Sophia. You're so sweet."

"I had to say that because she's one of my best friends," Sophia joked at a whisper, leaning in toward Aubrey's shoulder. Aubrey laughed. She couldn't help it. As much as she wanted to hate Sophia for being Grayson's ex, the girl seemed kind of cool. Not that she was surprised. Grayson probably wouldn't have dated her otherwise.

"Come on, Soph," Layla said, narrowing her eyes. "Let's go put on our skates."

"I thought you were cutting in line," Grayson said as they stepped away.

"Yeah, I'm not hungry anymore," Layla said.

Me neither, Aubrey thought, seeing right through Layla as if she was Plexiglas. Obviously she had cut in only so she could shove Sophia in Grayson's face and ruin their date.

"Bye!" Sophia said, allowing herself to be led

away. "I'll see you soon?"

"Yeah. Bye," Grayson said vaguely.

For a long moment, Aubrey stood in silence, listening to the boys in front of her as they confused the poor woman behind the counter with their constantly changing order. She glanced up at Grayson and found him staring straight ahead as if someone had just blinded him with a camera flash.

Okay, this is awkward, Aubrey thought. *Ask him something. Get him to talk. This silence cannot go on.*

"So, Sophia is . . . ?" she said, even though she knew the answer. *He* didn't know that she knew.

"My ex-girlfriend," he said, still staring. "She goes to Brown. I haven't seen her since August."

"Ah," Aubrey said again. "So that must have been weird."

"Weird? What? No," Grayson said, finally looking at her. "No. That's over. Beyond over. I was just surprised, that's all. It's fine. I'm fine."

Yeah. Too bad you still have that deer-in-the-headlights look going on.

"We can cut this short if you want," Aubrey

said, simply because she wanted to be the person who said it. If he suddenly decided he wanted to go home, she wasn't sure she could handle the disappointment.

"No. Absolutely not," Grayson said, taking her hand again. "I'm having fun. Aren't you?"

"Definitely," Aubrey replied, forcing a smile.

"Next!" the woman behind the counter called out, sounding harried.

"So we're good?" Grayson asked as he pulled out his wallet.

"We're good," Aubrey replied.

She glanced over her shoulder at the crowded lake as Grayson ordered their hot chocolate, trying to pick out a black ski jacket and suede coat skating around together.

The only question is, will we still be good after I hunt down your sister and scratch her eyes out? Aubrey thought.

Chapter 9

Aubrey moved through her dance steps with robotic stiffness on Friday morning, trying to keep one eye on the wings, where Grayson and Sophia had been chatting for the last fifteen minutes. Madeline called out some kind of direction, but it was entirely lost on Aubrey. All she could do was imagine what the two exes might be saying. Was Sophia telling him she'd made a mistake? That she wanted to get back together?

"Aubrey! What are you doing? You're supposed to move back, not forward!" Madeline shouted.

Aubrey whipped her head around just in time to see Dana bearing down on her. They collided with a jarring slam and both of them hit the floor.

"Sorry," Dana said, as the music continued to

blare through the speakers.

"No, I'm sorry," Aubrey replied, disentangling her legs from Dana's. "It was my fault."

"Please. I'm a total klutz. Do they have to make this dance so complicated?" Dana said with a laugh as she helped Aubrey up.

"It's *not* complicated," Layla said, horning in. "You two just don't know your right foot from your left."

Aubrey instinctively glanced over at Grayson to see if he'd overheard Layla's comment. She was simply dying for the day that she exposed herself for the bitch she really was. But Grayson was too wrapped up in Sophia to have heard.

"All right, everyone! Let's take five, and when we come back we will take it from the top!" Fabrizia announced, clapping her hands above her head.

Quickly, the girls huddled together and headed backstage to get warm.

"You coming?" Christie asked Aubrey, grabbing her jacket off the floor near the back curtain and shoving her arms into the sleeves.

"Actually, I was going to go talk to Grayson," Aubrey said, pointing over her shoulder at stage right.

Christie's mouth set in a line as she glanced past Aubrey's shoulder. "Looks like someone already beat you to it."

Aubrey's heart sank as she turned around. Grayson and Sophia were on their way down the stage steps together, heading away from Aubrey. As they reached the bottom stair, Sophia tripped and Grayson touched her arm to steady her. They both laughed in a familiar way and then he led her down the aisle in front of the stage and around back. Where were they going? And why did they have to be alone?

"Everything okay, FL?" Layla asked facetiously as she traipsed by, heading backstage. "You look like you're going to lose your breakfast."

Aubrey opened her mouth to respond, but nothing came out. What was she supposed to say to that? She *did* feel like she was going to throw up. Too bad she couldn't do it on cue and aim for Layla's feet.

"Aubrey, come on. You're going to freeze," Christie implored.

"Just a sec."

Aubrey watched the spot at the corner of the stage where Grayson and Sophia had disappeared and willed him to come back. She willed him to tell Sophia it was over, that he had moved on, and that the girl he had moved on with was probably waiting for him onstage right now. But he didn't reappear. And the longer she stood there, the more the cold penetrated her skin, until she finally had to give up and go backstage for some warmth with everyone else.

As much as it pained her to admit it, even to herself, it looked as if Layla *was* a person she didn't want to mess with. Unfortunately, the realization had come way too late.

"Do you think they're getting back together?" Aubrey asked, hating the pathetic tone of her voice. It was Friday night and she hadn't seen or heard from Grayson since he'd walked off with Sophia that morning. She lay on top of her unmade bed, fully clothed in a sweater and jeans, her cell phone clutched against her chest, silently mocking her. She had already left Grayson two messages and almost gone for three before Christie convinced her it was too much. But why hadn't he called her back? As she stared up at the ceiling of the room she was sharing with Christie, she willed her phone to ring, but it didn't oblige.

"Please. No way," Christie replied as she paged through last year's *Seventeen* prom issue on her own bed. Neither Christie nor Aubrey had settled on a dress for the pageant yet, and time was running out. Christie spent half her time perusing magazines and the internet, looking for ideas. Aubrey had done zero research herself. She just figured that one of these days she and Christie would go shopping again and she would just pick something out then. It wasn't as if it mattered.

At least it *hadn't* mattered. Not before Sophia had shown up on the scene. Now Aubrey was thinking it might be a good idea to actually *think* about which dress she wore. Because Sophia, obviously, was going to look like a supermodel when she handed over her crown.

"What do you think of this?" Christie asked, holding the magazine open to a photo of a girl in pink satin.

"It's nice," Aubrey said with a glance.

"I know the pink is kind of . . . *pink*, but I like pink," Christie said, laying the magazine down in her lap again.

"You know you'll look good in anything. And how could you say 'no way'?" Aubrey asked, laying her arms down flat on the bed with her palms up. "I mean, did you see her? She's perfect. Totally gorgeous, totally sweet . . ."

"And totally his ex," Christie replied with a sigh. "They broke up for a reason. Do you really think that Grayson's the kind of guy who just bumps into his ex-girlfriend once and turns into total mush?"

Aubrey rolled onto her side to face Christie, propping her head up on her hand and placing her cell on the sheet in front of her. "Knowing what I know about him, I'd definitely say no, but you weren't there, Christie. You didn't see how he looked at her."

"I'm sure he was just surprised to see her there," Christie said. She slapped the magazine closed and swung her legs over the side of the bed. "You can't expect him to have *zero* feelings when his ex shows up out of nowhere."

"So you admit it! He still has feelings for her!"

Christie rolled her eyes and groaned as she stood up and paced over to her dresser. "How do I know? I've never even had a boyfriend!" she blurted.

Aubrey blinked. Christie had sounded a tad impatient there. "Are you okay?" she asked.

"I'm fine. I'm just . . . stressed out," Christie said, looking at herself in the mirror. "I have to find a dress for the pageant and a dress for the ball, not to mention a *date* for the ball. . . ." She stared off into space, chewing on her thumbnail. Then suddenly she looked down at her nails and tucked them under her arms. Snow princesses, after all, could not have gnawed-up nails.

"Jonathan hasn't asked you, then?" Aubrey said gently.

"No. He hasn't," Christie said, looking at the floor. "At least you guys have *had* a date."

"Christie, I'm sorry. I totally suck," Aubrey said. She couldn't believe she'd spent all this time whining about Grayson, whom she'd just met, when Christie was still pining away for a guy she'd been crushing on for years.

"Whatever. It's not your fault," Christie said. She turned and grabbed her baton off the floor next to her dresser, avoiding eye contact. "I have to go practice."

"Okay. But, Christie . . . don't worry," Aubrey said, causing her friend to pause at the door. "I'm sure it's all going to work out."

"Yeah. I guess," Christie said.

Then she slipped into the hall, closing the door quietly behind her. Aubrey dropped back on her bed, placing her cell on the night table. Forget Grayson. For the moment, anyway. Aubrey would never have even come to this place and met Grayson if it hadn't been for Christie. And with all the stress going on in the girl's life right now, she deserved a date with the guy she liked. Aubrey decided right then and there that she was going to make that happen.

She just had to figure out how.

"Come on, upper right!"

Aubrey slapped her tenth puck at the hockey

goal and it flew off into the night, at least two feet above the hole. She tipped her head back and stared up at the stars. "Crap! Why can I not hit the upper right?"

"Don't worry, kid! You'll get it!" one of the carnival workers shouted from atop the Ferris wheel, waving a flashlight in her direction.

"Thanks!" Aubrey shouted back, clutching her stick with both hands and skating in a little circle. "You can do this," she muttered under her breath. "Just don't think about anything else. Concentrate."

She skated over to the edge of the pond to retrieve her pucks, using her stick to corral them together. After searching the inn for Jonathan, who apparently was not on shift that night, Aubrey had finally given up and come outside to practice. Shooting pucks was a perfect way to get out her aggression about Layla and Sophia and Grayson and the Chamberlains, but being on the pond was also distracting. She kept catching herself glancing over her shoulder at the woods—the spot from which Grayson had emerged that first morning—as if she expected him to come striding out toward her. Unfortunately, every time she looked she saw nothing but trees.

"Okay. Just try to get *one* puck in the upper right," she told herself as she set up again.

She reeled back and hit the first puck. It smacked into the tarp and bounced across the ice. She took a deep breath and tried again. This one went way wide. Aubrey gritted her teeth. Pucks three, four, five, and six all missed. Every muscle in her body coiled even tighter with each failed try. Aubrey was just pulling her stick back to hit number seven, when she felt someone skate up behind her.

"Whatcha doing?"

"Oh my God!" Aubrey gasped, her skates nearly slipping out from under her. She whipped around to face Grayson, her hand to her chest. He had his hockey stick and backpack with him. Apparently he'd come to the pond to shoot around as well. "What are you doing? Trying to kill me?"

Grayson laughed and skated off, making a wide circle around her and her goal. "Looks like you're practicing for the hockey shot competition."

Aubrey stared at him, her heart still in her

throat. He was simply smiling and skating around as if nothing was wrong. As if he hadn't totally vanished with his ex-girlfriend that morning and gone radio silent ever since. He stopped short behind her line of pucks, spraying ice up over her skates, and shot number seven directly through the center hole.

"Very nice," Aubrey said sarcastically. "What are you doing here?"

"Oh, I just had dinner up at the inn with a friend of mine," Grayson replied.

There was a huge lump in Aubrey's throat. Was this "friend" Sophia?

"Who?" she asked.

"His name's Brody Landry. He's this old bachelor guy who does some work around the resort sometimes. He's always heard about how good the food was at the inn, so I said I'd bring him," Grayson replied, skating around in circles with a grin. "He was definitely impressed."

Aubrey watched him, baffled. Grayson was bringing his parents' employees to eat at the inn? Why? And why did he seem so inordinately psyched about it? Of course, these weren't the most pressing questions on her mind, so she decided to ask what she really wanted to ask.

"Why didn't you call me back?"

Grayson's brow creased. He fished in his pocket for his cell phone and looked at the screen. "Damn. Dead again," he said. "When did you call?"

"Forget it," Aubrey said with a sigh. "You're supposed to charge those things, you know."

"People are always telling me that. I just never seem to remember," Grayson said. He tucked the phone away, skated another circle around her, and shot the eighth puck through the upper left hole. "So are you going to compete?"

Aubrey couldn't believe this. All that stressing about him not calling her back, and he'd simply let his battery run out. She thought back to the first time she'd met Layla, when the girl had complained about her brother's inability to answer his phone. Maybe she shouldn't count on his cell from here on out. If there was going to *be* a here on out.

"Yep," she said finally. "That's the plan."

"Cool. From what I saw, you're pretty good," he said. "But it's too bad I win every year," he added with a cocky smile.

Aubrey narrowed her eyes. Apparently the ego thing was something he and his sister had in common.

"Not this year," she shot back.

Grayson's grin widened. "We'll see about that."

Then, without even taking a breath, he slapped five pucks in succession, hitting each of the five holes. It was like watching a hockey-drill DVD on fast-forward. When he was done he stopped and leaned on his stick, looking at her all self-satisfied. His smile was semi-adorable, semi-infuriating. Where *was* he all afternoon? She knew he hadn't spent *all* his time with Sophia, because she had come back to rehearsal, but he never had. And where had he been *since* rehearsal? Had the two of them met up somewhere?

Aubrey wanted to ask all these questions, but she knew she would seem like a pathetic loser if she did. So, with no other options in mind, she turned and skated toward the goal and tugged it to the edge of the pond.

"What're you doing? Backing down from a challenge?" Grayson teased.

"No. I've just practiced long enough," Aubrey replied, kicking a few pucks in front of her.

"Oh, come on! Let's see what you've got!" Grayson said.

"You already saw when you got here," Aubrey replied, dropping the goal off on the dirt. "I think I'll save the good stuff for the night of the competition."

Grayson laughed and started to help gather the pucks. "All right, then. I can respect that."

As they worked, Aubrey refused to look at him. She was sure that if she did he would be able to see the hurt and confusion in her eyes. But she could feel him staring at her the entire time and her face started to grow warm under his gaze. Was he going to explain what was going on with him and Sophia? Was he trying to find the words to say he was sorry, but he couldn't see Aubrey anymore? Was that why she was being forced to endure this painfully awkward silence?

"You know, I gotta say, I'm surprised that you're participating in this whole pageant thing," he said suddenly.

Aubrey stood up straight, feeling as if she'd just been slapped. "Why? Because I'm not as perfect as Sophia?"

Grayson stared at her, shocked. Aubrey wished, suddenly, that she could go back in time and say anything but that. Talk about sounding pathetic.

"Um . . . what?" Grayson asked.

Aubrey skated toward the edge of the pond and dropped down on the cold dirt to unlace her skates. "Nothing. Forget I said anything."

"Yeah, like that's gonna happen," Grayson said, skating up in front of her. "First of all, Sophia is not perfect."

Aubrey snorted, staring down at the scratches in the surface of the ice as her cold, shaking fingers slowly worked her laces. "Yeah, right."

Grayson turned and sat down next to Aubrey, his leg touching hers. He lay his hockey stick aside and pulled his knees up, wrapping his arms around them.

"She is *anything* but perfect," he said. "But forget about her. The only reason I said what I said was . . . I think you're way too cool to be in the Snow Queen Pageant."

The laces dropped from Aubrey's useless fingers. She looked over at Grayson and found that his face was mere inches from hers. Her heart skipped an excited beat. "But I thought you liked pageant girls."

Narrowing his eyes, Grayson pretended to ponder this. "I used to. But I think I'm evolving."

Aubrey giggled. "Okay, then . . . what were you and Sophia talking about this morning?" she asked, hoping her nervousness didn't come through in her voice.

"Oh, that," Grayson said, his eyes twinkling. "Is that what you're all upset about?"

"I'm not upset!" Aubrey lied. "Just asking."

"Okay, well, Sophia told me she thinks our breakup was a mistake and she wants to get back together," Grayson said matter-of-factly.

"Oh," Aubrey said, looking out at the ice again.

Her eyes smarted and she told herself it was from the wind, even though the air was still. Grayson reached over and touched her face with his gloved hand, nudging her chin so that she had to look at him again.

"But I told her no," he said firmly, looking Aubrey in the eye. "I'm over it. Over her. Seeing her again has only confirmed that."

"Seriously?" Aubrey said.

"Seriously," Grayson replied. "I mean, what kind of person takes a week off from college to come back home and give away a fake diamond tiara?"

Tell me how you really feel, Aubrey thought happily. She pressed her lips together to keep from laughing and Grayson blinked, embarrassed.

"No offense," he added quickly.

"None taken," she replied. She pulled her own knees up under her chin to mimic his pose and found that she was much warmer this way. "Since you've been totally honest with me, I guess I should be totally honest with you."

"About . . . ?" Grayson asked, raising his eyebrows. He actually looked tense. As if he was afraid she might tell him that she also had an ex who was in the picture. Too sweet.

"The pageant. This stupid, ridiculous pageant," she said, happy that she was finally able to say it out loud. "The only reason I'm in it is because Christie said she couldn't do it without me. And it's her lifelong dream to be Snow Queen, so . . . what's a best friend to do?"

Grayson laughed, a cloud of steam rising from his lips into the night. "Really? That's why you're competing?"

"Yep," Aubrey said. She tilted her head and looked out across the ice. "You pegged it. I *am* way too cool to be a pageant girl," she joked. "And, you know, now we have added incentive . . . since she's planning to give the prize money to Rose and Jim. I have to help Christie win. There's a lot at stake, you know?"

"I think it's really amazing that you'd do that for your friend," Grayson said earnestly. "Endure all that hair spray and eyeliner and those insane high heels—"

"Not to mention the bitchiness and backstabbing and catfights," Aubrey put in. Not adding, of course, that his sister had been the instigator of most of these things.

"Of course. Let's not mention those," Grayson joked. He looked her in the eye. "Seriously, though, Christie is lucky to have you. And so are Rose and Jim."

Aubrey's heart skipped crazily. "Thanks."

"And it's lucky for me, too," Grayson told her.

Aubrey looked over at him, resting her chin on her arm. "How so?"

"Well, if she didn't have you for a best friend, you wouldn't be here," Grayson said, shifting slightly so he could face her better. "And I'm really glad you're here."

"Why?" Aubrey asked, her heart starting to pitter-patter. She had a feeling she knew the answer, but she wanted to hear him say it.

"Because if you weren't here, I couldn't do this," Grayson said.

Then he leaned in ever so slowly and touched his lips to hers. Aubrey's eyes fluttered closed as her heart flipped and cartwheeled and bounced around like a rubber ball. Grayson was kissing her. Ten minutes ago she had thought he was getting back together with Sophia, but now he was kissing *her*. It was all so crazy and surprising and incredible she felt like laughing. Then she got a faint taste of his cherry Chapstick and she couldn't help it. She smiled even with her lips pressed against his. Grayson smiled, too, and they both leaned back to laugh.

"I've been wanting to do that ever since that

first morning," he said.

"I've been wanting you to do that ever since that first morning," she replied giddily.

"Well, we should communicate better," Grayson said with mock seriousness.

"Definitely," Aubrey replied, nodding. "But not right now."

She grabbed Grayson's jacket, pulled him to her, and this time the kiss went on and on.

Chapter 10

"This is going to be our most fabulous winter carnival to date!"

Aubrey cheered for Rose's announcement along with Christie, Jim, Charlie, Jonathan, and a few other workers from the inn, lifting their mugs of coffee in a toast. It was Saturday morning and they had all gathered at the center of the carnival grounds so that Rose and Jim could do their walk-through and check out everything before the carnival began the next day. It was an annual ritual, and Aubrey was happy to be included. And she was impressed that everyone was managing to stay so chipper and positive when they had no idea how the Chamberlains' lack of participation was going to affect the carnival's business. She was about to mention this to Christie, when she noticed her friend watching Jonathan longingly over Aubrey's shoulder. Aubrey took a deep breath. It was about time to deal with these two already.

"You should go talk to him," Aubrey whispered to Christie as the group began to walk.

"Right now?" Christie said, hiding her lips behind her coffee cup. "It's six A.M. I look like death."

Aubrey rolled her eyes. Christie, in fact, looked as perfect as always with her shiny hair falling over the shoulders of her red jacket, her cheeks tinged with pink from the cold.

"You look beautiful. Just go over there and say hi. What's the worst that could happen?"

"He could laugh in my face," Christie said.

Right then, as if on cue, Jonathan let out a peel of laughter so loud everyone stopped talking. Christie looked as if she was going to faint.

"Sorry! Charlie was just telling me the story of his latest, greatest snowboarding crash," Jonathan told the group.

Everyone chuckled and continued to walk. Charlie's arm was tucked against his body in a new sling to help keep him from straining his freshly sprained wrist. Aubrey wouldn't have minded hearing the story herself, but right then she could have wrung both Jonathan's and Charlie's necks for their bad timing. Clearly Aubrey was going to have to get Jonathan to take the plunge and ask Christie out. It was never going to happen if Christie had to do it herself.

"So, Aubrey, do you have a favorite carnival ride?" Rose asked, slipping her arm around Aubrey's shoulders.

"I've always been a big fan of the games, actually," Aubrey said as they passed by the swings. "I like to go home with as many humongous stuffed animals as possible."

"Got a competitive streak in you, huh? I like that," Jim said with a nod.

"Oh, she *definitely* does," Christie chimed in.

Aubrey smiled as she thought back to last night. After kissing Grayson for what seemed like hours, Aubrey had finally told him she had to get to sleep so she would be fresh for today's rehearsal. Then, once he was gone, she had spent another hour shooting pucks. So what if they had kissed? That didn't mean she couldn't smoke him in the hockey shot competition.

"Rose, is it okay if I head back to the inn? I want to get in some twirling practice before rehearsal," Christie said, tossing the last of the coffee out of her mug.

"Sure, hon. Whatever you need," Rose said.

Aubrey shot Christie a withering look. "Come on, Christie. Don't go!"

Christie checked over her shoulder and saw Jonathan and Charlie closing in on them. "I'll see you later!" Then she jogged off as if a band of scary clowns were approaching, rather than the guy she liked. Aubrey sighed and took another sip of her coffee. How did the girl ever expect to be happy if she didn't even try?

Lucky for her, she had a friend who was willing to try for her. So what if Christie had begged Aubrey not to say anything to Jonathan? Sometimes a girl had to do what a girl had to do. And if *she* didn't do something soon, this romance was never going to get off the ground.

"Let's check out that new ride—the Tilt and Twirl," Jim suggested. "I want to see it run a few times before any of our guests get on it."

He walked ahead and Rose clucked her tongue, shaking her head fondly. "That's my

Jim. Always Mr. Double-Checker."

She patted Aubrey on the shoulder and followed after her husband. Aubrey took a deep breath and walked over to Charlie and Jonathan, who had paused to make faces in front of a fun house–style mirror. Way mature.

"What are you guys doing?" Aubrey asked.

"Having some fun. What are *you* doing?" Jonathan replied.

Aubrey heaved a sigh and pulled her hat down lower over her brow as the wind started to kick up around her. "Charlie, can I talk to Jonathan alone for a second?"

The two boys exchanged a baffled look.

"Sure," Charlie said finally. He supported his sling with his good hand as he shrugged. "I'll catch up with Rose and Jim."

He jogged off, leaving Aubrey alone with Jonathan on a wide patch of dirt between the merry-go-round and one of dozens of snack bars. Aubrey could hear some hammering in the distance and a power tool was running somewhere nearby, but otherwise, there was nothing but silence. She suddenly realized that she hadn't actually spoken to Jonathan much since her arrival and felt the full weight of the awkwardness between them.

"So . . . what's up?" Jonathan asked, repeatedly knocking his fists together.

Okay, just get it over with, Aubrey told herself.

"It's about Christie," she said. "Why haven't you asked her out yet?"

Jonathan instantly turned beet red. "What? What makes you think I want to ask out Christie?" he said, glancing past her shoulder nervously.

Aubrey looked behind her. There was no one there. "It's totally obvious," she said. "You like her, she likes you . . . why don't you ask her to the winter ball?"

"She likes me? Really? Did she tell you that?" Jonathan asked, suddenly all alert.

Aubrey stared him down. "Just ask her, Jonathan. I'm sure she'll say yes."

"I don't know." Jonathan took a few paces away from her and kicked at some hay that had been strewn along the edges of the path. "I mean, I work for Rose and Jim. What if they didn't approve?"

"Is that what's holding you back? Please! I'm

sure they just want their granddaughter to be happy," Aubrey said. She walked over to him and slapped him hard on the back with her free hand. "You can do this, Jonathan. I know you can."

Jonathan glanced at her over his shoulder and tilted his head with a reluctant expression. "I don't know. . . . "

"Well, I do!" Aubrey replied, growing frustrated. What was wrong with him and Christie? Why couldn't these people just go after what they clearly wanted?

"We'll see, okay? Maybe," he said, backing away from her. "I'll think about it."

"I'm not going to drop this, Jonathan! From now on I'm making it my mission to get you two together!" she said.

"Why do you care so much about this?" he asked, lifting his palms as he continued to back away.

Because her friend deserved a nice guy. Because she and Christie had never been to a dance together and she thought it might be fun. Because now that she was happy with Grayson, she wanted to help Christie become just as happy. Not that she could explain this all to him right now.

"Because I do!" she replied.

"Whatever that means." Jonathan lifted his hand in a wave, then turned and speed-walked around the corner where Rose, Jim, and Charlie had disappeared. Aubrey took a deep breath and tipped her head back to look at the clear, blue, snowless sky. She could just imagine the four of them walking into the winter ball together—her and Grayson, Christie and Jonathan. Grayson would look so handsome all dressed up, and Aubrey would find herself some killer gown that would make both Layla and Sophia green with envy. It would be the most incredible night ever.

Not that Grayson had asked her yet, but she was sure he would. He didn't want to be with Sophia or anyone else. He wanted to be with her. After last night, Aubrey was completely sure of that fact.

"Now if only it would snow," she said to herself, searching in vain for a cloud.

Then everything would be just perfect.

* * *

"Well, here we are. End of week one and still no snow," Aubrey complained as she and Christie walked down the plushly carpeted hallway toward the private rehearsal space behind the amphitheater. Every panoramic window they passed by afforded the same exact view—big blue sky, bright shining sun, bare, brown mountains. "Everyone kept saying there was snow in the forecast for the end of the week, but do you see a flake?"

"No, I don't see a flake," Christie replied.

"No flakes!" Aubrey said, throwing her hands up as she continued to walk. "Why do the weather people even bother? I mean, seriously. Of all the pointless professions in the world, that has to be the most—"

Suddenly Aubrey heard loud dance music and she stopped in her tracks. Someone was playing the music that Christie was using for her baton-twirling act.

"Oh my God. Do you hear that?" Aubrey asked, her heart sinking to her toes.

"Yeah," Christie said, going pale. "Did I leave my iPod in the rehearsal room?"

"Come on," Aubrey said.

She whirled around and headed for the supposedly soundproof rehearsal room. As she approached she realized that the door was slightly ajar, which was why they could hear the music all the way down the hall. Not wanting to be too obvious, Aubrey tiptoed over to the door and peeked inside, tugging Christie with her. When she saw the girl dancing her heart out in the middle of the rehearsal space, her vision prickled over with angry red dots.

"Layla?" she blurted, throwing the door wide.

"Aubrey! Hey!" Grayson said, his eyes lighting up at the sight of her.

She glanced over at him and Fabrizia, both of whom were standing in the far corner. Until that moment she hadn't realized they were there. Their presence was going to make it a lot harder to wrestle her nemesis to the floor.

"Hi," Aubrey said, unsure of how to proceed. Then she saw the haughty smirk on Layla's face and couldn't hold back. "What are you doing?" she asked. "That's Christie's music."

"What?" Layla said, all wide-eyed and innocent. Her forehead was beaded with sweat as she walked over and turned off the stereo. "I had no idea."

"Yes, you did. You totally had the idea," Aubrey said, attempting to keep her voice steady. "You were here when Christie was rehearsing the other day. You knew it was hers. Right, Christie?"

Everyone looked at Christie, who was standing near the door looking shaken. She opened her mouth, but nothing came out. Aubrey wanted to kill Layla for upsetting her friend like this. Christie was the sweetest person on the planet. She was just trying to compete in a stupid pageant. Why couldn't Layla just leave her alone?

Finally, Christie nodded. "She was here," she said weakly.

"Layla, is this true?" Fabrizia asked, holding one gloved hand over her heart. Like the very idea of Layla cheating might cause a sudden coronary.

"Of course not! Why would I want to use the same music as one of my competitors?" Layla asked, tossing her thick mane of hair over her shoulder.

"You are such a liar," Aubrey snapped.

"Aubrey," Grayson said, holding out a hand as if to stop her from doing something she'd regret. Aubrey felt the sting of betrayal, that he would believe Layla over her.

But remember, she is his sister. And she does have that innocent-angel act down pat, Aubrey told herself.

"Well, I guess it's your word against mine," Layla said, looking at Aubrey and Christie.

For a long moment, no one said a word. Then, finally, Grayson blew out a sigh. "Layla, I have a hard time believing Christie and Aubrey would make up something like this. Maybe you heard it here with them and then . . . forgot where you heard it?"

Layla's jaw dropped slightly and then she laughed. "Fine. I saw her rehearsing to it. But I didn't know that it was definitely the music she'd be using for the pageant. Besides, I've been rehearsing this choreography since last summer. It's not like I heard the music for the first time that day and said, 'Oh! I want to use that.'"

Aubrey didn't believe her. She was sure that Layla had decided to use it that day. And she was also certain that the girl had left the door to the soundproof room open on purpose, knowing that Christie would arrive for her designated time slot and hear it. Layla knew that Christie had confidence issues and this was her way of throwing her off her game. Which, apparently, was working. Christie looked as if she wanted to flee but was too upset to move.

Aubrey looked at Fabrizia for a decision. As far as she was concerned, it was up to the director to sort this out.

"Well, I suppose you could both use the same music, although I do not recommend it," Fabrizia said, lifting her fingers to her chin as she pondered the problem. "It is always far better to stand out to the judges."

"Don't worry, I'll stand out," Layla said with a smirk, looking Christie up and down.

"Oh, that's really nice," Aubrey snapped.

"I just mean that I'm sure our interpretations will be different enough," Layla said, her voice pitching up an octave as she glanced at her brother. Grayson, of course, seemed to accept this explanation. "I don't have a problem with it if Christie doesn't have a problem with it."

Aubrey narrowed her eyes. All she wanted to do was grab Layla's iPod and crush it under her foot. But she couldn't do that. Not with everyone watching her. Not with Grayson watching her. How was it possible that he couldn't see Layla for what she really was? At that moment she would have given anything to have Grayson squarely on her side. But instead, he was looking at Christie expectantly as if waiting for her to amicably agree to Layla's benevolent proposal.

"It's fine," Christie said, her voice watery. "I'll be fine."

Aubrey glanced at her watch. "Christie and I have the rehearsal room in five minutes. We'll be outside."

"Thanks, Christie!" Layla sang as Aubrey tugged Christie out the door.

Outside, with the door safely closed, Aubrey let out a frustrated groan and leaned her forehead against the smooth glass of the nearest window. The pane was cool and it felt good against her overheated skin. Calming.

"I don't believe this," Christie said, slumping against the wall. "What am I going to do?"

"You're going to pick another song," Aubrey said firmly.

"But how? There's no time," Christie said. "How could she do this?"

"She's doing it because she knows you can beat her," Aubrey said, looking her friend in the eye. "She's afraid of you."

Christie scoffed. "Please. Layla's not afraid of anything."

"Yes she is. She's afraid of seeing Christie Howell wearing the Snow Queen crown," Aubrey said, turning around and staring daggers at the door of the rehearsal room. "And we are going to make her worst nightmare come true. All you have to do is find new music."

"And perfect a new routine," Christie added, looking dubious.

"In less than a week," Aubrey added.

She and Christie sighed as one, a heavy sense of doom settling over them. Aubrey had never hated Layla more.

Chapter 11

"That's it. I have to drop out of the pageant," Christie said, shoving aside the silver curtain on her dressing room. She was wearing a deep red dress with a plunging neckline and rhinestone detailing.

"Why? That looks nice on you," Aubrey said, even though the gown was way too sparkly for her tastes.

Apparently, pageant dresses were supposed to be sparkly. Every single gown Christie had tried on had featured rhinestones or sequins or both. Aubrey had chosen her own dress over an hour ago—a plain black strapless with a single rhinestone snowflake brooch holding the sash at the side of the waist. It was elegant and didn't make her look as if she was trying too hard. But she hadn't even shown it to Christie yet, because the girl had been too busy whirlygigging around the boutique, trying on every dress in sight.

"Really? Because I think it makes me look like one of the *Real Housewives of Atlanta*," Christie said, turning to look in the three-way mirror. "I'm sixteen. I'm not supposed to look like I'm forty," she added, lifting up the slim velvet skirt and letting it fall again, trying to poof it out a bit.

"Then why do you keep trying on dresses that are made for forty-year-olds?" Aubrey asked, standing up from the velour couch on which she'd been parked for the last hour. "These dresses are not you."

"I know!" Christie groaned, dropping down on the couch and leaning her head back. "But these are the kinds of dresses the girls wear for the pageant. They're all slinky and sexy and sophisticated. . . ."

"Or just plain *old*," Aubrey said, wrinkling her nose in distaste at the pile of Christie's discards. She thought back to that morning's encounter with Layla and felt a jolt of inspiration. "So all the girls wear dresses like this?"

"Yeah. Dark colors, velvet, slits up the back.

It's pretty standard," Christie said, toying with the chiffon skirt on one of the dresses she'd rejected.

"So why not do something entirely different?" Aubrey suggested.

Christie's brow crinkled. "What do you mean?"

"You remember what Fabrizia said." Aubrey walked over to a rack filled with pastel-colored gowns. "You want to stand out to the judges—make them remember you."

"Yeah . . ." Christie said, sitting forward.

"So . . ." Aubrey pulled out a big pink gown with a poufy skirt and delicate spaghetti straps, similar to the one Christie had pointed out in her magazine the other day. She held it up to her chin with one hand and held the skirt out with the other to show its volume. "Stand out."

Christie's eyes lit up at the sight of the pastel pink dress. Tiny silver sparkles sprinkled the skirt, so that they caught the light when it moved.

"I don't know," Christie said. She got up from the couch and approached the dress with a smile. "Pink isn't really a winter color."

"Maybe not, but it's *your* color," Aubrey said. "You look beautiful in pink. You'll look like a princess. And I bet that something demure will really appeal to some of the older judges."

And maybe, just maybe, it'll give you the edge over Layla, Aubrey thought, imagining Layla's devastated face when she heard Christie's name called as the new Snow Queen.

"Just try it on," Aubrey said, handing the hanger to Christie. "Please? For me?"

Christie grinned. "Okay!"

She hustled over to the dressing room as fast as her tight skirt would allow her and snatched the curtain closed.

"Hey! I never saw your dress," Christie called out over the sounds of zipping and unzipping.

"It's nice. You'll like it," Aubrey told her, lifting the black velvet dress to inspect it. "I think it'll serve my purpose."

"Your purpose?" Christie asked.

"Yeah. My plan is to score higher than Layla, but lower than you," Aubrey told her friend. "Which shouldn't be too hard, considering I have no talent."

"Oh, come on! What about that song from

South Pacific? That was good," Christie called out.

"Who's singing a song from *South Pacific*?" the shop owner, Clarissa, asked, pausing as she walked by. "I *love* that musical."

Clarissa had been helping Christie pick out dresses all afternoon and had only stepped away to answer the phone. A tall woman with broad shoulders and curly brown hair, Clarissa had been a friend of Rose's ever since she'd opened her store twenty years ago. At least that was what she'd told Aubrey when Christie had introduced them. Like Jason at the ski shop, she had offered to lend both Aubrey and Christie their gowns for the pageant. Apparently Rose and Jim had put up her entire family at a huge discount when she'd gotten married a few years ago, and Clarissa was ready to return the favor.

"I am. Maybe," Aubrey replied. "Unfortunately, I sound ridiculous singing it."

"Oh, I'm sure that's not true," Clarissa said, sitting down on the arm of the couch next to Aubrey. "I think you two girls are going to blow away the competition. At least I *hope* you will. Everyone in this town is just sick of the Chamberlains getting everything they want."

"Really? I thought it was just me," Aubrey said with a laugh.

"Oh, please, honey. We're all rooting for Christie . . . and you, of course. Any friend of Christie's—"

"Thanks," Aubrey said. "Just don't get your hopes up when it comes to me. I am totally talentless."

"You are not talentless," Christie protested from behind the curtain.

"Maybe not. But everyone in that audience is going to think I am," Aubrey replied. *Including Grayson,* she added silently, shuddering at the very idea of him hearing her sing.

"Well, it's too bad you can't pick out dresses for everyone," Christie said. "Because you definitely have a talent for that."

She stepped out of the dressing room and Aubrey's jaw dropped. The color, as always, was perfect for Christie, showing off her olive skin and jet-black hair. The fitted bodice enhanced her small frame without being too slinky, and the skirt swished elegantly when Christie walked.

"My goodness, Christie! That dress was *made* for you!" Clarissa cooed, clasping her hands together.

"Really?" Christie asked, beaming.

"Definitely," Aubrey said with a grin. "That is a pageant winner."

"You weren't kidding. That was the best spaghetti and meatballs I've ever had in my life," Aubrey said, placing her hand over her stomach as she and Grayson emerged from Leonardo's Ristorante that night. It was a crisp, clear evening, and the sidewalks in town were packed with people moving in and out of restaurants or window-shopping. Grayson took Aubrey's hand and held it as they navigated the busy walkway. Aubrey's heart leaped happily, just like it did every time he touched her.

"I figured they probably don't do a lot of hearty Italian food in southern Florida," Grayson said.

"Not really. We're more of a fish-and-vegetable society. Unless you go Cuban," Aubrey said. "Then there's a whole rice and beans and cheese thing added to it and it's heaven. If you ever come to Florida I'll take you to Cuba North. You'll *love* their sampler platter."

"It's a deal," Grayson said. "The next time I'm in Florida, you're on."

Aubrey's smile widened. It may have been totally unrealistic, but she felt as if she and Grayson had just made a plan for the future. As if they had mutually agreed they wanted to stay together for more than just this week. And she kind of liked that feeling.

"So, how's the preparation for the pageant going? Is Christie going to take down the competition?" Grayson asked.

Aubrey laughed. "I hope so," she said. Then she hesitated. "I feel kind of weird talking to you about this. I mean, Layla's part of the competition she wants to take down."

"My sister can take care of herself," Grayson replied, pausing so an elderly couple could get by. "Of course I'd be happy if Layla won, but there's a lot more riding on Christie winning."

"Well, we went shopping for evening gowns today, and the one Christie picked is definitely a showstopper," Aubrey said happily. "The judges won't be able to take their eyes off her."

"Really? I always thought all those dresses were kind of rote," Grayson said.

"Exactly," Aubrey replied. "That's why Christie went with something different. She's going to wear pink. Light pink. She looks like a fairy princess."

"Really? That's a bold choice," Grayson said, stopping in front of a cozy-looking coffeehouse.

"I know, but it's so her. She was obviously uncomfortable in all those slinky little dresses. This way she'll be confident and composed," Aubrey said, smiling as Grayson opened the door for her.

Inside, the small coffeehouse was jam-packed with people, mostly couples cuddling over warm mugs and yummy-looking desserts. A glass case along one wall displayed all kinds of muffins and cookies and tarts, and a huge cappuccino machine chugged away behind the counter. Jazz music played over hidden speakers, and the lights were so low it was difficult to see whether any of the tables were free.

"That's a good thing," Grayson said as he stepped into the café behind her. "Since all the dresses looked the same to me, I always scored the girls on how comfortable they looked walking across the stage. You know, whether their smile was natural or forced, whether it seemed like they were terrified of tripping in their heels or whether they knew they could handle it."

Aubrey tilted her head. "Thanks for the tip. I knew that dating a judge was a good idea."

Her heart stopped for a second, hearing the boldness of her words. Neither of them had actually used the word "dating" yet, but it didn't seem to affect Grayson.

"Oh, so you're using me, then?" Grayson teased.

"Isn't it obvious?" Aubrey teased back.

"Well, don't tell anyone I gave you inside info," Grayson said, leaning in close as he surveyed the tiny shop, looking for an empty table. "Wouldn't want you to get disqualified or anything."

"God forbid," Aubrey joked. Actually, getting disqualified might not be a bad idea at this point. The pageant was in less than a week, and Christie was doing fine. Maybe she could handle the rest of it on her own. It would definitely save Aubrey from the humiliation of having to sing in front of all those people.

But no. She couldn't quit now. She wouldn't give Layla the satisfaction. Besides, she had promised Christie she would be there for her and she didn't want to go back on her word.

"So...what are *you* wearing?" Grayson asked, looping his arms around her waist. Evidently he hadn't seen an empty table, because he seemed content to stay put.

Aubrey grinned. "Wouldn't you like to know?"

"I don't know. Maybe it's better to be surprised," he said, leaning toward her. Aubrey's heart skipped, anticipating a kiss. She hoped there wasn't too much garlic in the spaghetti sauce.

"There's a table opening up over there, you two."

A passing waitress nudged Grayson's elbow and knocked them out of their gooey-eyed embrace before their lips could touch. Grayson stood up straight and cleared his throat.

"Yeah. Thanks," he said.

Giggling under her breath, Aubrey led the way, weaving around the tables and chairs toward the small round booth in the corner.

"So, there's a lot going on this week, huh?" Grayson said as the waitress appeared with menus. Extensive menus. Aubrey looked hers over in shock. Who knew there were so many different flavors of coffee in the world? "Lots of events."

Aubrey blinked. His voice sounded leading. Was he going to ask her to the ball now? She dropped the menu and looked up at him, trying to keep the giddy anticipation out of her eyes.

"Busiest vacation I've ever had," she replied nonchalantly.

Grayson laughed. "Seriously." He leaned his elbows on the table and rubbed his hands together. "So I was thinking . . ."

Aubrey's heart pounded. She bit her lip to keep from grinning and told herself not to sound too eager. Take a second to reply. Play it cool.

"Want to hit the carnival with me tomorrow night?" he asked. "The hot dogs are always freshest at the beginning of the week."

Aubrey's face fell along with her heart, but she recovered quickly. He was asking her out on a date, just not the right one. But the ball wasn't until Thursday night. They had some time. Not a lot of time, but some.

"Sure," she said. "Sounds like fun."

Grayson smiled. "Cool."

"You guys know what you want?" the waitress asked, reappearing with her pad and pencil.

"Not yet. Sorry," Grayson replied. "Can you give us a few minutes?"

"No problem."

Aubrey watched her go with a sigh. She knew what she wanted. A plain coffee and a date with Grayson for the Winter Ball.

Unfortunately, Grayson seemed to need some more time to decide.

Aubrey sat backstage on Sunday morning, her posture straight, her knees locked together, trying not to move a muscle so her strapless dress wouldn't shift on her and expose something she didn't want to expose. When she had first slipped into the gown in the dressing room, her heart had fluttered with excitement over the idea of Grayson seeing her walk across stage all elegant and feminine. But after fifteen minutes in the thing, she had learned that every time she so much as turned her head the top felt as if it was going to fall right off. Maybe this hadn't been the best gown selection after all. Maybe she was trying too hard.

"You look killer in that. You should always wear black," Dana said, pausing on her way to the full-length mirror, which every girl in the place had walked past at least once. Her gown was a deep emerald color with a halter neckline and a slit that exposed her entire leg.

"Thanks," Aubrey said, perking up slightly. "You look good too. That color totally brings out your eyes."

"You think?" Dana said happily. "Thanks!"

Aubrey sat back and smiled. So maybe she hadn't picked the *worst* gown in the world. Did she really look killer?

"So, where's Christie?" Dana asked.

"Oh, she had to run to the bathroom," Aubrey told her. "But just wait until you see her dress."

Just then, Christie emerged from around the edge of the curtain. She looked as if she was floating on air, her pink, poufy skirt swishing across the black plank floor. A few girls actually gasped at the sight of her. Sophia stepped out behind Christie, grinning from ear to ear.

"Oh my gosh, Christie! Look at you!" Dana breathed.

"Doesn't she look amazing?" Sophia asked, reaching up to pat Christie's updo. "I just did her hair in the bathroom."

Aubrey glanced at Sophia as all the other princesses gathered around Christie to check out her dress. "You're helping Christie? What about Layla?"

Sophia cleared her throat and stepped over to Aubrey's side so she could lean toward her ear. "I know what Layla's been doing and it's not fair," she whispered. "I figure my helping Christie kind of levels the playing field."

Aubrey blinked in shock. "But isn't Layla your best friend?"

"Yeah, but that doesn't mean I agree with her about everything," Sophia said, straightening up. "Besides, Christie's always been sweet to me. She doesn't deserve to be sabotaged."

"Wow. I'm impressed," Aubrey said.

Sophia shrugged. "Just because I'm your boyfriend's ex doesn't mean I'm evil."

Aubrey laughed. Sophia really *was* a nice girl. And mature, considering she'd hung around even after Grayson had turned down her offer to get back together. If the same thing had happened to Aubrey, she would have been on the first flight home.

"Do you like it?" Christie asked, breaking away from the pack to show Aubrey her hair.

"It looks *amazing,*" Aubrey said. "Nice work," she added to Sophia.

"Thanks," Sophia replied with a smile.

"You look like a fairy princess!" Dana breathed, touching the skirt with her fingertips.

"It's so . . . different," Rebecca added, in a tone that verged on annoyed.

Aubrey glanced around and saw that all the other girls were whispering about Christie, but not in a bad way. They looked put out, jealous even. As if they were irritated they hadn't thought to veer away from the norm. Christie noticed it too, and smiled conspiratorially at Aubrey. This was totally going to blow the judges away. She could feel it.

"Ladies! I'd like to see all my little princesses

out here, please!" Fabrizia shouted from center stage.

Aubrey's stomach executed a nervous flip as Christie grabbed her hand and squeezed. Grayson was out there somewhere. Suddenly her mouth went dry and her palms felt clammy. For the first time he was going to see her in something other than jeans.

"I hope they have the heat lamps pumped up. I'm freezing," Dana said as they lined up in their preordained order.

"Hey, where's Layla?" Christie asked.

"I guess she's still in the dressing room," Sophia said, glancing over her shoulder.

"Today, ladies!" Fabrizia called out.

"Here goes nothing," Rebecca said. Then she led the girls out onto the stage.

As Aubrey stepped out from behind the warmth and protection of the curtains, she had to concentrate to keep from holding on to her bodice to make sure it would stay up. She also willed herself not to look out at the audience. She didn't want to appear too eager. But finally, the whole line had to turn and face the seats, and when Aubrey did her gaze went automatically to Grayson, who was seated, as usual, in the front row. Her heart burst when she found that he was staring right at her, a smile on his handsome face.

"Wow," he mouthed.

Aubrey giggled, then slapped her hand over her mouth. Grayson simply shook his head in what appeared to be awe. Okay. So the dress *was* killer.

"Sorry I'm late!"

Everyone turned to find Layla fluttering out of the opposite wings in a pale yellow gown with a huge skirt and demure neckline, her hair drawn back in a girlish bun. Aubrey felt the stage tilt underneath her as tiny prickles of gray clouded her vision. She glanced at Christie, who looked utterly devastated, and ire bubbled up inside Aubrey's chest like a surge of lava from a volcano. She looked out at Grayson in the audience and wanted to smack the smile right off his face.

He had told Layla. He had told Layla about Christie's pastel princess dress. It was the only explanation. How could he do this to Christie? To *her*? What was he trying to do, play both sides? Didn't he realize this was war? That the Spotted Owl was at stake?

Layla was just passing in front of Aubrey, when all the anger and confusion and hurt gurgled to the surface. Without even thinking about it, Aubrey reached her foot out and brought it down right on the long train at the back of Layla's dress. There was a snag and then a loud *rip*. Suddenly Layla tripped forward and fell onto her knees. Half the girls in the line gasped. Aubrey looked down at her foot and saw a jagged swath of light yellow fabric caught on her heel. The outer layer of Layla's skirt had completely torn away.

"You bitch!" Layla shouted, shoving herself off the ground.

"First her music and now her gown," Aubrey shot back. "Do you ever think for yourself?"

What happened next was all a blur. Layla swiped at Aubrey. Aubrey took a few dumbfounded steps back. Sophia ran out of the wings and grabbed Layla's arm, trying to pull her in the other direction. All the other girls skittered backward, squealing, screaming, or laughing. But Aubrey simply stood there, unsure of what to do, until Grayson came bounding up the stage. Aubrey half expected him to yell at her for marring his sister's gown. Obviously, *obviously* he was on Layla's side in all this. But when he turned to face Aubrey, he was laughing.

Aubrey blinked, confused. He was *laughing*?

"How is this funny, Grayson!?" Layla shouted, lifting what was left of her skirt in both hands. "She totally trashed my dress!"

Then she turned and ran off the stage, Rebecca scampering behind her.

Grayson dried tears of merriment from his eyes and sighed, looking at Aubrey. "You really shouldn't have done that," he said, barely containing his mirth.

"And *you* really shouldn't have shared our personal conversation with your sister!" she snapped. "Obviously our date tonight is off."

Then she turned her back on his stunned expression and, holding her dress up with both hands, stormed off the stage.

Chapter 12

*T*hat afternoon the sky was blanketed with gray clouds. Gray to match Aubrey's mood. In the back of her mind she knew that this was a good sign for snow, but she no longer cared. She was too busy being seriously angry and hurt.

As Aubrey shot puck after puck after puck on the pond, using the iced-tea bottles to mark the edges of the goal since she hadn't had the energy to drag out the real one, all the carnival rides twirled and whirled and buzzed and hummed. The workers were doing their final test runs before the carnival opened up to the public in a few hours, and the air was filled with the scent of fried foods and popcorn. Merry shouts sounded over the bopping notes of organ music coming from one of the rides. The anticipation in the air was palpable. And it all made Aubrey want to cry.

"Stupid Chamberlain jerks," she said through her teeth. She reeled back and slammed a puck with her stick. The puck went zooming across the ice and slammed into one of the iced-tea bottles, upending it. The bottle rolled across the ice until it finally came to rest under the tread of Grayson Chamberlain's boot.

Aubrey's heart stopped at the sight of him. Stopped and shriveled into a black knot. "What are you doing here?"

She skated over to the edge of the pond and started to gather up her pucks. Grayson bent and picked up the iced-tea bottle, tossing it from hand to hand.

"I didn't tell Layla anything," he said with no preamble.

Aubrey scoffed as she skated by him, tossing a few of the pucks toward the center of the ice. She put too many on the stick, however, and they flew out in all directions.

"Yeah, right," she said.

"Well, I didn't tell her on purpose," he said, stepping toward her. "This morning I was up early and Fabrizia was in the kitchen making tea, so I told *her* about Christie's dress because I thought it was a cool idea. Layla must have come down and overheard."

Aubrey's face burned as she made another pass at the pucks. She wasn't sure whether or not to believe him.

"Honestly, I can't believe she stole the idea," Grayson said, looking down at the iced-tea bottle. "I'm starting to think that Layla's taking this whole thing a bit too seriously."

A laugh burbled up in Aubrey's throat, but she held it back. *Starting* to think? Where had Grayson been the last week? But she didn't feel like trying to tell him about all the things Layla had done to her and Christie. She was sure he would just defend his sister, and she didn't have the patience to listen to it right now. She took a deep breath and stopped short, spraying ice all over the toes of his hiking boots. Looking into his eyes, she could tell that he really was feeling conflicted and upset. What was she supposed to do here? Let it go and trust him again, or go with her gut—her gut, which was telling her that when it came down to it, he was a

Chamberlain? When it came down to it, all he cared about was his family. Which meant doing whatever he could to help Layla win. Which meant that Christie would lose, the Howells would never get the money they needed, and the Chamberlain Ski Resort and Spa would run the Spotted Owl out of business.

"What are you thinking?" Grayson asked tentatively.

"I don't know." Aubrey looked away, watching the gray clouds as they moved slowly across the sky.

"I wish you would trust me," Grayson said.

"I barely know you," Aubrey replied. "Look at it from my side. I told you something in confidence and less than a day later, it's thrown back in my face."

"Look, all I can say is . . . I really do want Christie to win. I want the Howells to save the inn, I want to keep my job there, and I want you to not hate me," Grayson said, stepping right up to her. "You either believe those things, or you don't."

Aubrey looked up into his eyes and her heart

flipped. Why did he have to be so damn gorgeous? And why did he have to look so damn earnest?

"Can't we just pretend all of this never happened?" Grayson asked. "I'd really still like to go to the carnival with you tonight."

His words sent a little skitter of excitement through Aubrey's veins and she found herself smiling against her will. She was still attracted to him, even if she wasn't entirely sure she trusted him.

"All right, *fine*," she said, relief rushing through her lungs as she let go of as much of her anger as she could. "But you have to buy me whatever junk food I want and you're not allowed to judge."

"Deal," Grayson said with a grin. "It does smell seriously amazing," he added, looking around.

"Good. Now get out of here," Aubrey said, pushing her hockey stick against his chest. "I have more practicing to do."

"Okay, okay," Grayson said, lifting his hands in surrender. He walked over and replaced the iced-tea bottle across from its partner on the ice.

"I'll see you tonight."

As he walked off, Aubrey stood still on the ice and watched him go. Part of her wanted to smile, but she also felt an odd sense of trepidation. Was she doing the right thing, letting him back in? Or was she just allowing herself to be duped by a shady Chamberlain? If Christie were to lose the pageant because of some detail Aubrey let slip, she would never forgive herself.

So just don't let anything else slip, Aubrey thought, turning toward the goal and lining up behind her row of pucks. She pulled back and shot one as hard as she possibly could. It raced across the ice and sliced right between the two bottles.

Just don't trust the guy you're dating. She tilted her head back and groaned in frustration. Yeah. That was a really good idea. Going out with a guy she couldn't trust. A cold wind kicked up and she stared at the sky.

"Okay, if it starts to snow right now, I can trust him," she whispered to herself, her words nearly drowned out by the noisy carnival rides. "One flake. Come on, just give me one flake."

But the sky remained obstinately gray and

flakeless. Aubrey groaned again and got back to her shooting.

"Is it just me, or have you been kind of quiet tonight?" Grayson asked as the Ferris wheel made its fifth trip toward the sky. The once-again cloudless, starlit sky.

It's not you, Aubrey thought. *Why do you want me to talk? Want me to give you more ammo you can hand over to your sister?*

"Is everything okay?" Grayson asked, nudging her leg with his knee.

"Everything's fine," Aubrey replied, looking out across the carnival grounds.

Whether or not Grayson's parents were working to keep tourists away from the carnival, the place was happening. There were lines for every ride, and the game counters were crowded with people. Kids raced around with cotton candy, clutching reams of tickets, and there were prize teddy bears everywhere, so big they blocked the faces of the people toting them from view. As the wheel dipped and then headed for the sky again, Aubrey saw that the workers were setting up bleachers around the pond near the woods, getting ready for the hockey shot competition, which would happen in a few days.

"Really? Because it seems like you won't even look at me," Grayson said flatly.

Aubrey glanced over at him then, but found that she couldn't hold his gaze. She felt as if all her misgivings would be obvious in her eyes and she didn't want to get into another serious conversation. She wished things could go back to the way they had been yesterday, but she wasn't sure how she could make that happen.

"I'm just tired," she said.

"Tired," Grayson repeated dubiously. He actually sounded annoyed, which surprised Aubrey, considering the fact that *she* was still somewhat annoyed with *him*.

"Aubrey, I really think we should talk about this."

"Talk about what?" Aubrey said, raising her eyebrows and trying to appear as if she was clueless.

He tilted his head. "You *know* what."

The ride started to slow. Suddenly Aubrey was even more eager to get out of the tight Ferris wheel seat. It seemed to take forever for the bucket to inch forward. Just then, she spotted Christie down on the ground, waving her arms over her head. "What's that about?" she asked, happy to have an excuse to change the subject.

"I have no idea," Grayson replied, glancing over the side.

As their car inched toward the operator, who was letting people off, Christie ran around the side of the fence to get as close to Aubrey as she could.

"Guess what?" she shouted giddily. "Jonathan just asked me to the Winter Ball!"

Aubrey's face lit up and she forgot all about what was going on with Grayson. "No way!" she replied happily. "That's amazing!" She turned to Grayson. "I'm sorry, but I really don't feel like getting into this right now. And as you can see my best friend needs to talk to me, so—"

As soon as the worker released the safety latch on their seat, Aubrey pushed herself out and ran down the ramp to join her friend, as happy to be sharing a light moment with Christie as she was to be free from Grayson and all the heaviness. Christie caught Aubrey up in a hug and jumped up and down.

"What happened? I want every detail!" Aubrey exclaimed, pulling Christie over to a wooden bench near the ride's exit. Grayson strolled over and hovered a few feet away, giving the two girls some space.

"Well, he told me that he wanted to ask me, but he wasn't sure if Rose and Jim would be cool with it," Christie said breathlessly. "And then he said that *you* convinced him it would be okay!"

Aubrey bit her lip. "Are you mad that I talked to him?"

"No! Not at all! Honestly, I was so happy. I was starting to think that you didn't care and I—"

Aubrey blinked. She put her hand over Christie's. "Wait a minute. You thought I didn't *care*?" she asked.

There was a long, awkward pause as Christie looked down at their gloved hands. "Well . . . I mean . . . every time I tried to talk to you about it you got distracted by something or someone," Christie said, lowering her voice as she glanced over at Grayson. "I just feel like we haven't had much time to talk since we've been here, and when we do it's all about the pageant."

A warm blush lit Aubrey's face and she kicked at the ground with the toe of her boot, feeling chagrined. "I know we've been busy. . . . I know *I've* been busy," she said. "But that doesn't mean I don't care about you! Please! You're the whole reason I'm here. Nothing's more important than you."

Christie grinned and squeezed Aubrey's hand. "I know," she said with a nod. Then she lifted her sparkling eyes. "I can't believe Jonathan asked me out!"

"I know!" Aubrey squealed and hugged Christie again. "I'm so happy for you!"

Grayson finally moseyed over to them and cleared his throat. "Hey."

"Hey, Grayson!" Christie said giddily. "Did you hear? Jonathan and I are going to the Winter Ball together!" she announced, looking meaningfully between him and Aubrey. "It's this Friday, you know."

Aubrey's pulse raced and she looked away, feeling like a total moron. It was so obvious that Christie was trying to prod Grayson into asking

Aubrey to the dance, which was so lame. Aubrey knew that she had done the same to Jonathan, but at least she hadn't done it right in front of Christie.

"Yeah, I know," Grayson said, shoving his hands into the pockets of his wool coat. "Listen, Aubrey, I think you're right. I'm kind of tired too. Maybe we should just call it a night."

Aubrey's heart fell and she felt Christie slump in disappointment. That was his reaction to the obvious prodding from her best friend? Cutting the current date short?

"Um . . . okay," Aubrey said. She was so stunned no other words came to mind. She knew their date hadn't been perfect, but was he really going to ditch her like this, right in front of Christie?

"I'll see you at rehearsal tomorrow." He leaned in and gave her a quick peck on the cheek. "See you, Christie."

"Bye, Grayson!" Christie said, trying to sound chipper.

He gave them one last tight smile before disappearing into the ever-shifting crowd. Aubrey slumped back on the bench and blew out a breath. "What the heck was that?"

"I don't know." Christie seemed genuinely baffled. "Did he totally miss my hint?"

"Maybe," Aubrey said.

But she knew that Grayson wasn't that stupid. He had to have known what Christie was doing and he'd just ignored it. Obviously he didn't want to go to the Winter Ball with her. But why? He was the one who had betrayed her trust. Wouldn't taking her to a ball that she *had* to attend because of *his* family's dumb rules be a good way to make it up to her?

"Come on," Christie said, standing. "You need a sugar fix, stat."

Aubrey nodded and followed after her friend. How had this all happened? A few days ago everything had been going right. But now every little thing felt seriously wrong.

Chapter 13

"*I* can't believe he didn't show up. Not even for five minutes," Aubrey ranted, dropping down on the cushy chair near the fireplace in the Spotted Owl's lobby. Her feet hurt from strutting around in heels all morning and dancing all afternoon, her head hurt from all the concentration it took *not* to kill Layla, and her heart hurt from Grayson's very obvious absence. "I mean, what kind of assistant director *is* he? We have less than a week until the pageant. How irresponsible can you be?"

"Fabrizia said he had to run a pageant-related errand," Sophia said, perching on the edge of the opposite chair. "I guess he just didn't make it back in time to stop by."

"Exactly," Christie added, dropping her bags

near the bottom of the staircase before she joined them.

"Yeah, right. You're working on the pageant now," Aubrey said to Sophia. "Do *you* know about any all-day errands he was supposed to run?"

Sophia looked guilty. "Not exactly."

"So he *is* avoiding me!" Aubrey wailed.

"I'm going to go get us some hot chocolate while we work on our interview skills," Christie announced, standing. "Extra marshmallows?"

"Sure," Aubrey grumbled.

"Sophia?" Christie asked.

"Whipped cream for me," Sophia replied.

As Christie strolled off behind the counter, Aubrey toyed with the fringe at the end of her white scarf and sighed. An awful, dark feeling had been swelling inside her chest all day long, and it was only intensified by the many knowing, triumphant smirks Layla threw in her direction as the hours wore on.

Something had gone wrong on that date last night. Aubrey had realized it the moment Grayson had walked away from her at the carnival. She knew that she hadn't been her usual, fun self, but she'd still been mulling over everything that had happened yesterday morning. Couldn't Grayson understand that?

"So . . . what happened between you two?" Sophia asked tentatively, shrugging out of her suede coat. "Did you have a fight?"

Aubrey glanced over at her, feeling a bit hesitant. Was it weird to talk to Grayson's ex about him?

"It's okay if you don't want to tell me, but . . . maybe I can help," Sophia said. "I've known him a long time. Even before we started going out, we were always friends."

Aubrey blew out a sigh, trying not to feel jealous of Sophia's long history with Grayson. The past didn't matter. Only the present and the future.

"We kind of had a fight yesterday . . . and then we made up, but . . ." Aubrey paused and stared at the fire crackling in the fireplace. "But I don't know, I guess I wasn't totally over it yet when we went out last night, and I think I was kind of rude to him."

"Ah," Sophia said with a nod. "That could be awkward."

"I'm such an idiot," Aubrey said, bringing her hand to her head. "I always do this. I act like a jerk and only realize later that I was wrong. When it's *too* late."

Her mother was always calling her on this behavior. Warning her to calm down and process before she said or did something she would eventually regret. Which was, of course, what she had done last night. And by the time she'd woken up this morning she had realized that she trusted Grayson. That there was no way he would have sabotaged Christie—and the Spotted Owl by extension—on purpose. All she had to do was think back to that first day on the pond—how he'd spoken about loving his job and the Spotted Owl, all before he knew Aubrey at all, all before he had any ulterior motives to convince her of this—and she realized he was telling the truth.

"Who said it's too late?" Sophia asked.

"Oh, please. He was totally avoiding me today. It's obvious," Aubrey said.

She had even tried to call him on his cell phone during breaks, but he hadn't picked up—a fact she would have loved to attribute to his general cell spaciness, if she didn't have that awful sinking feeling taking over her chest.

"Maybe he was," Sophia said, causing Aubrey's heart to sink even further. "But that doesn't automatically mean he's over you. Sometimes Grayson just needs time. You know, to think through how he feels. To, you know . . ." She looked up at the wood beams in the ceiling, trying to come up with the word.

"To process?" Aubrey said, a slight flicker of hope springing to life inside her chest.

"Yes! That's it. To process," Sophia replied with a grin.

Aubrey smiled. So maybe she and Grayson were more alike than she realized. She couldn't expect Grayson to give *her* time to think, but not pay him the same favor. It stunk that she had to lose a whole day with him, especially when she had less than a week left on the mountain, but what was done was done. Tomorrow he would be back at rehearsal and the two of them would talk and everything would get sorted out. Unless, during his processing, he decided to process her right out of his life.

"Thanks, Sophia," Aubrey said. "You're pretty cool for my boyfriend's ex."

"And you're pretty cool for my ex's girlfriend," Sophia laughed.

"Three hot chocolates, right off the stove," Christie announced, backing through the door with a tray full of steaming mugs. "Now let's get to work."

"Okay," Sophia said, standing up and taking her mug from the tray. "Now, when it comes to the interview, brevity is key. Don't start rambling or you might lose your train of thought and it'll get really uncomfortable really fast."

"Brevity. Got it," Christie said, sitting down at full attention.

Aubrey leaned back with her hot chocolate and let her mind wander. Sophia was here to help Christie, after all, not her. And she was much more interested in looking forward to tomorrow. She would just have to get to Grayson first thing in the morning and apologize. It wouldn't be easy, but this time she knew she was wrong and she knew it had to be done. Everything was going to be fine. She was sure of it.

Aubrey was so pent up with nervous energy on Tuesday morning, she had to stop in the bathroom and take a few breaths before continuing on to the amphitheater. She had told Christie to go ahead—her best friend had never been late for anything in her life, and the very idea made the girl nauseous—and ducked into one of the bathrooms off the resort lobby. Inside, she stared into her own eyes in the mirror, took a deep breath, and held it.

"It's going to be fine. Just talk to him," Aubrey told herself.

She just wished she knew what kind of reception she was going to get. Would he smile at her or give her the cold shoulder? Would he listen at all? Or maybe she was just making a big deal out of nothing and he would walk right over to her and give her a big, good-morning kiss.

Aubrey sighed. She would have been slightly more confident about this possibility if he had returned any one of her many phone calls from the day before. But maybe he simply didn't get the messages. It was always a possibility.

"Okay. Let's do this," Aubrey said to herself, putting on her low, guttural game voice—the one she used to psych herself up before roller-hockey games back home. She pulled her hat on over her ears, turned, and strutted out of the bathroom and into the hallway, the picture of confidence. Even if she didn't *feel* completely confident, at least she could project it.

Aubrey came around the corner into the long hallway that led to the back of the resort and slowed her steps. Two shadowy figures stood near the end of the hall, dark against the blinding sunlight that poured through the glass door behind them. Aubrey was yards and yards away, but even from this distance, she could make out Christie's petite form and Layla's taller, more imperious one. Christie's shoulders were slightly slumped while Layla was obviously prattling on.

A surge of adrenaline shot through Aubrey's heart and she sped up. She did not like the look of this.

"I'm just trying to help. You don't have to cry," Layla said as Aubrey approached.

"What's going on?" Aubrey asked, glancing at her friend. Christie swiped a tear away from her face with her gloved fingers. "Why are you crying?" she asked. Then she whipped around to face Layla, her eyes flashing. "What did you do to her?"

Layla's jaw dropped and she placed a hand against her chest. "I didn't do anything! I was simply trying to *suggest* that Christie come up with a different talent for the pageant. Twirling is *so* thirty years ago."

Aubrey's fingers curled into fists. What she wouldn't have given to be able to punch Layla right across her perfect jaw.

"Not where we come from," Christie said, clinging to the strap on her bag.

"Exactly. Where we come from, girls line up to try out for the twirling corps," Aubrey lied, crossing her arms over her chest. "And Christie is the best twirler on the team."

"That's nice," Layla said in a tone that was anything but. "But up here in New England, you'll get laughed off the stage."

Christie looked at Aubrey desperately. Aubrey's anger seethed in her veins. Suddenly, every little thing that Layla had done or said since Aubrey had arrived in Vermont came rushing back. Ever since Aubrey had first laid eyes on the girl she had been rude, conniving, and fake. It was because of her that Aubrey was even in this awful position with Grayson, not to mention the fact that she'd done everything she could to try to cheat Christie out of winning the pageant. Layla was a selfish jerk. And someone had to stop her.

"You are such a bitch!" she snapped at Layla.

"No, Aubrey! It's fine. She's right," Christie said, reaching for Aubrey's arm. "Maybe I should—"

"No, Christie, she's *not* right," Aubrey replied, shrugging off her friend's hand and looking Layla squarely in the eye. "She's a manipulative, lying jerk who's just trying to get under your skin and make you feel self-conscious."

"Oh, really?" Layla said, crossing her arms over her chest and squaring off with Aubrey. She moved so that her back was to the door and Aubrey's was toward the lobby.

"Yes, really," Aubrey replied, tilting her head. "And don't think I don't know why you're doing it."

"Why is that, do you think?" Layla asked.

"Because you *know* that Christie is your main competition for the crown!" Aubrey shouted. "You're so worried that she's going to beat your pathetic little butt you're trying to sabotage her in more ways than one! Well, don't think for a second that I'm going to let that happen. There's no way a shallow, heartless bitch like you is going to win Snow Queen. You can quote me on that!"

Aubrey half expected Layla to slap her across the face. Or at least to shout back at her. But instead, and much to Aubrey's shock, Layla's big blue eyes suddenly filled with tears. Aubrey was so stunned she actually took a step back.

"What are you—"

"What the hell is your problem?" Grayson blurted, coming up behind Aubrey.

Aubrey froze at the sound of his voice. In a flash she realized what he must be thinking about what he'd just heard. In his mind, he had just watched Aubrey ruthlessly tear down his sweet little sister—reduce the girl to tears, even. Her heart pounding painfully, Aubrey looked at Layla and saw the snickering behind her tears. Layla had seen Grayson coming. She had backed against the door so that Aubrey would *have* to put her back to Grayson. She had engineered this whole thing. And it had completely worked.

"Are you okay?" Grayson asked Layla. He brushed by Aubrey and Christie, his ski jacket swishing, and put his arm around his sister. Layla turned her face into his chest and her shoulders trembled as she sobbed.

"I *will* be," she said through her crocodile tears.

Aubrey had to say something. Something to explain this ridiculous charade away. "Grayson, I—"

"I don't want to hear it, Aubrey," he snapped. Aubrey's heart skipped a beat. She had never seen such venom in his eyes before. "I know that steal-ing Christie's gown idea sucked, but did you really have to make her cry? It's just a freaking dress."

"No! You don't understand. That's not what this was about! And . . . she's faking!" Aubrey said lamely. "Can't you tell she's faking?"

Layla's sobs grew louder at this accusation and Grayson narrowed his eyes. "You're such a hypocrite. I thought this pageant didn't mean anything to you. Clearly that was a big lie."

"It wasn't. Grayson, I swear. I was just . . ."

She took a deep breath, thinking back to the things she'd just said to Layla. Realizing how horrible they must have sounded to her brother—her brother, who thought she was just a sweet little thing who wanted to win a pageant. Whose worst crime was maybe listening in on a conversation between him and Fabrizia. He was never going to forgive her for this. Not as long as he believed in Layla's innocent façade. Layla had ruined everything. Everything.

"I was just trying to protect my friend," Aubrey said finally, stoically.

"It's true, Grayson," Christie said meekly. "It was all just a . . . a misunderstanding."

Grayson's mouth set in a grim line. "It's okay, Christie," he said. "You don't have to try to explain."

Aubrey swallowed hard. His hidden meaning was obvious to her. He still thought Christie was a sweet girl and that she was obviously just making excuses for her psycho-bitch friend.

"Come on, Layla. Let's get you out of here," Grayson said, shoving open the door.

Once outside, he didn't look back, but Layla did, with a victorious smile. Aubrey's blood boiled in her veins. She had known she was right about Layla faking, but having it confirmed in such a way made her want to scream. Why couldn't Grayson have just seen that look? Why was he so blind to his sister's faults?

"Christie, I may have to kill her," Aubrey said through her teeth.

Christie put her arm around Aubrey. "Believe me, Aubrey, I totally understand."

Wednesday afternoon, Aubrey trudged into the Spotted Owl's lobby, still out of breath from her workout on the pond, sweat clinging to her skin underneath her layers of clothing. She had just had her best on-ice workout yet and should have been feeling giddy and confident about that night's shootout competition.

Unfortunately, no matter how many pucks she shot perfectly or how many hours she spent trying to work out her aggression, she only felt sad. Sad and angry and beyond ready to hop a flight home.

"How'd it go?" Christie asked. She had been walking across the room next to Sophia, practicing her posture with a book on her head, which she now let fall into her hands.

Christie looked beautiful and snow-bunny perfect in a white turtleneck sweater, long dark braids, and red corduroys, while Sophia could have been a model in her clingy, gray cashmere dress. Aubrey felt like an ogre in comparison. She fell onto the couch at the center of the lobby, letting her equipment clatter to the floor.

"Fine," she said, kicking her legs out and letting her clunky boots fall open. "Whatever."

"I'm sure you're going to win," Christie said, walking over to join her. She sat down next to Aubrey with her perfect posture and smiled. "You'll win the hockey thing and I'll win the pageant and we'll both go back to Florida all triumphant."

"Good attitude, Christie. Attitude is half the battle," Sophia said, walking over to stand behind Aubrey.

"Yeah," Aubrey said with a sigh. "Whatever."

Christie pressed her lips together and sat back on the couch. She shot Aubrey a tentative look, and all the hairs on the back of Aubrey's neck stood on end. Clearly, there was something Christie wanted to tell her or ask her. Something she wasn't sure Aubrey wanted to hear.

"What?" Aubrey asked hesitantly. She sat up a bit straighter and looked at Christie, then Sophia, her breath shortening. Had Grayson called? Had he stopped by?

"Ummm . . . we were just thinking . . . " Christie said, toying with one of her braids as she glanced up at Sophia. "About the Winter Ball?"

Aubrey's stomach turned and she groaned. Right. The Chamberlains reared their ugly heads once again. Why did they have to have so many stupid events and so many stupid rules? She shouldn't be required to attend some ridiculous dance just because she was in the pageant.

Not to mention being forced to have a date for said dance, as if it was some kind of debutante ball. What was this, 1950?

"What about it?" Aubrey asked, even though she now knew where this conversation was headed.

"You still need a date," Sophia said, walking around the back of Aubrey's chair to perch on the arm.

Christie bit her lip. "Jonathan has a few friends who—"

"No! No setups," Aubrey blurted. "I do not want to spend the entire night making small talk with some guy I don't know."

"Yeah, but there's no one on this mountain you *do* know," Christie protested, pulling her knees up onto the couch to sit sideways. At the same moment, Jim came walking out of the office and settled in behind the desk with his coffee.

"I'll take Jim!" Aubrey said brightly.

Sophia laughed. "Um, no."

The door to the office had not swung closed when it was suddenly shoved open again and out stepped Charlie. Aubrey's heart leaped.

"I'll take Charlie!"

Christie turned around to look at the desk and Charlie froze in his tracks.

"Not bad," Sophia said, looking him up and down.

"Take me how?" Charlie asked.

"Not bad? He's perfect!" Christie cried, jumping up. "Why didn't I think of that?"

"Think of what?" Charlie asked, clutching his sling and looking a tad fearful. "Where are you taking me?"

Aubrey stood up, cleared her throat, and tried to ignore the cold sheen of sweat congealing on her skin. "Charlie, will you go to the Winter Ball with me?"

Charlie's eyebrows shot up. "As friends? Because I have a girlfriend."

"Yes, as friends," Aubrey said through her teeth.

"Then I'm in," Charlie said with a nod.

"Good."

Aubrey dropped down on the couch again, biting back tears as all the images of her and Grayson walking into the ball together flitted away into the fire and burned into nothing. It wasn't romantic, but at least she had a date. All she had to do was get through the next few days. Before she knew it she'd be on her way home again and she could put this whole, bizarre, crappy trip behind her.

I'd just better get to see some snow first.

Chapter 14

It seemed as if everyone in Vermont had shown up to watch the hockey shot competition that night. As Aubrey stood between two other competitors—guys twice her size—near the edge of the pond, her ankles quaked beneath her. That afternoon she had been determined to win this thing, or at least to beat Grayson. Now, with the stands packed with unfamiliar faces, with Layla, Rebecca, and their friends crowded into the front row, with all the cheers and jeers being tossed at the contestants, she realized she might just be happy if she kept from falling on her face.

No. No, you will not be content to simply not fall, she told herself. *You are going to win. Win, win, win.*

"Oh, too bad!" the announcer shouted over

the loudspeaker. The guy at center ice had hit only three of the targets with his ten pucks. "Nice try, though, dude. We'll be here again next year."

The crowd laughed, and Aubrey felt an uncomfortable warmth creeping up her neck from under her scarf and taking up residence on her face. She would die if she didn't hit all the targets. Just die. She glanced over at Christie, who was standing near the announcer's booth along with Jim, Jonathan, Charlie, and Sophia. They all flashed her confident smiles and Jim gave her a thumbs-up. Rose was back at the inn, manning the desk, but she had given Aubrey a hug for luck before she'd left. She felt buoyed by their support and took a deep breath, focusing her attention on the goal.

Right down, left up, right up, left down, center, she told herself, tipping her head back to look up at the starlit sky. This was the order in which she planned to hit her shots, and the mantra had been running through her head all day. As her breath made little puffs of steam in the air, she repeated it over and over again. *Right down, left up, right up, left down, center. Right down, left up, right up, left down, center.*

"Next up, local favorite and three-time hockey shot competition champion . . . Grayson Chamberlain!" the announcer called out.

Aubrey's heart first leaped, then took a nose-dive into her shoes. Grayson skated out to the sound of uproarious cheers, which he acknowledged with a wave of his hand. Every muscle in Aubrey's body clenched as she tried not to feel anything for him—nothing good, nothing bad. She wanted to be indifferent to him. But as he lined up behind his row of ten pucks, she found herself recalling his ire yesterday morning. Remembering how he so easily fell under Layla's spell and wouldn't even listen to her. Thinking of the five messages she'd left him that afternoon, none of which had been returned. And suddenly, she was seething.

"Give 'em hell, Grayson!" someone shouted, earning a round of laughter from the stands.

Fall on your butt, Grayson, Aubrey added silently.

She was reminded of that old saying, "It's a thin line between love and hate." She had never understood how that was possible until now.

Grayson pulled back his stick. As he made contact with the first puck, Aubrey found herself wishing he would fail. Let him feel as crappy as he'd made her feel yesterday. But the first puck whizzed across the ice and right through the center hole. Everyone cheered. The second puck hit the top left target. Again, everyone cheered. The third puck sailed through the top right target. There were gasps of amazement. After that, Aubrey knew it was over. Grayson could hit the last two shots in his sleep. And he did. One, two. No problem. The crowd went wild.

"Five for five in less than thirty seconds!" the announcer crowed. "It's a new winter carnival record!"

Grayson slapped a few hands as he returned to his spot in line. Aubrey half expected him to smirk at her as he skated by, but he looked straight ahead instead, pointedly ignoring her presence. Somehow, this stung even worse than a taunt would have.

"And now, all the way from sunny Florida, Aubrey Mills!" the announcer shouted.

There weren't quite as many cheers for

Aubrey, since no one there knew who she was. But Christie and the crew tried to make up for it, shouting and clapping as loud as they could. Aubrey took one step out onto the ice and her right ankle wobbled. Her heart hit her throat, but she recovered quickly. Still, that was not a good sign. If she couldn't even skate to the center of the pond, how the heck was she going to shoot?

You're just nervous, she told herself, glancing over at Layla, Rebecca, and their friends, who were whispering about her behind their hands. *Get a grip. You can do this. You've prepared. You're going to kick ass.*

But when she lined up behind her pucks, the goal looked impossibly far away. And the holes in the board seemed tiny, like a puck wouldn't even fit through them. A cold wind whipped by, bringing tears to Aubrey's eyes and blurring her vision. She blinked them back but still felt disoriented. Her heart pounded in her chest.

Don't mess this up. You can't screw this up, she thought.

"Hey, FL!" Rebecca shouted. "Get on with it already!"

Aubrey scowled over her shoulder, pretty

sure that Layla had told Rebecca to say that. *She* couldn't have taunted Aubrey, of course. Not with Grayson and half the town present. As she turned around again, her eyes fell on Grayson, and her blood stopped. He was staring at her, but when she looked at him he quickly glanced away. Suddenly, Aubrey felt as if she was going to throw up.

"Anytime now, Ms. Mills," the announcer said.

More laughter. Aubrey could have wrung the guy's neck, even though she'd never met him.

Just do it, she told herself. *Get it over with.*

Feeling zero confidence, Aubrey pulled back and shot the first puck. It zipped right through the bottom right opening. The crowd cheered. Aubrey blinked, surprised. Not the shot she'd intended to make first, but it was something. She squinted at the target and shot the next puck. It whacked against the board and ricocheted toward the crowd.

A lump formed in Aubrey's throat as the crowd let out a groan. *It's okay,* she told herself. *You were never going to go five-for-five like Grayson. Just keep going.*

She slammed the next puck, lifting it off the

ice. It sailed through the top right hole. Usually her worst shot, it was done.

"Yes!" Christie cheered.

The crowd applauded, back on her side again. Aubrey bit back a smile. She went for the top left. The puck sailed over the net. Another groan. She tried again. Over the net again. Five pucks down, only five to go, and three more targets to hit. Aubrey's confidence started to wane. As she lined up behind the next puck, she could feel Grayson watching her. Feel Layla laughing at her.

Don't let them do this to you, she thought, as her eyes welled up again, this time on their own. *Don't let them shake you.*

But when she pulled back again, she felt her ankle wobble and her heart stopped. She threw her arms out, but it was no good. This time, she was going down. And she did. Hard. Her butt hit first, then her skull cracked against the ice. For a moment, Aubrey actually saw stars—big blue and pink ones, not the ones that were actually winking down at her from overhead. She heard the crowd react with a suck of breath and wished the ice would melt under her. Wished it would melt and just swallow her up and then close over again. Anything to be free of this humiliation. And then, just as she was starting to feel the pain at the back of her head, Grayson appeared.

"Are you all right?" he asked.

Aubrey stared at him, mortified. She was more embarrassed about falling in front of him than she was about the hundreds of other spectators. Didn't he realize that? What was he doing, rubbing it in her face?

"Here. Let me help," Grayson said. He knelt down and put one hand behind her back, helping her sit up. Aubrey felt thankful and embarrassed and annoyed all at once. But maybe he wasn't rubbing it in her face. Maybe he still cared about her and just wanted to help her get out of this moment as quickly as possible. Maybe he *had* gotten her messages and wanted to hear her side.

But then she saw him glance over her shoulder at the stands and smile. A cold realization came over her, even as she was still burning from the embarrassment. He wasn't out there because he cared about her. He was out there because it was the right thing to do. Because he wanted to look like the gentleman and hero in front of the community. He *was* just like his sister and parents. A big, obnoxious fake.

"Oh, so you won't take my calls, but as long as you've got an audience, you're there for me," she said, shoving him off her. She tottered to her feet and when he moved to help steady her, she batted his arm away. "I'm fine," she snapped, even as a new explosion of pain radiated across her skull.

Grayson's face turned to stone. "Fine."

He skated to the edge of the ice, retaking his position in line. Aubrey glanced around at the expectant faces, all of them wondering what she would do next. Some of them, she knew, were waiting for a breakdown—hoping for some kind of soap-opera drama. Well, she wasn't going to give it to them. She bent down, picked up her hockey stick, and shot the last four pucks right through the center hole, not even bothering to try for the harder shots. Then, before the confused announcer could even think of what to say, she dropped her stick and skated off the ice, taking the sparsely populated north bank—skating away from the spectators. Layla's laughter followed her the whole way.

It was the most humiliating moment of her life.

As she hobbled over to a bench in her skates to wait for Christie to find her, Aubrey felt exhausted. Exhausted, defeated, and angry at Grayson. Why couldn't he have just left her alone? The fact that he'd tried to help her only confused her even more. Was he really just trying to play the hero, or did he still care about her? Was he having second thoughts about what he'd said to her yesterday? Or did he just like to help a damsel in distress? Rose and Christie kept maintaining that Grayson was a good guy, different from his family. Were they right, or had he had them both fooled all this time, just as Layla was fooling him?

It was too much to sort out, and above it all, she had just lost. Lost big-time. Lost in the most spectacular, embarrassing way possible. Lost to Grayson Chamberlain. Aubrey closed her eyes, wanting to cry for a hundred different reasons and just hoping that it wouldn't happen until she got back to the privacy of her room at the inn.

* * *

"'I'm gonna wash that man right outta my hair, I'm gonna wash that man right outta my hair, and send him on his way!'"

Aubrey looked at her huge, fake smile in the mirror, dropped her arms, and groaned, doubling over at the waist. Was she really singing a song about washing a man out of her hair? Was she *really* going to strut around onstage pretending to wash her hair in front of hundreds of people and sing this stupid old song? Off-key, no less?

Grayson would definitely think the song was about him. And Layla would definitely laugh her ass off.

But at least she'd have zero chance of winning and beating out Christie by mistake. There was always a bright side.

"This sucks," Aubrey said to the gleaming wood floor of the rehearsal room. "How did I get myself into this mess?"

But she knew how. She had gotten into this for her friend. Her friend who wanted this more than anything even *before* she knew that winning would mean saving her grandparents' business.

But she'd *stayed* in it because she wanted to see Layla go down. Because she couldn't quit and let the girl think she'd won. For better or for worse, she was in this thing to stay now. And she had to make the best of it.

Aubrey stood up again and looked herself in the eye with determination. Maybe not happiness, but determination. She would sing the dumb song. Who cared? It wasn't as if she was ever going to see any of these people again. It wasn't as if anyone on this mountain cared about her or anything she did. A picture of Grayson flitted through her mind and her heart panged, but she let it go.

Moving on.

Aubrey took a deep breath and started to sing. "'I'm gonna—'"

There was a rap on the door. Aubrey jumped for it, more than happy to give herself a break. But when she whipped the door open, her throat closed over. Grayson was standing in the hallway, looking all gorgeous in a navy-blue turtleneck sweater, his blond hair gelled into a perfect tousled look.

"Hey," he said quickly.

Aubrey tried to read his tone. Was that a reluctant "hey," a tentative "hey," a hopeful "hey"? Then she decided that it was too short of a word to read. Besides, she didn't care anymore. After the spectacle on the pond last night, she would have preferred to never have to face Grayson again.

"Hey," she replied, looking away.

Grayson glanced past her into the room as if checking to make sure she was alone. Satisfied, he shoved his hands into the front pockets of his jeans and looked her in the eye.

"Can we talk?"

Aubrey's heart leaped and she clucked her tongue, annoyed at herself. Her goal was to get off this mountain without any new drama. And talking to Grayson meant just that. Drama galore. No matter what he had to say to her, he still thought that Layla was Miss Perfect and that Aubrey had berated her needlessly, and he was never going to believe otherwise. How could they ever get past something like that? And why even bother when she was going to be here for only three more days?

"There isn't really anything I feel the need

to talk about," she said, turning away from the door and striding to the center of the room. She stared at her reflection in the mirror, trying as hard as she could not to look at Grayson's. Still, from the corner of her eye she could tell he was standing there in the doorway, watching her.

Just go away, she thought. *Stop torturing me.*

"Are you sure about that?" he asked finally.

No.

"Yes," she said, forcing herself to look him in the eye. "I'm sure." Grayson looked so hurt that Aubrey felt a surge of regret. But it was always better to be the dumper than the dumpee. And besides, he was the one who had refused to listen to her. Her pride was still smarting from that.

"Look, I think it's better if we just be friends," Aubrey said.

Grayson looked up at her, his eyebrows raised. "Friends," he repeated.

"Yeah."

He blew out a breath through his nose and looked at the floor. When he glanced up again, there was an almost amused light in his eyes. Similar to the amusement she had seen that first morning on the ice. But this time, it was tinged with sadness. What did all of this mean? Had he expected her to apologize all over again? Was he amused that she didn't seem to feel the need? Where was *her* apology?

"Well, then, as your friend, can I make one suggestion?" he asked.

Aubrey hesitated. Where was this going, exactly? "Sure."

"Scrap the singing," he said. "It's not that I don't think you're good, it's just . . . you should do something you really love. Something you're comfortable doing. Something that makes you happy. If the judges see you all lit up from the inside, you can't lose."

A lump formed in Aubrey's throat. There was nothing she could do that made her light up from the inside. "Like what?" she asked finally.

Grayson smirked. "You'll figure it out." He tapped his hand against the doorjamb and reached into the hall. "You . . . uh . . . left this on the ice last night," he said, holding up her hockey stick. He placed it against the wall inside the door and leaned it there. "Wanted to return it to you."

The lump in Aubrey's throat widened and

tears stung her eyes as she recalled in vivid detail all the humiliation of the competition.

"Thanks," she managed to say, the word but a croak.

"No problem," Grayson said.

Then he smiled one last time, closed the door, and was gone.

Chapter 15

"*If* everyone would please be seated for a moment, we have a special guest who would like to make an announcement!"

Aubrey glanced at Christie as Fabrizia stepped aside and welcomed Mrs. Chamberlain onto the stage from the wings. All the snow princesses sat down dutifully on the floor as the benefactress of their pageant strode in front of them, her black high heels clacking against the floorboards. Out in the audience, Rose loitered along with several parents, all of them cold and some of them visibly irritated, having arrived fifteen minutes ago to drive their daughters home. Rehearsal had already gone late, and now there was this added delay. Aubrey felt a rush of foreboding down her spine. For some reason she had a feeling that Mrs. Chamberlain's unexpected presence did not mean good things. A glance at Layla confirmed it. The girl was grinning like the cat who'd just gulped down the canary *and* all the canary's eggs. If Layla was happy about whatever was coming, Aubrey knew she would hate it.

"Good afternoon, everyone. I'll make this brief," Mrs. Chamberlain announced, tugging the lapels of her fur coat closer to her neck. "We have decided to start a new tradition this year. For the Winter Ball tomorrow night, all pageant contestants will be required to wear white gowns."

"What?" Dana blurted.

There was a murmur among the parents in the audience. A few of the girls gasped in glee, and Aubrey heard Rebecca make a comment about how chic it would be, all of them dressed somewhat alike and set apart from the rest of the crowd. Aubrey, meanwhile, started to panic. She didn't have a white dress and neither did Christie. Did all these other girls have dozens of gowns of every color just waiting to be trotted out?

"Mrs. Chamberlain, is that really necessary?"

one of the moms in the audience called out.

Apparently not, Aubrey thought.

Mrs. Chamberlain's lips screwed into a sour pucker before she turned around. She looked down at the audience and sighed. "My event, Joyce, my rules," she said. "Of course, if you'd like to withdraw your daughter from the pageant—"

"No! Mom!" one of the girls wailed. "You can't do that!"

Joyce, who reminded Aubrey a bit of her own mother with her short brown hair and modest clothing, narrowed her eyes at Mrs. Chamberlain. "It's fine. We'll figure something out."

"That's all, girls! Looking forward to seeing you tomorrow night!" Mrs. Chamberlain said brightly.

Everyone started chatting as they rose to their feet. Aubrey grabbed Christie and pulled her toward the front of the stage. "What are we going to do?" she whispered. "We don't have white dresses."

"I know," Christie said, looking ill. She tugged her hat on over her forehead as she scurried down the steps. "I can't believe they're doing this at the last minute."

"Well, it *is* her event," Aubrey said under her breath. "*Her* rules."

Rose stood up from her seat and gave the girls a dubious smile as they approached up the aisle. All around them, other girls were finding their moms or dads and talking about this new requirement. Already Aubrey heard a group of girls planning a shopping trip to the mall that night.

"Unbelievable," Aubrey whispered. "Do they all have endless amounts of money?"

The cash her mother had sent her to spend on the pageant was already gone—spent on makeup and shoes and jewelry and the costume for the opening number—and she wasn't about to ask for more. Already this thing had cost her family hundreds of dollars, all for something she hadn't really wanted to do in the first place.

"This is the biggest event of the year for these girls," Rose replied with a shrug. "I suppose their parents are willing to pay through the nose for it."

"What are we going to do, Rose?" Christie

said, wringing her gloved hands together. "Aubrey and I are toast."

"Luckily I happen to have a white gown back home. I wore it to my coming-out party back in Atlanta," Rose said. "It's vintage by this point, but I think if I make a few adjustments it'll do for one of you."

"Really?" Christie breathed. Then she glanced at Aubrey. "But which one of us?"

"You should take it, Christie," Aubrey said. "I don't want to steal your grandmother's dress out from under you."

"But what will you wear?" Christie asked.

Aubrey took a deep breath and glanced down the aisle at Layla and Grayson, who were obviously listening in on their conversation. All at once, she felt utterly defeated. Maybe it was time for her to call it quits. She had never let anyone run her out of a competition before in her life, and the thought made her feel nauseous, but there was a first time for everything. Besides, Christie would be okay without her. She had come this far.

"Christie, I hate to say it, but maybe it's time for me to back out," she said.

"No!" Christie wailed, grabbing Aubrey's hand. "You can't leave me now!"

"I don't think I have a choice," Aubrey said.

From the corner of her eye, Aubrey saw Layla walking toward them, leaving Grayson behind in the aisle. Her whole body stiffened, anticipating Layla's triumphant smile. But she could take it. All she had to do was stand there and not say anything, and soon it would all be over.

"Aubrey, hey," Layla said, her hands behind her back. Aubrey blinked. Was it just her, or did that sound tentative? It certainly didn't sound like an evil victory laugh.

"Um, hi," Aubrey said warily.

Layla and Grayson exchanged a look, then Grayson quickly distracted himself with something on his clipboard. What the heck was this about?

"Listen . . . we couldn't help overhearing your . . . dilemma, and I think I can help," Layla said.

Aubrey snorted a laugh. She couldn't help it. It was a knee-jerk reaction. Rose gave her a little nudge with her elbow to quiet her and Aubrey cleared her throat, standing up straight.

"I'm sorry, *you* want to help *me*?" Aubrey said.

"I have a white gown you can use," Layla said, lifting a shoulder. "It was my prom dress last year, but I think it'll look really pretty on you. If you're interested. Consider it a peace offering."

"Oh my God! Yes! Yes! She is *totally* interested!" Christie trilled, jumping up on her toes.

"Christie!" Aubrey admonished.

A cold wind whipped Aubrey's hair back from her face and she felt as if it was a sign from the universe. A sign telling her not to trust this girl.

"A peace offering," Aubrey repeated dubiously.

Layla rolled her eyes. "Look, I'm sorry if I've been overly competitive," she said, crossing her arms over her chest. "It's just . . . this is my family's thing, and all I've ever wanted is to win it. But someone has convinced me that the only way to win right is to compete against the best people," she added, glancing over at her brother, who was deliberately looking in the other direction. "And you two are the people to beat. So I don't want you to drop out, okay?"

Aubrey blinked, confused by a rush of under-standing. Layla was doing this because Grayson had convinced her to. He was trying to help her. But why? He knew she didn't really care about being in the pageant. Unless he really didn't believe that anymore. He had said as much that morning they had argued in the hallway. Did he actually think she wanted to win this thing now? Part of her wanted to turn Layla down and just walk away, just to prove to him that she didn't care. But then Christie was clinging to her hand, staring at her hopefully. And Layla was basically challenging her to stay in the com-petition and try to beat her. It was all too much for her to take.

"All right, fine," she said. "I'll take the dress."

"Yay!" Christie cheered.

"I'll drop it off tomorrow morning," Layla said with a smile.

"Thanks," Aubrey said with some difficulty.

She glanced over at Grayson as Layla walked away, hoping to shoot him a silent thank-you as well, but he had already turned his back on her and was headed down the aisle toward the stage.

* * *

Friday morning, Aubrey awoke with a start. The room was bathed in sunlight, and Christie was snoozing away in the next bed. For a moment, her heart was all in a panic, wondering why the alarm hadn't gone off, and then she remembered: no rehearsal today. The first morning since arriving in Vermont that she didn't have to be up early to get her butt to the Chamberlain for hours of prancing and strutting and singing. She took a deep breath, leaned back into her pillows, and sighed.

There was a light rap on the door. Aubrey glanced at Christie, who blinked herself awake. They regarded each other for a moment, confused. Then Rose stuck her head inside the room and smiled apologetically.

"Sorry if I woke you girls, but Aubrey, I thought you'd want to get a look at this as soon as possible." She stepped over the threshold with a white gown wrapped in a clear plastic bag. "Layla just dropped it off."

"Let's see!" Christie trilled, suddenly more than awake. She jumped out of bed and rushed over to her grandmother, grabbing for the bag's zipper. Before Aubrey's feet had even hit the cold wood floor, Christie had extricated the dress and was holding it up against her own body.

"Oh my God, Aubrey! It's gorgeous!"

"Beautiful," Rose added with a nod, taking a step back to check it out. "What do you think, Aubrey?"

"I think it's amazing," Aubrey replied. She was, in fact, stunned.

The bodice of the dress was strapless and looked as if it was made out of dozens of grosgrain and satin ribbons, crisscrossing the front and tucked in all over, but this was the only detailing. The skirt was plain silk and fell in an A-line to the floor, with just a slight train in the back.

"Try it on so we can see if we need to make any adjustments," Rose suggested, nudging Aubrey forward.

Christie handed the dress over and Aubrey took it into the bathroom to change. The gown slipped over her waist easily and zipped right up in the back. Its only flaw was that it was slightly large in the chest area, but the length and waistline were perfect. She stepped out, holding the bodice against her chest.

"Oh my God. I am *so* jealous," Christie said, her eyes bright. "No offense, Rose. Your dress is nice, but *that* is, like, Oscar-worthy."

"You think?" Aubrey asked, trying not to smile too hugely. After all, she wasn't supposed to care about this stuff.

"Absolutely," Rose replied. She stepped over to Aubrey and pinched the bodice in the back, cinching it to Aubrey's body. "And we can fix this with just a few stitches. No one will be the wiser. I'll go get some pins." She patted Aubrey on the back and slipped from the room, leaving Aubrey to hold the dress up again.

"I gotta say . . . Layla really came through for you," Christie said, dropping down on the edge of her bed as she continued to eye Aubrey with envy. "Honestly, I thought she was going to bring over some torn-up rag or something, but that is amazing."

"So did I. I'm in complete shock," Aubrey replied, stepping closer to the full-length mirror on the wall.

She could imagine herself all made up with her hair piled atop her head and knew that she was going to look great. Maybe even pretty. Instantly she wondered what Grayson would think when he saw her, and she smiled automatically, but then her heart fell. She wasn't sure that Grayson would even be there tonight, and he certainly wasn't going to be there for her.

"This was really nice of her," Christie said.

"I know," Aubrey said, eyeing herself sadly. "I guess I'm *just friends* with both the Chamberlains now."

Chapter 16

"*I*'m going to *kill* Charlie!" Christie said, pacing back and forth in front of the couch in the center of the Spotted Owl's lobby. Aubrey rested her elbow on the armrest, her chin in her hand, and watched her friend as she walked to and fro, wearing a tread into the burgundy throw rug. Christie's dress was actually quite pretty. It was all satin with cap sleeves and rhinestones adorning the bodice in a curlicue pattern. The skirt fell to the floor in a wide A-line that made her tiny waist look even tinier and swished around her feet as she walked.

"Christie, it's okay," Aubrey said. "He's going to be here. Just chill."

"How can I chill?" Christie said, opening her palms to the ceiling. "We are going to be *so* late!"

Aubrey sighed and glanced at Jonathan, who was waiting by the front window, looking out at the drive. He rolled his eyes in an indulgent way and Aubrey forced a smile, wishing Rose wasn't working the dining room that evening. She could have calmed Christie down, Aubrey was sure. As of that moment, Aubrey didn't have the energy to try. She was too busy wishing this night were already over.

"Why are you so calm? We've been waiting for almost an hour!" Christie said, dropping onto the opposite couch.

Because all I can think about is how I wish I was waiting for Grayson, Aubrey thought, feeling lame. *Because I wish this ball had happened* last *weekend, before all the crap hit the fan, so that we could be going together.*

"Because I'm not worried. Charlie is a stand-up guy," Aubrey said, lifting her head. "If he's late, I'm sure he has a good reason."

"Uh-oh," Jonathan said.

Aubrey's heart squeezed at his tone. "What?"

"He does have a good reason," Jonathan replied, glancing over his shoulder at Aubrey.

"And it's that he *can't* stand up."

"What?" Aubrey and Christie blurted in unison.

Aubrey pushed herself up from the couch, her satin skirt tickling her legs as it fell around her ankles. The door to the inn opened wide. Jim came through first and held the door open for Charlie . . . who was on crutches. He hobbled into the room, his right leg in a full cast, and shot Aubrey a sheepish look.

"What happened?" Christie wailed. "Are you all right?"

"I'm fine, I'm fine. Aubrey, I am *so* sorry," Charlie said, clip-clopping toward her. "We tried to call, but something's wrong with the inn's phone."

"Which I'm going to figure out right now," Jim said, making a beeline for the front desk. "Has it not occurred to you that the phone hasn't been ringing for the last few hours?" he asked the stricken-looking worker behind the desk. "Where's Rose?"

"I'll go get her, sir," the girl said, scurrying off toward the dining room.

"What did you do this time, man?" Jonathan asked, slapping Charlie on the back.

"Tried a three-sixty," Charlie said, looking chagrined.

Jonathan frowned. "Dude, that's, like, basic stuff."

"I know. I think I'm officially done with snowboarding," Charlie said, lowering himself onto the couch with a groan. He looked up at Aubrey and raised his eyebrows. "I'm so sorry I won't be able to take you to the ball."

Aubrey swallowed a lump of dread that was creeping up her throat. Dateless. She was dateless. For a dance at Grayson's parents' resort. But she shoved her selfish thoughts aside for the moment.

"It's okay. I'm glad you're more or less all right," she said, putting her hand on his shoulder. "That's all that matters."

"No! No, that is not all that matters!" Christie wailed. She whacked Charlie over the head with her satin clutch purse. "How could you go snowboarding on the day of the ball? You knew Aubrey was counting on you."

"Calm down, Christie!" Aubrey said with a gasp.

"Yeah. Where's my levelheaded, sweet little cousin?" Charlie asked, lifting his hands to defend himself against another swipe with the purse.

"I kind of like it," Jonathan said with a laugh, crossing his arms over his tuxedo shirt.

Christie blushed and lowered her arms. "Sorry. It's just . . . who's going to escort Aubrey? Who's going to dance with her during the Snow Princess Spotlight Dance?"

"The Snow Princess Spotlight Dance?" Aubrey asked. "What is *that*?"

"Oh. Didn't I mention that?" Christie said, biting her bottom lip.

Aubrey moaned and dropped down next to Charlie. This was going to be so awful she could practically taste it. Being announced with no guy on her arm. Having to stand on the outskirts of the dance floor while everyone else participated in some Snow Princess Spotlight Dance. What if Grayson *was* there? He would get to witness her ultimate-loser status firsthand. And Layla and Rebecca and all the other girls—they were going to *love* this.

"You cannot go without a date," Christie said.

And then, just like that, something inside Aubrey snapped. She had never *needed* a guy before. Not for anything. And she wasn't about to start needing one now.

"Yes, I can," she said determinedly. She stood up and smoothed the front of her skirt. "Jonathan, get your car."

"Yes, ma'am," Jonathan said with a grin.

"What? Aubrey, no. You can't go to the Winter Ball as a snow princess without an escort," Christie said, shaking her head. "It's unheard of."

"So? In three days I'll be back in Florida. What do I care what any of these people think of me?" Aubrey said, reaching for her ski jacket. She slipped it on over her formal gown and zipped it up, knowing it looked ridiculous and not caring. "I'm only doing this for you, anyway, and you have a date. It doesn't matter that I don't. And if anyone there says it does matter, they can kiss my butt."

"You go, girl," Charlie said, snapping his fingers.

"Yeah, don't do that," Christie told him, bringing a blush to his face. She looked at Aubrey and sighed. "Come on, Aubrey. I'm sure Jonathan can find *someone* to go with you."

Aubrey took a deep breath, trying to ignore the sadness that suddenly filled her heart. "I don't want just someone," she said, thinking of Grayson. "So I'm not going with anyone."

A horn honked out on the drive and Aubrey handed Christie her black wool coat. "Come on, Chris," she said, feeling a flutter of pride and self-confidence over her decision. "Let's do this thing."

The Grand Ballroom of the Chamberlain Ski Resort and Spa looked like the inside of a glittering snow globe. Everything was white and sparkling and pristine. Millions of glitter- and rhinestone-covered snowflakes were suspended from the ceiling, and gleaming ice sculptures adorned the center of every table. Along the walls, white poinsettia plants were crafted into huge arrangements in the shapes of evergreen trees, and white twinkle lights adorned each arrangement. The chairs were decorated with white velvet swags and yards of white and silver beads. In the center of the dance floor, a huge snowman inside an actual snow globe turned slowly on an automated lazy Susan, fake snow swirling around his head.

"This is insane," Aubrey said, taking in all the exquisite gowns and perfectly fitted tuxedos.

"This is the Winter Ball," Christie said with a sigh.

They stood at the top of a wide set of stairs that spread out in front of the three double doors leading into the ballroom. For a moment, Aubrey felt overwhelmed and completely out of her element. What was she doing here, at a posh event like this, in a state so far from home, with barely anyone to talk to? But then she looked at Christie's excited smile as Jonathan took her arm and started down the steps, and she remembered.

All she had to do was get through the next few hours and the pageant tomorrow. And when they got home, Christie would owe her one. A big one.

Realizing how very alone she suddenly was, Aubrey lifted the sides of her skirt and carefully descended the stairs. She was almost to the bottom, when she felt someone watching her, and looked up to find Grayson standing on the other side of the dance floor, holding a glass of sparkling cider. Her heart caught as she looked into his eyes. He was so ridiculously gorgeous that he stood out even in a sea of handsome men in formal wear. His tie was long and white and tucked into a white vest under his black jacket. If someone had plucked him out of the ballroom and dropped him on a red carpet somewhere, he wouldn't have looked a bit out of place.

Time seemed to stand still as they stared at each other. But then someone grabbed Grayson's arm and offered his hand in greeting, and the moment was over. Aubrey's foot, which had been hovering off the last step, finally hit the ground, and she almost lost her balance before catching herself. She took a deep breath and thanked her lucky stars for that. The last thing she wanted to do was fall in front of these people—in front of Grayson—again. But when she glanced once more over at the spot where he'd been standing, he was gone, having been absorbed by the crowd. She felt a pang of disappointment and realized she'd been hoping he would come over to greet her, say something perfect that would negate the last two days. But apparently, he had no interest in clearing things up, making it better.

Apparently he had no interest in her.

"All right, ladies! Everyone here? All lined up in alphabetical order?"

Aubrey held her breath while Mrs. Chamberlain strode down the line of princesses and their escorts, checking them over as if they were dressed-up cattle. It was nine o'clock, the moment all the snow princesses had been waiting for. Soon they would each be announced and escorted to the center of the floor where they would all dance with their partners and be admired by the rest of the ball's attendees. Aubrey tried to ignore their whispers and stares, which were growing more fevered by the moment. Everyone was starting to notice that one of the princesses was dateless. And to make matters worse, Fabrizia and Grayson had just emerged from the ballroom and were now hovering near the front of the line. Apparently they were going to participate in this charade in some capacity. Perfect. Just perfect.

"Good . . . good . . . nice," Mrs. Chamberlain was saying as her discerning green eyes flicked over the couples. She was getting closer, and the hallway in which the princesses were loitering was getting warmer. Aubrey closed her eyes and said a little prayer that the woman would somehow not notice her lack of a date. When she opened them again, Mrs. Chamberlain was gazing down at her with obvious confusion. "Miss Mills, is it?" she said, her words clipped.

"Yes." Aubrey detested the meek sound of her voice. She cleared her throat and tried again. "Yes?" she said, raising her chin. She saw Grayson glance over at the sound of her voice.

"Where might your escort be, Miss Mills?" Mrs. Chamberlain asked, folding her hands in front of her at waist level.

Christie glanced over her shoulder at Aubrey from a few spots ahead in line. Her eyes were horrified, but her mouth twisted into a supportive smile. As if she was watching Aubrey drown, but wanted to make her feel okay about it.

"I don't have a date," Aubrey said loudly, clearly. She didn't want anyone thinking she was ashamed of this fact. Of course every girl on line started to whisper anew, and a few of them even laughed.

"No date." Mrs. Chamberlain was non-plussed. She guffawed and looked around as if she was searching for the hidden camera. For someone to jump out from behind the potted evergreen against the wall and yell, "Gotcha!" But no one did. "How is it going to look, one of our princesses being announced without a date?"

"Maybe it'll look like I'm independent," Aubrey shot back, her face burning nonetheless.

"Don't fool yourself," Mrs. Chamberlain replied. "I'm all for girl power, but this is not the time. All anyone is going to see when you walk out there alone is a pathetic little—"

"Mom!" Grayson snapped.

Aubrey's heart squeezed. The word cut the air like the buzz of a chain saw, and everyone fell silent. Aubrey was still recovering from the insult that was about to be hurled at her by a supposedly mature adult, which made it difficult to process the shock of Grayson striding down the hallway toward her. He buttoned his jacket as he moved and when he arrived at his mother's side, he took the woman's arm and gently, but firmly, moved her aside.

"I've got this," he said, offering Aubrey his arm.

Aubrey looked up at Grayson. His blue eyes were questioning. Maybe even wary.

"If you'll let me," he said.

Her heart pounding a mile a minute, Aubrey automatically glanced at Christie. Her friend's jaw was hanging open and she nodded her head eagerly like a puppy dog.

"I don't need a pity escort," Aubrey said, hanging on to her pride.

"The pity would be passing up the chance to dance with the prettiest girl in the room," Grayson replied, his eyes softening.

Aubrey warmed from head to toe, but this time in a pleasant way—not in a searing, sizzling, humiliated way. The hallway was as quiet as a library on a Saturday night.

"Um . . . okay, then," Aubrey said, linking her arm through Grayson's. She may still have been baffled by him, annoyed at him, and in need of a long conversation with him, but she could recognize a white-knight rescue when she saw one, and she wasn't about to turn it down. For the first time in the last ten minutes, she felt as if she could breathe again.

"Thank you, Grayson. I appreciate your helping out," Mrs. Chamberlain said, standing up straight. Aubrey and Grayson exchanged a smile. They both knew he hadn't done this to help out his mother. "Now let's get this show on the road."

Chapter 17

"Miss Aubrey Mills, escorted by Mr. Grayson Chamberlain!"

Fabrizia raised her gloved hand with a flourish to punctuate her announcement, and Aubrey and Grayson stepped forward. Aubrey couldn't help laughing as she and Grayson descended the marble stairs together and moved toward the center of the dance floor, joining the other couples in a wide circle. The guests applauded as they strolled by, and Aubrey saw a few women admiring her gown. It was like something out of a fairy tale. All that was missing was the tiara.

"I'm sorry about my mother," Grayson whispered as the next couple was announced and the room erupted in applause again. "She's not used to people voicing their own opinions. She usually just gets her way."

"Tell me about it," Aubrey said, looking around at the other princesses in their white gowns.

"I'm glad you didn't have a date, though. I kind of like swooping in and saving the day," he said, adjusting his lapels in a proud way.

Aubrey rolled her eyes and tried not to smile. "For the record, I did have a date. It just so happens he broke his leg."

Grayson laughed as the final couple completed the circle on the dance floor. "Charlie?"

"Yep," Aubrey said, grinning.

"That guy needs to take up a new hobby," Grayson said as the music started. "Like Scrabble."

Aubrey laughed and he took her hand, pulling him toward her. Her heart stopped beating as she pressed against his chest and she suddenly remembered she was a horrible dancer. All around her the other couples started to sway back and forth, keeping time with the music and smiling in a poised way. Aubrey froze, petrified.

"Just follow my lead," Grayson told her confidently.

"You sure your toes are up for this?" Aubrey asked.

"These shoes have steel toes," he joked.

Holding her hand and waist firmly, Grayson started to move. Aubrey tripped over her own two feet, but he held her even more tightly and kept her from going down. Luckily her dress was long enough that no one could see her feet fumbling around beneath her, and soon she and Grayson settled into a rhythm. It wasn't as if they were supposed to be waltzing for real. All they had to do was step back and forth and turn in a slow circle. Aubrey soon found, much to her pleasure, that she was capable of at least that.

"Just for the record, I was going to ask you to this thing, but then my parents informed me that as the pageant emcee I had to announce the couples, so I couldn't be *in* one of the couples," Grayson told her.

"Oh. That makes sense, I guess," Aubrey said. "It's a good thing Fabrizia was around to take your place."

"Yeah, although I'm not sure anyone here

has understood one syllable out of her mouth," Grayson joked.

Aubrey laughed. "Secret? I don't know what she's saying half the time she's giving me directions."

"Secret?" Grayson replied. "Neither do I."

They grinned at each other as they twirled around the dance floor and Aubrey realized that she didn't feel awkward or tense. She simply felt relieved. Relieved that things seemed normal between them again. Even if she was unclear about the reason.

"I'm thinking we need to scrap this whole 'just friends' thing," Grayson said suddenly, looking down at her. The snowflakes overhead sparkled in the winking lights. "It's not working for me."

Aubrey's heart fluttered. "It's not working for me, either."

"I feel like everything that's happened over the past few days has been one big misunderstanding after another," Grayson said with a hint of a smile.

Relief rushed through Aubrey, making her feel lighter than air. "I know!"

"Like, did you really think I only tried to help you off the ice because people were watching?" Grayson asked.

"I don't know. Not really," Aubrey said, feeling ashamed of the way she'd acted. "I was just so freaked out that I fell. I don't know what I was thinking."

"Well, I really just wanted to help. And I wanted to apologize for the other day," Grayson said, his expression serious. "I shouldn't have gone off like that. Layla explained the situation and now that I have all the facts—"

"You mean she admitted that she was trying to sabotage Christie?" Aubrey interrupted, surprised. "Wow. She really *has* turned over a new leaf."

Grayson hesitated as Aubrey kept moving, and soon their steps were all off-kilter. It took a moment for Grayson to catch up and the intervening confusion left Aubrey feeling flustered. She looked up at him and tried to smile. "What was that?"

"What do you mean, sabotage?" he asked, his brow knit. "I'm talking about your mother."

Now it was Aubrey's turn to stop dancing.

She paused in the center of the dance floor and took a step back, still holding on to Grayson's hand. She needed the extra space so she could really see his face and make sure he wasn't losing it.

"My *mother*? What about my mother?" Aubrey asked.

She saw a few of the other princesses shoot them confused and concerned looks as they waltzed by, but ignored them. All the hairs on the back of her neck were standing on end and goose bumps popped up along her arms. She had a feeling that something was very wrong here.

"It's okay. Layla told me the whole story," Grayson said under his breath, trying to tug her back toward him. Aubrey didn't move, however. She simply arched her eyebrows at him. Grayson rolled his eyes. "You know, about how your mother was a pageant queen and you've never won one, so it's really important to you to win at any cost. With that kind of pressure on you I can understand why you might snap at someone like Layla."

Aubrey's mind was reeling faster than the

dancers whirling around her. Layla was just fabricating stories out of thin air now. Where did that girl get the nerve?

"Grayson, I don't even . . . I can't even . . . " Aubrey began, fumbling for which of the many lies to refute first. "*None* of that is true!"

Grayson clucked his tongue and pulled her to him, starting to dance again. Aubrey was so dumbfounded that she allowed him to lead her around the floor for a moment while she collected her thoughts.

"It's *okay*," he said in what felt to her like a condescending tone. "I just don't understand why you downplayed the importance of the whole thing. You don't have to act with me."

"Act? *Me?* I'm not the one who's acting!" Aubrey blurted, her voice cracking in anger.

"All I'm saying is, it's in the past," Grayson continued as if she hadn't spoken. "As long as you promise not to mess with my sister again, we're cool."

This time, Aubrey stopped in her tracks and tore herself out of Grayson's grasp. She could feel dozens of eyes on her as the music hit its crescendo, but all she could see was Grayson.

Grayson, standing there in the center of the floor, his brow knit in utter confusion. So this was why he'd tried to help her out with her talent, why he'd convinced Layla to be nice to her and lend her a dress for tonight. He thought she was a total pageant psycho who wanted to win the crown more than anything. He thought she had lied right to his face.

"You are such an idiot!" Aubrey seethed through her teeth. "Your sister is the one who's acting and she has you totally snowed!"

"Aubrey—"

"I cannot believe that you're swallowing all this crap she's feeding you!" Aubrey ranted. "All she has done since Christie and I arrived is try to sabotage Christie and keep you and me apart! She's the one who tied Christie's shoes together that day so she would fall. She *stole* Christie's music, bogarted her gown idea, and tried to convince her that her talent was passé. *And* she brought Sophia back here to get back together with you so that you would dump me. The girl is a total jerk and you refuse to see it!"

Grayson laughed in an unkind way. "My sister would never do those things."

Aubrey groaned and threw her hands up. A few of the other princesses stopped dancing and paused to stare. Layla, however, continued to whirl and twirl with the adorable boy she'd come with, either oblivious to the scene or ignoring it because she knew she'd pretty much orchestrated it.

"Do you even hear yourself?" Grayson added. "God, you *are* willing to do anything to win."

Tears stung Aubrey's eyes. She couldn't believe that Grayson refused to listen to her. That he refused to see who she really was. She took a step toward him as the music drew to a close.

"You know what, Grayson? I don't want to be just friends with you or anything else," she spat. "You can take your apology and shove it."

"Your snow princesses, ladies and gentlemen!" Fabrizia announced. "Aren't they lovely?"

There was a brief silence as those closest to the dance floor recovered from Aubrey's last few words, and then the room was filled with applause. Grayson's jaw clenched. He turned around and shoved his way through the crowd, leaving Aubrey alone once again.

But this time, she was more than happy to be left.

As if the announcement of the contestants and the spotlight dance weren't enough pageantry for one evening, Aubrey soon found herself lined up on the stage in front of the band along with her fellow princesses, waiting to introduce herself. Her stomach was in knots over the confrontation with Grayson, and the stage lights were making her sweat. All she could think about was getting out of this stupid gown, putting on some sweats, and hitting at least fifty thousand roller-hockey balls against a nice concrete wall, if she could find one. Maybe more. However many it would take to make this awful, disappointed, sick feeling go away.

"Thank you, Miss DiLauria," Fabrizia said as Dana finished up with her fun facts about herself. "And now, Miss Rebecca Lawrence."

Aubrey scanned the strange faces of the crowd, wondering how many of them had witnessed her fight with Grayson—wondering what they thought of the princess with the attitude. Then her eyes fell on Grayson himself. He was over by the edge of the stage to the left, and it looked as if he was embroiled in a serious argument with his mother and a tall man with gray hair who had to be his father. His dad said something to him, and Grayson stood up straight as if he'd been slapped. Then, without another word, he turned and stormed out of the room, letting the ballroom door slam behind him.

Good riddance, Aubrey thought. She didn't want to be in his presence for one moment more.

"Thank you, Miss Lawrence," Fabrizia said, glancing over at Aubrey. She realized with a start that she was next and that she had yet to figure out what she was going to say. Fortunately, it didn't seem that difficult. All she had to do was tell the people her name, age, where she was from, and at least one interesting thing that set her apart from the other princesses.

How about "I'm Aubrey Mills, sixteen, from Florida, and what sets me apart from the other princesses is I want to kill Layla Chamberlain?"

What she couldn't figure out was, why had Layla agreed to lend her this gorgeous dress? Aubrey had thought the girl had changed, but if that was the case, she wouldn't be making up lies about Aubrey behind her back. The whole thing just didn't add up.

"And now, Miss Aubrey Mills!" Fabrizia announced.

Aubrey plastered on a fake smile as she walked along the line of contestants toward the microphone at stage right. She was about three feet away from Fabrizia's side, when she felt a tug behind her. She tripped a bit, there was a loud ripping sound, and suddenly a whoosh of cold air enveloped her legs.

"Oh my God!" Christie shouted.

Aubrey looked down. The entire skirt of her dress was gone. She was standing in the middle of the stage, in front of hundreds of people, wearing nothing but a bodice and her yellow cotton underwear. All of these facts had just registered with her brain, when the crowd started to gasp and laugh. Christie raced forward and stood in front of her, blocking the audience's view of her by holding her own skirt out at both sides for more coverage.

Aubrey whirled around, her heart in her throat. The skirt of her dress lay in a heap on the floor, pinned under the heel of Layla

Chamberlain's shoe.

"You rip my dress, I rip yours," Layla said with a smirk.

And suddenly, it all became clear. This was why Layla had given her the dress. She had rigged the skirt so that it would tear away easily. She hadn't turned over a new leaf at all. Anger, hurt, shock, and despair all welled up inside Aubrey's chest as she glared at her sworn enemy. The girl was more wicked than Aubrey had ever imagined.

And of course, Grayson was not there to witness it.

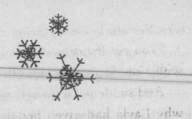

Chapter 18

*A*ubrey didn't sleep at all that night. And not because she was replaying her latest humiliation over and over again in her mind, but because her adrenaline was pumping as if it was hooked up to a generator. Layla's latest and most public revenge had awakened the very monster Aubrey had been trying so hard to keep chained up inside of her. She had awakened Aubrey's competitive beast.

And now, nobody was safe.

I am going to win this thing, Aubrey told herself as she scrubbed her face in the shower the following morning. *No. I'm not just going to win, I am going to crush the competition. I am going to flatten all those sorry princesses beneath my big, heavy feet.*

She stared into her eyes in the mirror, savoring the determination and confidence reflected there. Yes, she knew that winning meant beating Christie as well, but as of last night all bets were off. She would give the Howells her prize money when she won, even though her mother might kill her. It would assuage some of her guilt over taking Christie's crown. But she had to take it. She had to show Layla that she was the better girl. And the better girl would win.

She would even give Christie the tiara when all was said and done. She just had to hope that Christie would understand.

Aubrey wrapped a dry towel around her head and padded back into her room. Christie was downstairs having breakfast, so Aubrey was alone to do what she needed to do. She dropped down on her unmade bed and pulled her laptop toward her. Bringing up her favorite search engine she typed in the words "common pageant interview questions." She planned to memorize every question asked of every major pageant contestant over the last five years and come up with the perfect answer. It didn't matter if it took all morning. This was war.

"Hey," Christie said as she walked in. "Aren't you hungry? There's French toast."

"Maybe later." Aubrey didn't look up from her computer screen. She ignored the grumble her stomach let out.

"So . . . how are you feeling?" Christie asked tentatively, perching on her own bed. She zipped up her pink hoodie and crossed her legs yoga style. "You barely said anything before bed last night."

"M'fine," Aubrey mumbled, scrolling through a list of questions she'd found on a former contestant's website.

"Okay," Christie said dubiously. "Well, Sophia suggested we do something today, just you and me. You know, to keep our minds off the pageant tonight. Like maybe go for a hike or a ski, or oh! We could hit that new mall everyone's talking about! She said that it's very important that I be relaxed going into tonight."

Aubrey let out a sigh. Christie's enthusiasm was getting right under her skin. She was trying to concentrate. What kind of questions would Grayson ask tonight? Would it be something about philanthropy or hopes for the future, or would it be something more Snow Queen–specific? Like how to preserve the wildlife of Vermont or something?

"Aubrey?"

"I'm kind of in the middle of something here," Aubrey snapped.

There was a prolonged, uncomfortable silence. Then Christie's feet hit the floor. "What are you in the middle of?"

"I'm trying to figure out what they're going to ask us tonight," Aubrey replied in a huff. "I have a million things to do today to prepare for the pageant, so no. I'm sorry. I can't go to the mall with you."

She looked up for the first time and saw the disappointment and confusion on Christie's face. Her heart panged, but she ignored it. Her adrenaline washed the guilt away as if it was nothing.

"Since when are you taking this pageant so seriously?" Christie asked, her voice quiet.

"Since I have to kick Layla Chamberlain's ass," Aubrey replied, hitting a few keys on the keyboard to find a new page.

"But I thought . . . I thought you were helping *me*," Christie said, confused.

"I was. I mean, I am." Aubrey groaned.

"Don't you get it, Christie? You were there. You saw what she did to me. There is no way I am letting that girl beat me tonight."

"Wow. You have totally gone over to the dark side," Christie said, getting up and walking in front of the bed. "If you see my friend Aubrey, tell her to call my cell. I'm gonna call Sophia and see if *she* wants to go to the mall."

"Hey! You're the one who made me do this," Aubrey pointed out.

Christie paused with her hand on the doorknob. "Yeah. I know. And apparently I've created a pageant monster."

She left the room, closing the door with a bang, and Aubrey rolled her eyes before returning to her work.

Later that morning, Aubrey stood in front of the full-length mirror in her room and started to sing. She had been avoiding this task all morning, not wanting to disturb the other guests, but finally she realized she had no choice. There was no place better to rehearse inside the inn, and she had to rehearse. Her talent was, as far as she was concerned, her weakest event. She needed to find some way to make it work.

"'I'm gonna wash that man right outta my hair . . . I'm gonna wash that man right outta my hair . . .'" Aubrey's voice trailed off. She sounded awful. Tired and uninteresting and off-key. She took a deep breath and tried again, attempting to put more energy into it. "'I'm gonna wash that man right outta my hair, and send him on his way!'"

Suddenly an image of Grayson in his tuxedo flitted through her mind, and a lump instantly formed in her throat. She paused and stared at her reflection. Why did he have to be so blind to his sister's manipulations? Last night could have been amazing. They could have danced and talked and maybe even snuck off for a kiss by the fire. They could have made everything okay and erased all the crap that had happened over the last few days. But no. He had to believe in Layla the Teenage Witch. She thought of the way he'd looked at her when she'd told him the story about her mother was a lie, and her heart felt as if it was breaking all over again. She groaned and dropped back on her bed, staring up at the ceiling fan overhead.

"God! I wish I *could* wash that man right outta my hair," she said to herself.

Maybe she should go back to singing "On My Own." But it was a harder song. And the tone of that one was even more pathetic than her current choice. "'On my own, pretending he's beside me . . .'" There was no way she was singing *that* and letting Grayson think she was pining for him.

She took a deep breath and turned her head to the side. Suddenly, her heart caught. There, standing against the wall between the closet door and the window, was her hockey stick. The one Grayson had returned to her the morning after the hockey shot competition debacle. Aubrey sat up straight, her heart pounding, remembering what he'd said to her.

You should do something you really love. Something you're comfortable doing. Something that makes you happy. If the judges see you all lit up from the inside, you can't lose.

And then, he'd left her with the hockey stick. Had he been trying to tell her something? Had he actually tried to suggest that she shoot hockey balls for her talent?

Suddenly, Aubrey's chest inflated with hope and she jumped up off the bed and grabbed her hockey stick. Could she do it, or would she be laughed off the stage? She knew that hockey wasn't a normal pageant talent, but this was Vermont. The people here appreciated a good hockey player, didn't they? And besides, it would feel so good to show off her skills—to make up for that awful mishap on the ice the other night.

She had to get her hands on some hockey balls, stat. They would work much better on stage than pucks. And she needed a new goal, too. Looked as if she was going to be calling her mother and begging for a little more leeway with the emergency credit card. But it would all be worth it. She would be up on that stage doing something she loved, something that she was comfortable doing—rather than singing with a fake smile on her face just waiting for the whole thing to be over.

Aubrey paused in the doorway, realizing with a pang how much Grayson had helped her. She wished she could call him and thank him. Wished he wasn't such a moron when it came to his sister. But maybe, when he saw her out onstage tonight, he would know that even though they were both still angry, even though they might never be friends again—she was grateful.

Then, Aubrey grinned. Because thanks to Grayson, she was also one step closer to taking his sister down. Aubrey slammed the door and ran for the lobby.

"Is everything okay between you and Christie?" Rose asked Aubrey as she navigated the small parking lot behind the amphitheater that evening. Usually the lot was closed to anyone but staff, but the Chamberlains had made an exception for the princesses that night so that they could get right backstage and start prepping.

"Apparently not," Aubrey said under her breath, clutching her bags in her lap. When Aubrey had come downstairs to ride to the pageant with Christie, Rose had told her that her friend had already hitched a ride with Jonathan. Christie hadn't even told Aubrey that she was going over early. Clearly their little tiff that morning had meant more to Christie than it had to her. But Christie *knew* Aubrey. She knew that when Aubrey got into her competitive zone no one could talk to her. That was just the way Aubrey was.

"Well, I hope you girls haven't let this pageant get between you," Rose said, putting the car in park in front of the wide pathway that led to the backstage door. "It would be silly to let something so frivolous ruin a friendship."

Aubrey's blood boiled at her use of the word *frivolous*. In less than twenty-four hours, this pageant had become the most important thing in her world. But she managed a smile as she reached for the door handle.

"I'm sure we'll be fine," she said. "Thanks, Rose."

"Break a leg!"

I'd like to break Layla's, Aubrey thought.

But she smiled again as she removed her hockey stick and the goal from the backseat. "Thanks!"

Aubrey slammed both doors and waited for Rose to pull away. Then she shoved her stick through the strap on her duffel bag, slung her gown and snowsuit in their plastic bags over one arm, and gripped the top of the hockey goal with her free hand. Dana and Rebecca strolled by her as she hobbled her way toward the door, awkwardly carrying all her things, but she simply smiled at them and kept moving. She didn't want to hear anyone's comments or questions or criticisms. She just wanted to get inside, get on with this competition, and win.

Turning sideways at the backstage door, Aubrey managed to jostle everything inside and let the heavy door slam behind her. Once she was through, she dropped the goal and her bag, leaned against the cinder-block wall, and took a deep breath. Carrying her stuff might turn out to be the most difficult event of the night.

The door behind her whipped open again and Grayson strode through. He was wearing a wireless headset and talking into it as he looked down at his clipboard. Aubrey's heart seized up at the sight of him and she stood up straight.

"Yes, Fabrizia, I'll head backstage and make sure everyone has arrived." He paused when he noticed the hockey goal blocking his path, then looked over and saw Aubrey for the first time. His expression went blank. "I'll buzz you once

I have the list," he said into his microphone. Then he hit a button on his earpiece and was silent.

"Hey," Aubrey said, swallowing hard. It was torture, being this close to him. Knowing all he had to do was believe in her and they could be together. Knowing his jerk of a sister was keeping them apart. "I hate to do this, but I have to change my talent. You're the one I need to tell, right?"

Grayson blinked. He looked down at the hockey goal again, at her stick, at her hockey bag. When he looked up again, his expression had softened a bit. "Yeah," he said. "But it's too late to get it into the program."

"I know. But I'm hoping that won't be a problem," she said. "Because I am *not* going to sing."

Aubrey saw the faintest hint of a smile twitching at Grayson's lips and felt a surge of hope. But then, just like that, the blank face was back again.

"It's fine. I'll change the script," he said, drawing himself up straight. "You'd better get to the dressing room. I'm about to go take attendance."

Then he turned and strode off down the long, cold hallway, leaving Aubrey behind with her two tons of stuff. She took a deep breath and blew out a sigh.

"It'll all be worth it," she told herself, reshouldering her bag and grabbing the goal. "It'll all be worth it just to watch Layla lose."

Chapter 19

Aubrey stood in the wings in her street hockey gear—black hockey pants, bright red Under Armour top, black helmet, severely beat-up, used Rollerblades—and ignored the stares and laughter of her fellow contestants, all of whom were wearing frilly dresses or sparkly dance outfits. The audience murmured in interest and confusion as one of the stagehands set up Aubrey's hockey goal on the opposite side of the stage and placed the hockey balls in a line about twenty yards out. Aubrey peeked around the curtain and saw several people checking their programs, turning them over as if the explanation for all this would be typed on the back cover. Clearly, Aubrey was not going to be singing a song from *South Pacific*.

"And now, we have Miss Aubrey Mills, whose

talent is . . . hockey," Grayson said into his microphone.

There were a few laughs, and the murmuring grew louder. Aubrey took a deep breath, closed her eyes, and told herself to focus. She could do this. She had gotten through the opening dance number without tripping herself or anyone else, had managed to stroll around the stage in her evening gown without snagging her heel on the skirt or tugging up the bodice, and had breezed right through the snowsuit competition. She knew that her talent was way cooler than any of the other girls' with their yodeling and gymnastics and ballet. Ironic, considering that as recently as that morning she had been sure that this was the one event in which she was going to tank. But things had changed. She opened her eyes again, focused on the goal, and skated onstage.

For a moment, she thought about saying something by way of introduction, but nothing came to mind. She decided to just stun them with her skill. Let the hockey stick speak for itself.

She pulled back and shot the first three goals

into three different corners of the net—*bam, bam, bam*. The murmuring in the audience stopped. Then she quickly skated an arc around the back of the goal, sped over to the balls again, and shot another, smack into the top right corner. She stopped on a dime, turned around, and raced the other way, hazarding a glance at the judges as she went. They all sat in the front row with their clipboards, transfixed. Clearly they had never seen anything like this before. At least not on this stage.

Aubrey made another round, raced to the balls, and hit another two goals. There was one ball left. She popped it up onto the blade of her stick and juggled it. A wave of impressed whispers and gasps made its way through the audience. Grinning now, Aubrey popped the ball up into the air, reeled back, and whacked it out of midair like a baseball. The ball whizzed across the stage and stuck in one of the net's holes. Perfection. The crowd went wild and Aubrey kicked one skate behind her and performed a quick curtsy, which just made them laugh and applaud even harder.

I have this in the bag, Aubrey thought, looking

down at the judges, who were smiling at one another and making notes. Now all she had to do was score big in the interview competition and she was sure that crown was hers.

"Miss Aubrey Mills, ladies and gentlemen!" Grayson called out, striding back onto the stage.

Aubrey gave a quick wave, then turned and skated off the stage, blowing right by the other princesses, who were no longer snickering at her. In fact, they all looked rather ill. They knew they had just seen their scores knocked down a peg.

"Aubrey."

Christie stepped out from behind a curtain with her baton. She was wearing the sparkly gold and red twirling uniform of their school's marching band and she looked, as always, adorable. Still, Aubrey's heart caught temporarily at the sight of her friend. They hadn't spoken since that morning.

"That was . . . great," Christie said. "When did you decide to change your talent?"

"Today," Aubrey said, lifting one shoulder. "I gotta get back and change."

"I'm up next," Christie said, glancing out at

the stage. "I'm *so* nervous."

"I'm sure you'll do fine, Christie," Aubrey said quickly. "I'll see you after."

She turned her back on Christie's stricken expression and skated for the dressing room. The schedule was beyond hectic. Christie should have known there was no time for chit-chat. If she wanted to be a winner, she would have known that.

Sitting on her stool in front of her mirror, Aubrey flipped through the huge stack of index cards on which she'd written all the potential interview questions she could find. On the back of each one was an articulate, winning answer that was sure to impress the judges. The interview was the last event of the night and, like the talent competition, the scores were weighted more heavily than the scores for the evening gown and snowsuit competitions. The talent show wasn't quite over yet, but if the lukewarm responses of the crowd were any indication, Aubrey had taken that hands down. If she had scored in the top five in gown and snowsuit, and could win the interview portion, she was sure this pageant would be hers.

Aubrey glanced up as Christie walked into the room. Her friend hesitated at the door, then came over and dropped her baton on the counter in front of her mirror.

"How'd it go?" Aubrey asked.

"Fine," Christie said, reaching back to unzip her outfit. "I'm going to change back into my gown."

She didn't make eye contact with Aubrey once. Not directly, not in the mirror, not at all.

"Who's out there now?" Aubrey asked.

"Layla," Christie replied. "She's the last one."

Aubrey rolled her eyes. "Of course she is. Give the big, memorable finale spot to the girl who's *supposed* to win."

Christie said nothing. She simply turned and walked behind the dressing curtain, grabbing her gown and hanger off the hook as she went. Aubrey felt a knot forming in her stomach. She knew that Christie was upset with her because she hadn't wanted to spend the day together, but how could Christie not understand that Aubrey wanted to concentrate on the pageant? Christie had seen what Layla had done to her. She knew that Aubrey was a competitor. Wasn't it obvious that she had to take Layla out? And wasn't it even more obvious that, in order to do that, she would have to work her butt off?

Suddenly, the crowd erupted with cheers. It was so loud that all the chatter around Aubrey stopped and the princesses looked toward the open door of the dressing room in shock.

"What just happened?" Dana asked, sitting down on her stool to Aubrey's left.

"Layla just finished her dance number," Rebecca replied flatly, holding a cordless curling iron in her hair.

Aubrey felt a hot rush of annoyance. She slapped her study cards down on her counter and got up, whipping her own gown down from its hook.

What are they doing out there, giving her a standing ovation? she thought bitterly. *It's just a little hip-hop.*

She ducked behind the changing curtain just as Christie ducked out the other side. Aubrey clucked her tongue. Was Christie avoiding her completely, or had the timing been just a coincidence? Her hands shook with anger and frustration as she whipped off her hockey gear and stripped down to her bra and underwear. She was about to step into her gown, when she saw a big, white smear across the front of the skirt.

Aubrey blinked. That couldn't be there. She had to be seeing things. She brought the skirt closer to her face and touched the smear with her fingertip. It was ivory colored and greasy. Makeup. Someone had gotten foundation all over her evening gown.

"Who did this?" Aubrey shouted, storming out from behind the curtain. She didn't even care that she was half dressed. Her adrenaline, nervousness, and ire were all roiling together, and her skin burned. She held the gown up in one hand and glared around the room, her eyes feeling as if they were about to pop out of her head. "Which one of you ruined my dress?" she yelled.

Christie stepped forward. "Aubrey, calm down."

"I will not calm down! Someone is trying to sabotage me," Aubrey ranted, stepping forward. "Layla did it, didn't she? One of you had to see her do it. Just tell me!"

Rebecca and Dana exchanged a disturbed look.

"Tell me!" Aubrey shouted again.

Ever so slowly, Dana stood up from her stool and stepped forward. "Actually, Layla didn't do it. It was me. But I didn't do it on purpose. My makeup slipped out of my hand and it fell on your dress. You really should have put it back in a garment bag, you know. I—"

"How could you be such a klutz?" Aubrey shouted.

"Aubrey," Christie said in a warning tone, reaching for her arm.

Aubrey wrenched herself away. She started to imagine how ridiculous she was going to look, stepping out onstage for the interview in a stained dress. The judges were surely going to deduct points for this. She might never recover. And then Layla would win and all of this would be for nothing.

"They should disqualify you for this!" she ranted. Dana backed away nervously and all the other girls in the room gave Aubrey a wide berth.

"Aubrey," Christie said again.

"You owe me a dress! Go find me a dress!"

"Aubrey!" Christie shouted at the top of her lungs.

The room was completely silent. Aubrey turned and looked at Christie, and her overwhelming anger suddenly morphed into complete shock. Had Christie just yelled at her? That had never happened before. In fact, as far as she knew, Christie had never yelled at anyone, ever.

"Come with me," Christie said firmly. Then she gripped Aubrey's bare arm, grabbed her own silk robe with her other hand, and shoved it at Aubrey. "But cover up first."

Aubrey quickly slung the robe over her shoulders and allowed Christie to drag her into the hall. From the corner of her eye, Aubrey saw Layla striding toward them, looking all triumphant after her talent performance. Christie groaned at the sight of her, turned, and shoved open the door to the men's room, practically throwing Aubrey inside.

"What are you doing?" Aubrey blurted,

shoving her arms through the sleeves of the robe.

"No! No talking! I get to talk now," Christie said, raising a hand. "You, Aubrey, are completely out of control."

"What, that? I just—"

"No! Me! Talking!" Christie said, pacing in front of the urinals in her high heels and pink gown. "Look, I know that Grayson let you down. And I know what happened at the ball last night sucked. Layla has been just awful to you—"

"To both of us," Aubrey said.

Christie shot her a narrowed-eyed look that stopped her blood cold. She couldn't believe her sweet, upbeat friend could even produce such a look.

"Sorry," Aubrey said, looking at the floor.

"But you have not been yourself since we got here," Christie continued. "You're either completely focused on taking Layla down or you're completely focused on winning the hockey competition or you're completely focused on getting Grayson to like you. And now . . . now you've become a complete pageant psycho! How could you yell at Dana like that? You know she didn't mean to do it!"

Aubrey's head hung a bit lower. "I'm sorry, I just . . . look, you know I'm a competitive person."

"Yes. I know this," Christie said. "But I also know you're a good person. And you've always been a good friend. You've always cheered me on and supported me and I thought you were going to do that this week. But today—the most important day of the whole thing—you've suddenly become completely selfish. I mean, this is the biggest event of my life. And you didn't even wish me luck before my talent."

Christie tugged a paper towel out of the dispenser on the wall and toyed with it, twisting it into a tight roll. Aubrey blinked. Her heart felt as if it was shrinking down to the size of a pea. Had she really been that awful to Christie? But then, she realized with a start, she *must* have been. Because for the first time ever, Christie had confronted someone. Unfortunately, that someone was Aubrey.

"Well, I did one thing right," Aubrey said,

her entire chest constricting. "I got you to stand up for yourself."

Christie looked up at Aubrey, her eyes a blank slate. Was she still mad? Was she ever going to forgive her? Aubrey held her breath. And then, finally, Christie laughed.

"Yeah. I guess you did."

Aubrey stepped forward and hugged her friend, relief coursing through her. "I'm so sorry, Christie. I didn't realize."

"I know. And I could have said something sooner," Christie said.

"It's okay. It's *so* not your fault," Aubrey said, leaning back. She looked at herself in the mirror above the sinks, saw her heavy eye makeup and glossy lips and sprayed hair, and didn't recognize herself. She knew that this pageant thing wasn't her. It had all started because she wanted to be there for Christie. But instead of being there for her friend, she had totally upset her and ruined everything.

Exactly what she had promised herself she wouldn't do.

"That's it. I'm dropping out of this thing," Aubrey said. She felt her conscience resisting even as she said it, so unaccustomed was she to backing down or letting someone else win. But she had to do it. "I'm going to go tell Fabrizia I'm out."

She reached for the door, but Christie held on to her hand. "No! I don't want you to do that!"

"Why not? You said yourself I've become a total pageant psycho," Aubrey said, lifting a hand.

"I know, but I don't want you to quit. Quitting a competition right in the middle would kill you," Christie said with a knowing smile. "I just want my friend back."

Aubrey smiled in return. "Okay, fine. I won't quit," she said. "But I no longer care about winning. I said I was going to help you beat Layla, and that's exactly what I'm going to do."

Christie's brow knit with concern. "How? You're not going to try to sabotage her, are you? Because I don't think—"

"Oh, no. Nothing like that. Don't worry," she said. "But right now I have to go apologize to Dana."

Apologizing was never fun, but she knew she had to do it. Dana had not deserved the insane rant Aubrey had subjected her to. Once that was done, Aubrey really had to figure out how, exactly, she was going to help Christie win with only one event left. Because if she had been perfectly honest with Christie, she would have told her she had no clue.

Aubrey stood onstage, the spotlight baring down on her, and tried to keep the fake smile plastered to her face. It was difficult to smile for real when more than five hundred people were about to watch her answer some inane question asked by the very guy who had essentially chosen his lying sister over her. The guy who looked annoyingly handsome in his suit and tie, wielding his microphone.

All the questions were written on pieces of folded white paper and had been stuffed into a clear vessel that resembled an oversized fishbowl. As Grayson reached inside to pluck out her question, Aubrey's heart pounded with nerves. She hadn't come up with any sort of brilliant plan to help Christie win. What could she do at this point? Grab the bowl of questions and run, thereby preventing Grayson from ever asking Layla anything? Would Layla get a zero in the interview category if that happened?

Probably not. They probably wouldn't penalize Layla just because some nut job from Florida had made off with the question fishbowl. Especially since her family was running this thing.

Grayson had his question. He read it to himself before approaching Aubrey. Her hands were clutched behind her and she stood with her right leg behind her a bit, trying to hide the makeup smudge on her dress from the judges. She glanced out at the audience and, knowing where their seats were situated, easily found Rose, Jim, Jonathan, and Charlie, who sat in the last seat of their row with his cast jutting out into the aisle. Jim flashed her a thumbs-up as Rose and the guys looked on excitedly. She knew they were rooting for her, but obviously they were rooting for Christie even more. She also saw Jason Tucker from the ski shop and Clarissa from the evening-gown store and all the workers from the inn who were crowded behind Rose and Jim with handmade signs of support for Christie. Aubrey had the awful feeling that she had let them all down.

And then, suddenly, it hit her. Maybe she couldn't sabotage Layla, but she could sabotage herself. She knew that after the first three events she had to be somewhere near the top of the heap, if not *at* the top. But if she somehow tumbled out of the top spot, that would leave the door open for someone else to take it. Maybe even Christie.

It was a long shot, but it was something. It was all she could do. Beating Layla no longer mattered. Giving Christie the best chance to win was all she cared about.

As Grayson stopped in front of her, Aubrey turned toward the audience, allowing the makeup smear to be seen by all. She noticed a few of the judges grimacing and for the first time since she'd walked onstage, her smile was real.

"Aubrey, here's your question," Grayson said, holding his microphone in one hand and the scrap of paper in the other. "If you could change one thing about this country, what would it be?"

Aubrey's smile widened. This was one of the questions she had worked on today. And she knew she had the perfect answer. How she would have all the citizens of the nation open their hearts to one another and care for one another and be kind to one another, because change started with the individual, and blah, blah, blah. It was the answer Miss Teen Wisconsin had given last year and it had won her the title of Miss Teen USA. The words were on the tip of her tongue. She opened her mouth and spoke.

"I think we totally need to change the length of the school year," she said. "I mean, ten months? Really? Do we really need to be in school ten months out of the year?" she blabbered. She had no idea where she was going with this, but if Sophia was right about rambling being bad, then she was on the right track. The judges looked confused, which only spurred her on more. "I know that I've absorbed all the information I'm going to absorb by about January. Why not end the school year then and let kids spent the rest of the year earning their keep? Working minimum-wage jobs? Helping their families keep a roof above their heads. That's what I would change."

Aubrey nodded and looked up at Grayson

with a smile. He stared back at her, his brow knit in confusion, his eyes searching hers as if she'd just answered the question in some foreign language he didn't understand.

"Um . . . okay . . . thank you," he said finally. "Aubrey Mills, everyone!"

There was an unenthused smattering of applause, and Aubrey raised her hand in a perfect pageant-queen wave as she walked offstage, making sure her stain was turned toward the audience. Her grin was so wide she may as well have been striding off to thunderous cheers.

"What did you just do?" Christie asked as soon as Aubrey hit the wings. All the girls who had already been interviewed, including Christie, were gathered around, while those who had yet to be interviewed, including Layla, were sequestered in the dressing room, where they were unable to hear the questions and answers.

"I just threw the competition," Aubrey said with a grin. "And it felt good."

Chapter 20

"All right, ladies, the scores have been tabulated," Grayson said, holding three sealed, cream-colored envelopes up for the audience to see. "Inside these envelopes I have the names of the two runners-up as well as this year's Snow Queen!"

The audience applauded excitedly. It was, after all, the moment they had waited for in the open air on a frigid night for the last two hours. Heat lamps or no, it had to be pretty cold out there. Aubrey, however, felt warm from the tension and suspense. Her sweaty hands were squeezed by Christie on one side and Dana on the other, so hard she was sure her fingers were going to crack.

Please let Christie win, please let Christie win, Aubrey thought over and over again. She had never felt so nervous for someone else in her life. Not only had Christie always dreamed of this moment, but if she won the crown and the money, she was going to help Rose and Jim save the Spotted Owl. Plus Aubrey would get to see Layla have a nervous breakdown, which would be the highlight of this entire trip. It was almost too much drama to handle.

"Are you ready?" Grayson asked, turning to the side to face the line of seriously tense snow princesses. They all nodded and smiled politely, serenely, even though Aubrey knew that most of them were more than ready to tackle him to the ground and rip open the envelopes themselves.

"Okay, the second runner-up is . . ."

He opened the envelope and drew out the card. A strange look of surprise and what seemed like disappointment flitted across his face. Aubrey's heart nose-dived.

Please don't say Christie. Please don't say Christie. Please don't say—

"Miss Aubrey Mills!" Grayson announced.

Aubrey's eyes popped open before she even realized she had closed them. She came in third? Even after that ridiculous interview answer she had managed to come in third? Her heart leaped with excitement as she realized that *must* have meant she'd taken the talent competition. Dana released her hand and Christie reached in to hug her.

"Aubrey! This is amazing!" she said.

"I know! What do I do?" Aubrey asked.

"Go over and get your flowers," Christie instructed, giving Aubrey the tiniest shove.

Aubrey stumbled forward and found Grayson smiling at her—a little sadly, but still smiling—as the audience applauded. Her heart felt full as she walked past him. If they were still together, would he have reached over and kissed her? Would she have run up and hugged him? As it was, Aubrey averted her eyes and focused instead on Sophia, who walked out with a huge bouquet of white roses and handed them to Aubrey.

"Congratulations," she said. Then she leaned in and whispered in Aubrey's ear. "You had it in the bag until that interview answer."

All Aubrey could do was smile as Sophia led her upstage right and left her to stand there on her own, to wait for the next results. Suddenly she realized that she had participated in a competition and lost and it didn't bother her. She felt none of that searing agony, none of that what-if uncertainty she usually felt after a loss. She had done well. Really well. And she was proud of herself.

From her position, Aubrey could see all the other contestants and knew that they were waiting in agony—everyone except Layla, who looked as poised and sure of herself as a girl whose parents had paid for and run the pageant *should* look.

I swear if she wins I'm gonna—

"And now, for the first runner-up," Grayson said. "They tell me this was one of the closest results in the history of this pageant," he told the audience with a conspiratorial smile.

He tore open the envelope, held it up, and froze. Aubrey could feel the tension in the air and she knew that either Layla's name or Christie's name was on that card. Everyone in the audience probably thought it was Layla's name. They were sure that the Chamberlain boy wanted the Chamberlain girl to win. But Aubrey wasn't so sure. She was still holding on to the belief that Grayson wanted Christie to win and save the inn. Was it possible that he looked that stunned and upset because Christie had come in second? Why was it taking so long for him to read it? Maybe he didn't know *who* he wanted to win. Layla was, after all, his sister, but Christie deserved it and the Spotted Owl needed it. Maybe he didn't know what to hope for, and now that he knew the result he didn't know how to feel. The audience started to whisper and murmur. All the smiles on the faces of the snow princesses grew strained. Time seemed to tick on more slowly with each passing second until finally, Aubrey couldn't take it anymore.

"Get on with it already!" she shouted.

The audience dissolved into laughter. Grayson woke up from his catatonic state and looked over his shoulder at her.

"Thanks for that, Miss Mills," he said, which caused Aubrey's heart to flip over. Was he just being cute for the audience, or was he joking around with her because it was her? Then he cleared his throat and read, "The first runner-up for this year's Snow Queen crown is . . . Miss Layla Chamberlain."

It took a moment for anyone to react. Stunned silence was the overwhelming response. How could Layla Chamberlain not have won? This was her family's event. Her family's resort. Obviously this whole thing had been carefully constructed and planned so that she could wear the crown. No one could quite believe it. Not even Aubrey.

And then, Jim Howell stood up and started to whoop and holler. A few people laughed and then joined in, thinking, Aubrey was sure, that he was applauding for Layla's solid showing. Aubrey, meanwhile, knew that he was clapping because she had not won. Because the fix clearly was *not* in. Because whether or not Christie eventually took home the crown, in his mind, evil had just been defeated. Soon the entire audience was applauding, and a stunned Layla was forced to step forward and accept her second-place flowers. Grayson gave his sister a kiss on the cheek and whispered something in her ear, but she said nothing. Sophia gave Layla her flowers, then led her over to stand next to Aubrey and congratulated her, but still she said nothing. She simply stood next to Aubrey, a sourpuss on her face, and waited to find out who had beaten her at her own game.

It was all Aubrey could do to keep from shouting, "Nyah, nyah, nyah-*nyah*, nyah!" right in the girl's face.

"And now, for the moment we've all been waiting for," Grayson said, tearing into the final envelope. "This year's Snow Queen is . . . Christie Howell!"

"Yes!" Aubrey shouted, pumping her fist.

Rose and Jim jumped up from their seats and Jonathan followed, dragging Charlie up by the arm. Half the audience, in fact, was on its feet. Christie's hands flew to her face and tears sprung to her eyes as she stepped forward, triumphant big-band music blaring through the loudspeakers. Sophia strode over and placed a beautiful, glittering tiara atop Christie's dark hair. Then, over Christie's head, she slung the white satin sash, which read SNOW QUEEN in red sequins. Flashbulbs popped as Christie doubled over laughing, then straightened up again and waved to the crowd. Then all the princesses gathered around her, hugging her and congratulating her and checking out the crown. Aubrey had to fight her way to the center of the crowd, and when she finally found her friend, she threw her arms around her, nearly knocking the tiara free with her bouquet of flowers.

"Congratulations, Christie. I'm so happy for you!" Aubrey shouted over the mayhem.

"Thanks, Aubrey. Thank you so much for doing this with me," Christie said.

"Even though I almost ruined it?" Aubrey said with a laugh, leaning back.

"Yeah, but you didn't," Christie said, reaching up to reposition her crown. "I can't believe this is actually happening."

"Well, believe it," Aubrey said with a grin. "The best girl just won."

"First runner-up? This is such crap!" Layla screeched, storming into the bustling dressing room. She flung her roses at the first mirror she saw and white petals rained everywhere. All the snow princesses had already changed into their casual wear and were getting ready to find their families and head out to dinner or back home. Layla had disappeared somewhere right after the announcement, and Aubrey could only imagine that she had been whining to her mother or making the judges recount their scores. Whatever she'd been doing, it clearly hadn't made her feel any better.

"You!" she shouted, whirling on Christie, who was still wearing her pink gown and tiara, not yet ready to let the moment go. Layla stormed over to her, one finger raised toward Christie's nose. "You had this fixed! Your stupid grandparents know half the judges on the panel! How did they get them to vote for you? Pity? Blackmail? You're such a little cheater!"

Christie's jaw dropped, stunned, and she stumbled back a few steps, knocking into a fabric-steaming machine that was hanging near the wall. When Aubrey noticed the fear on Christie's face, something inside her snapped. She was not going to let Layla ruin this night for her friend.

"*She's* a cheater? Are you kidding me?" Aubrey blurted, getting in between Christie and Layla. "Why don't you just back off, you whiner?"

At that moment, Grayson stuck his head in

the room as if to check to make sure everyone was fully dressed before he walked in. He had already changed into a gray turtleneck sweater and jeans and was looking much more like his usual self, and still as drop-dead gorgeous as ever. Aubrey cursed her own bad luck. Of course he'd once again caught *her* looking like the bad guy, when seconds ago it had been Layla who was showing her bitchiest colors. But Grayson had walked in *behind* Layla, and she hadn't seen her brother yet. Suddenly, Aubrey was struck with a perfect idea.

"I mean, how dare you accuse Christie of fixing the competition?" Aubrey said to Layla. "Not only do your parents own this pageant, but you spent the entire week trying to sabo-tage *us*!"

"So what?" Layla said, crossing her arms over her chest. "It's not as if any of it worked! Not wearing that stupid yellow dress or steal-ing your music or trying to make you give up on twirling. Even that dinner party I threw for the judges turned out to be totally pointless!"

A few of the other contestants gasped when they heard this. Grayson's face went ashen.

Aubrey's heart was so happy it was doing cart-wheels.

"I spent a *fortune* on that meal, but did it matter? *No-o-o!* Clearly you two had something far bigger up your sleeves than any of my plans," Layla ranted. "So what did the Howells do, Christie? Pay off their friends to vote for you?"

"Layla!" Grayson blurted. His expression was one of shock and confusion. All eyes in the room darted from him to Layla and back again. No one wanted to miss a second of the back-stage drama.

Facing Aubrey and Christie, Layla's face fell. She swallowed hard and turned around to look at her brother, but there was no going back this time. He'd heard her admit that she'd tried to sabotage his friends. For once, he'd been there to witness her true self. Inside her chest, Aubrey's heart did a happy dance. Finally, finally, *finally*.

"Grayson!" Layla trilled, putting on her faux-sweet voice. "Hang on a sec. I just have to get changed and then we can go meet up in the restaurant with Mom and Dad."

"What the hell was that?" Grayson said, stepping up to her. "Did you really do all those things? And were you really just accusing the Howells of paying off judges?"

Layla's mouth opened, but no words came out. She glanced up at the ceiling as if trying to find some logical explanation for what he'd just heard, but clearly nothing was coming to her. "That?" she said finally, lifting a hand. "That was just a joke. I was *kidding* with Christie . . . right?" She glanced over her shoulder at Christie. "We were just joking around."

She shot Christie a prompting look and it was all Aubrey could do not to scream. Did Layla really expect Christie to back her up here? After everything she'd done? Christie took a few steps forward, drew herself up, and looked down her nose at Layla. With the gown and the tiara, she looked very regal at that moment.

"I'd rather not answer that question, because anything I have to say to you right now would be very unbefitting of the Snow Queen," she said diplomatically.

Layla's eyes narrowed and she let out an incredulous sort of noise. "Whatever. Come on, Grayson. Let's just go," she said, crouching to gather up her bags and shoes from the floor.

"Mom and Dad are waiting."

"Uh, no thanks. I don't think I'll be coming along," Grayson said, his jaw clenching. "The Howells just invited me to Christie's victory party."

"What?" Layla blurted, standing up straight.

"We're having a victory party?" Christie asked, excited.

"Yeah, so I wouldn't change out of that if I were you," Grayson said with a nod at Christie's gown. "I'm sure everyone's gonna want to see the Snow Queen in all her glory."

"Okay!" Christie said excitedly. "And all you guys are invited!" she said to the room. "Come one, come all!"

Layla groaned in frustration and stormed out of the room, leaving her brother, her friends, and all her crap behind. Aubrey was both amused by her exit and relieved to see her go. In her mind she heard the classic refrain played at the end of all her roller-hockey victories. *"Nah, nah, nah, nah! Nah, nah, nah, nah! Hey, hey, hey! Good-bye!"*

As the snow princesses started to chatter in excitement about the party, Grayson stepped over to Aubrey. "Can I talk to you for a second?"

"Sure," Aubrey said, her heart pounding. She glanced around for an escape route, but the girls were all blocking the door as they crowded out with their garment bags and duffels and makeup cases. Then Aubrey saw the changing curtain. She tipped her head toward it and smiled. "Follow me."

Together they ducked behind the curtain and, even though it was no less quiet back there, at least they were free from the prying eyes of all the other contestants.

"Aubrey, I'm so sorry," Grayson began, looking anguished. "I can't believe Layla . . . so she really did all those things you accused her of last night at the ball?"

"And more," Aubrey said, thinking of her skirt lying on the stage, her underwear exposed for the entire resort to see. But if he hadn't heard about that yet, she saw no need to tell him.

"I'm such an idiot. I was totally wrong about you. I thought you were trying to turn me against my own sister, when all you were doing was telling the truth," Grayson said.

"It's okay. I mean, she's your sister," Aubrey replied. "Considering what's been going on with your parents I can understand you not wanting to believe that Layla was—"

She stopped herself, not wanting to say something awful that she would regret.

"Being a total witch?" Grayson finished for her with a laugh.

"Your words, not mine," Aubrey replied.

"Well, she's always been good at getting what she wants," Grayson said. "I guess I just never realized *how* she always gets what she wants."

Aubrey took a deep breath. "Well, it didn't happen this time."

"No, I guess it didn't," Grayson said with a smile. He took a deep breath and blew out a sigh. "It's been a crazy couple of weeks, huh?"

"That's the understatement of the year," Aubrey said. When she had signed on for the trip to Vermont, all she'd wanted was to see some snow. Instead she had been roped into a beauty pageant, engaged in a war with a beauty queen, and fallen for a guy who had spent days confusing her.

"I wanted to tell you . . . I think it's really cool

what you did for Christie out there," Grayson said, looking into her eyes in a way that made Aubrey's heart flutter.

"What do you mean?" Aubrey asked.

"A shorter school year? That's really the biggest change our country needs?" he teased.

"Yes!" Aubrey protested, letting her jaw drop indignantly. But she couldn't help it. She started to laugh. She was just so happy to be near Grayson again, to be joking with him again. To know that he believed in her again. The laughter bubbled up and she couldn't stop herself. "Yes. That was totally what I meant," she sputtered.

"Well, this time I really *don't* believe you," Grayson said with a laugh.

"Well, this time I really don't mind," Aubrey replied, lifting her shoulders.

They just looked at each other, enjoying the lightness of the moment after all the heavy ones. Then Grayson slipped his hand into hers. The rough warmth of his skin sent excited tingles all up and down Aubrey's arms.

"Come on," he said. "We have a party to go to."

"There's just one thing I need to do first," Aubrey said, her heart pounding. She reached up, slipped her hand around the back of Grayson's neck, and pulled him in for a kiss.

Aubrey sat in the front row of the VIP bleachers on Main Street, saving the seat next to hers for Grayson. It was the last night of the winter carnival, and most of the town of Darling had gathered along the sidewalks for the event's big finale—a parade through town to the carnival grounds. Aubrey caught a few curious glances from the people settling in around her and knew that they recognized her as the second runner-up from the pageant. They were probably wondering what she was doing in the stands when she was supposed to be on the Snow Queen float. But they didn't ask, so she didn't say a thing. She was right where she wanted to be.

"Hey! I got your text," Grayson said, side-stepping his way down the aisle. Aubrey smiled up at him, feeling a bittersweet pang in her heart. It was their last night together. The last time she would see him all giddy to see her. He gave her a quick kiss and settled onto the cold bench next to her. "Did you really have to send it twenty times?"

"I wanted to make sure you got it," Aubrey said, slipping her arm through his.

"Understood," Grayson said as he surreptitiously cuddled in closer. "So, don't get me wrong. I'm more than happy to be here to keep you warm, but aren't you kind of supposed to be on a float right now?"

Aubrey laughed as the local high-school band marched by, playing selections from Usher's latest hits. "I talked to Christie about it and we agreed that I've done enough pageant stuff. Tonight I get to do what I want to do."

"And what you wanted to do was hang out with me?" Grayson said, pulling his head back to see her better. "I'm honored."

"Well, that, and I bet those girls are freakin' freezing right now," Aubrey joked.

"I'm more than happy to be your personal heater for the night," Grayson said, lacing his glove-covered fingers through hers.

"Thank you."

Aubrey placed her head on his shoulder and

sighed, her breath making a huge steam cloud in front of her. On the street in front of them, a group of middle-school kids danced around, waving pom-poms and ribbons and holding huge snowflakes over their heads. A band of clowns ran by and tossed candy at the spectators. Aubrey had to duck to keep from being brained by a Jim Dandy.

"You're going to miss this, aren't you?" Grayson said in a low voice. "I mean, where else can you cuddle with a hot guy, listen to a tuba playing Usher, and get attacked by candy-wielding clowns?"

Aubrey laughed and lifted her head. "Oh, so now you're a hot guy?"

Grayson raised his eyebrows, feigning surprise. "I'm not?"

"Love the modesty," Aubrey said. "No, I am really going to miss it here." She looked up at the pitch-black sky and sighed. "And I never did get to see any snow."

"Sorry about that," Grayson said. "I suppose that if I were a true Vermont gentleman I would have been able to figure out a way to control the weather patterns for you."

"Work on that for next year," Aubrey said.

"Next year?" Grayson replied, squeezing her hand. "Sweet."

Aubrey didn't want to have the conversation. The one about what they were going to do after she returned to Florida, whether they would keep in touch, whether they would try to be long-distance. It all seemed too messy and emotional and not how she wanted to spend her last few hours with him. But she could feel the questions hanging out there between them, expanding like a balloon that was going to pop painfully in both their faces the longer they let it go. She had to say something, but what?

"Grayson? Grayson, there you are!"

Startled out of her deep thoughts, Aubrey looked up to find Jim and Rose climbing up the steps and barreling toward them, along with a familiar-looking man in a black knit cap. Grayson stood up as they approached.

"So, do we have a deal?" he asked.

Rose reached up and hugged him. "Of course we have a deal! You are the sweetest boy on earth!"

"How did you come up with the idea?" Jim

asked, his eyes bright with excitement in a way Aubrey had never seen before—not even on the night that Christie had won the pageant.

"Okay, what deal? What idea?" she asked, standing as well. "What's going on?"

"Aubrey, I'd like you to meet Brody Landry," Grayson said, lifting his hand toward the man in the cap. "Remember when I brought a friend to dinner at the inn? This is him."

"Right! Nice to meet you," Aubrey said, shaking his hand.

"You as well," Brody replied.

"Brody owns Ace Plumbers," Grayson explained.

Suddenly Aubrey realized why he looked so familiar. He was the man in the coveralls whom Grayson had been speaking with at the Chamberlain that day.

"And he's just agreed to fix all our plumbing issues for free!" Jim said happily.

"What?" Aubrey gasped.

"Well, not for free," Brody corrected. "We've done a barter deal. I get to eat gratis at the inn once a week for the year, and they get all their pipes fixed up like new."

"Oh my gosh, Grayson! You did this? This is amazing!" Aubrey said, her eyes wide.

"Well, I knew the Howells wouldn't take charity, so I figured a trade would work," Grayson replied. "And Brody *loves* to eat."

"Do I ever," Brody said, patting his wide stomach with a laugh.

"It's a genius plan," Rose said, beaming. "Grayson, we can't thank you enough."

"And now we can use this year's carnival profits to buy a proper van for a shuttle for next year," Jim said. "Christie can use her Snow Queen winnings to put toward college instead of bailing out her old grandparents."

"She was more than happy to do it," Aubrey told him.

"I know. But we would have felt awful taking it," Rose replied.

Out on the street a float rumbled by carrying the local firefighters, and the crowd went wild.

"We should probably sit so everyone else can see," Grayson said, glancing over his shoulder at the stands. The five of them all crowded onto the bottom bench, which meant Aubrey was forced to cuddle close against Grayson.

Not that she minded.

"You totally saved the day," she whispered to him happily.

"It was the least I could do," he replied. "Besides, I like my job. If the inn went under, I'd be unemployed."

It wasn't exactly true and they both knew it. Grayson would always have a job at the Chamberlain. But he liked his job at the inn much better.

"Look! There's the Snow Queen float!" Aubrey said, pointing. Everyone else in the stands seemed to notice it at the same time, and some of the spectators stood up to snap pictures or just get a better view. The sides of the float were constructed like a castle with glittering white bricks and gray turrets topped by pink flags. All the snow princesses sat on risers at the front of the float, bundled up into coats, their hair and makeup elaborately done. Layla sat in the second row from the top, alone, a fake smile plastered on her face. Aubrey realized with a start that, as the other runner-up, she would have been forced to sit next to Layla for the entire parade. She let out a mental sigh of relief over dodging *that* bullet.

Then, in the top row, with a chair and a spot all to herself, was Christie. She wore her Snow Queen sash over her white wool coat, and her tiara was perched atop her long, dark hair. As the float made its way past the VIP section, the bleachers erupted in cheers, but no one shouted louder than Aubrey and the Howells and Grayson—unless it was Jonathan, who was down on the ground, wielding his video camera.

Christie laughed and waved at them, giving Aubrey a wink as the float drove past. Aubrey couldn't wait to get back to the carnival with Grayson and meet up with Christie, Jonathan, Charlie, and Sophia to enjoy the rides and games and food the way they were supposed to be enjoyed. She had a feeling this was going to be the best night of her trip.

"Well, let's leave these two alone," Rose said, patting Jim on his knee. "I'm sure they don't want to hang around with two old fogies like us."

"I should get going, too," Brody said, standing.

"No! You can stay," Aubrey protested.

But they were already on their feet. "You two kids have fun," Jim said. "You both deserve it."

"Nice to meet you again, Aubrey," Brody said, lifting a hand.

He walked off, followed by Rose and Jim. They strolled arm in arm, pausing here and there to chat with friends from town.

"So," Grayson said, looking at her.

A flutter of nervousness went through Aubrey. This was it. The Talk. "So," she replied.

"Did I mention I've decided to go to college next year?" he said unexpectedly.

Okay. So maybe it wasn't the Talk. All around them the crowd was starting to disperse. The Snow Queen float was the finale of the parade.

"Really?" Aubrey said.

"Yep. Gonna get me some higher education," Grayson said jokingly.

"Any idea where you're going to go?" Aubrey asked.

Grayson narrowed his eyes. "I'm thinking I need a change of climate," he said. "Maybe . . . University of Southern Florida?"

Aubrey's grin widened. "Oh, please. You couldn't handle the heat. Let alone the street hockey."

Grayson laughed and tilted his head back to look up at the sky. "You're probably right. And I know I'd miss the snow."

"The what?" Aubrey's heart leaped and she looked around. Sure enough, snow had started to fall, tumbling down from the sky in tiny white flakes. Already there was a dusting on the railing in front of her. Aubrey jumped to her feet, ripped off her glove, and held her hand out, letting the snowflakes drift into her palm. "Oh my God! It's actually snowing!" she shouted.

A few people around her laughed. Aubrey looked at Grayson in wonder. "You *are* the perfect Vermont gentleman!"

"Told you so," he said, stepping next to her.

Aubrey slipped her arms around his neck.

"You really are something else," she teased, recalling their conversation on the night he'd first asked her out. She'd felt so angry that evening as he'd demanded her apology. So conflicted. So stubborn. But now she was no longer any of those things.

"Something else good, or something else bad?" Grayson joked, placing his arms around her waist.

"Something else good," Aubrey said. "Definitely good."

Grayson smiled as he pulled her closer, touching his lips to hers. As they kissed under the cloudy sky, snowflakes tickling Aubrey's cheeks and clinging to her hair, all she felt was pure happiness.

From the beach to the slopes, **EMMA HARRISON** has the perfect read for every vacation.

The Best Girl

When the bride is a famous heiress, the location is a posh ski resort, and the bellhop is Hot Connor, Jane's best man—um, best girl—duties may not be as simple as she expected.

Tourist Trap

All Cassie Grace has to do is survive one more summer in her tiny tourist-trap town before getting out into the real world at last. But when Jared Kent, a wealthy "summer invader," shows up, Cassie's life is turned completely upside down.